Obsessed

Lila Casey Series

J Collins

Copyright & Disclaimer

Acknowledgements

Mark Collins, fashion designer & stylist, The Tailor's Shop, Royal Wootton Bassett, www.thetailorsshop.com
Thank you for all of your help with styling for all book covers and assistance with all other arrangements – without you this book would never have made it from my laptop to kindle!

Nigel Ferris, cover photographer, www.ferrisphotographics.co.uk
Thank you for the amazing composite photography on all book covers!

Simon Addis, model
Thank you for bringing Adam to life on all book covers!

Kyrie Roberts, model (Forsaken Desires www.modelmayhem.com)
Thank you for bringing Lila to life on all book covers!

Bill Edwards, The Tooth Fairy, Royal Wootton Bassett,
Thank you for creating our amazing vampire fangs used on all book covers!

Chapter One

The stairwell was very high and I was at the top level of the building. Okay, so ten stories doesn't sound that high, but I'm afraid of heights. Pathetic, isn't it?! Well, it's not all that irrational a fear because falling from a great height will, of course, kill you in a pretty nasty way. High stairwells are the worst especially when you can see all the way down to the bottom if you peek over the railing. When you're scared of heights... stairs take you up past the height you can tolerate and then you're forced to walk back down them, knowing that drop is just ahead of you. One stumble or trip and you're going dowwwn.

Anyway, so there you have it. Oh, don't worry, that's not all I'm scared of. I'm also terrified of lifts. Hence why right now I'm staring down towards hell from a great height wishing I'd never got out of bed this morning. What a choice – climb into a too-small box and plummet at speed relying on a single cable to stop you at the bottom (assuming it doesn't get stuck between floors or something like in the movies) or walk down, watching that dizzying drop just ahead the whole time.

Anyway, as I faced the stairwell which descended inextricably through the floor as if sinking into hell… I asked myself why I let myself get talked into going to the top floor. It wasn't for anything specific, just this feeling that I should try it at least once. The building had been grabbing my attention each time I passed it. And every time that urge to go inside, and up to the top floor, grew stronger. So today, I said to myself, go to the top floor for once in your pathetic life, Lila Casey, and see what wonders it holds… so I did. Mistake number one. Well to be fair, I've made more than one mistake in my life but this one seems like the biggie right at this moment.

Worse still that this dare came from me personally. There was no smug friend waiting at the bottom feeling certain I wimped out. I just got angry with myself staring up at the highly modern, glass building yet again. Why was I fascinated with this building? Why was I so scared of heights and stairs? Why had I had so many nightmares about them all my life?! Most people are scared of actual things, which seem more real, or likely… like the dark, monsters, ghosts, muggers, etc. But stairs?! The looks I have had from people over the years when I've said that. Especially when I follow it up with 'oh and lifts'. Did I really think I could live a life only on the bottom floor of everything?!

Anyway, see what I'm doing now? Stalling. Overthinking it. I have to get back down to the ground floor. That's where the street is and my walk home and

2

well, everything else. I'm not really hyperventilating… just breathing fast shallow breaths, which make me feel really light-headed… okay so I *am* hyperventilating. Sue me.

I sat in a plush leather seat in the expensive white lobby, which faced away from those stairs. Surely nobody would mind if I took a moment… A well-dressed, young, pretty woman approached me from behind the reception desk.

"Miss, are you okay? Do you have an appointment with Mr Drake?" I stared at her with spotty vision. She asked again with a doubtful look on her face, and I sucked in a deep breath to try and clear my head.

"I'm sorry. Wrong floor. I just need a minute." I gasped with what I hoped was my 'sorry to be any trouble' face. She pursed her lips at me, irritated. To her I was obviously just a time waster, not worth her valuable time – she was very perceptive…unfortunately.

"Well this is a busy office so don't loiter too long or I'll have to call security." She sniped as she walked away. I bit back a snappy retort. It wasn't her fault she was a lousy human being. Actually, it probably was, but still I decided to give her the benefit of the doubt. Besides I had no breath to snap back with yet.

While I waited for my panic to pass I watched the people come and go. My stupid dare had made me wander into a busy office full of very smart, attractive professional-looking young people. Typical – I couldn't pick somewhere full of mediocre-looking people dressed all in black, could I? No… nowhere I'd actually fit in. I caught my reflection in the modern glass table to my left. Longish black hair (well I was a redhead underneath the

3

black dye and the vivid red of several stripy sections), black eyeliner (not thick, goth black but just enough to try and emphasise my dark eyes) ... there really wasn't much else going on with my face but I could see why the woman had to check on me. I know the panic had made me pale and the black hair only made that look more shocking. Why had I dyed it black this week? Because I'd wanted to try it for so long, that's why. Another idea backfired...

I stood up and took a deep breath. Time to face my nightmare and head down those terrifying stairs. I heard a conversation behind me. The words 'crazy goth chick' were muttered and I grinned involuntarily. Finally, I had an identity. Okay, not really the one I'd have aspired to but still... take what you can get, that's what I say. As I turned to face those hell-bound stairs I walked into someone big. He grabbed me to stop me falling down and thankfully saved me from looking even more moronic. As I looked up into his face time stopped. Okay that's silly. What I mean is I forgot to breathe for a while. When I started again I gasped and he looked at me with concern.

"Miss, are you okay? Do you need help?" I tried to smile and shook him off.

"I'm fine, really. Please tell your boss not to worry. I'm not casing the place or planning to steal all his money. I just need to get back down there which should be easy but unfortunately for me these stairs are pure evil". Never babble like an idiot when you meet the hottest guy you've ever seen. I mean, really? Now he just knows I'm a crazy goth chick. And I'm not even a goth. He laughed.

4

"Don't worry about my money, I'm sure it's perfectly safe. Let's see about getting you down without having to brave these evil stairs though." He guided me firmly to an office and closed the door behind us. I looked around. Oh crap, he *is* the rich boss! Just my luck! Still if I'm going to faint into someone's arms, could I find hotter ones?

"Sorry to be rude, but I'm pretty sure this isn't downstairs…" I looked around the opulent office and grimaced. Could I be more out of place? In response, he handed me a glass of water. The glass was ornately carved and the light from the many windows shone through it and made patterns on my hand. I sipped a little water and let him direct me to a seat. A plush, cream, expensive-looking seat, which I immediately cheapened by sitting on it. He sat opposite me on a perfectly matched chair, leaning forward with his elbows on his knees.

"So, miss… um… I'm not sure 'crazy goth chick' is your actual name…."

I somehow smiled calmly, all the while mortified that this god of a man called me that. Damn that receptionist.

"I normally just go by Lila these days but your lovely receptionist wasn't to know that, bless her." Immediately I was mad at myself. What if that was his girlfriend and I've just insulted her? He laughed though, thankfully. Oh, what a wonderful sound when he laughs… and oh my God, I'm getting a crush… and tingles pretty much everywhere…

"Look I'm sorry about that. I was a bit out of sorts but I'm feeling tons better now and I really must go.

Thank you for your time. I imagine you're a very busy man." I stood up and handed the still full glass back to him, heading for the door before I could embarrass myself any more and wow, I must have zoned out crushing on him because he somehow beat me to the door. His hand covered the door handle before I could grab it.

"Please don't run. My next appointment has just been cancelled so I'm not busy at all. I'm actually enjoying the break from my routine."

His smile was huge and beautiful and I floundered for a moment. Where was I going? And for that matter, what was my name again? He leaned against the wall beside the door and folded his arms comfortably. At least they looked comfortable but who was I to judge without testing them myself? He grinned.

"Do you have some kind of inner monologue going on or are you just on something?" I laughed involuntarily, then blushed with shame, then laughed again but this time weakly.

"Sorry. My mind was elsewhere. I really do have to go." I reached for the door handle but his hand caught my wrist suddenly. I looked up into his deep blue eyes. How was I supposed to look away from them? He was so beautiful, chiselled and clean-shaven with neatly styled, light brown hair.

"I thought you wanted to go um... down?" He asked quizzically while I pondered his choice of words.

"Um... the stairs from hell are thataway right?" I pointed to the door.

He laughed as he led me away from the door and to a set of doors on the opposite wall, which I'd failed to spot while intermittently zoning out and being a weirdo.

"Oh. What's that?" I asked as he pressed a silver button on the wall. As the doors slid open to reveal a large lift, I got the idea and taking a deep breath and praying not to die in a freak lift-cable-snapping-incident, I stepped in. He stepped in with me.

"Oh, do I have to be escorted out?" I asked bewildered and, to be honest, a little flustered. He grinned as he leaned over and jabbed the button for the ground floor.

"No not at all. I just wanted to make sure you didn't freak out and break my lift or anything." The doors whooshed closed and I heard a quiet chuckle from him. Oh, so I was a joke?

"Hey, you don't know me, pal. For your information, I happen to have a very rational fear of heights, stairs and lifts. Yes, I know crazy goth chick and all that. But for the record, it's not goth anyway. It's steampunk. Or at least it would be if I wore the right clothes for steampunk but since all I did was the hair and my nails, I'm just a creepy freako so get used to it. Actually don't, cos the lift will stop at the bottom in a minute and I'll be gone. All without breaking your lift too." I really should learn when to breathe and shut up. Actually, learning to shut up is the most important one. Unfortunately, it usually takes me running out of breath to accomplish that though so sadly for me they're a package deal really.

He surprised me then because he jabbed a big red button, which apparently stopped the lift in its tracks and turned to face me. Oh hell, he was going to murder me in his secret lift and nobody would know. And oh wow, did I really care because he was really *hot*… okay seriously, Lila? What's wrong with me? If he's a serial killer I should totally care. I'm pretty sure about that… He waited for me to stop arguing with myself and look at him.

"First of all, breathe. I don't know how you get so many words out with one breath! Are you sure you're human? Second, no I'm not going to axe murder you. See?" He held up his empty hands. "No axe. Third, and this one's the most important, you intrigued me so I wanted to keep you here a few moments longer. I'm sorry if that freaked you out. You just seem so different from every other boring clone up there." He jabbed a finger upward I guess to the top floor. Or maybe the sky but that would be weird so I'm going with top floor.

"I intrigue you? And how did you know I was worried you'd kill me? And I didn't even think of axe murder but now I'm wondering if you've hidden one in the walls or your trousers…. And now you're looking at me like I'm hitting on you!" I went back over my words and I guess they were a bit ambiguous. He laughed aloud and leaned back so his elbows rested on the silver rail which ran around the three walls of the lift. He was wearing a crisp white shirt with grey suit trousers and a bright blue tie, which matched his lovely eyes. When he leaned back like that, I could see a hint of muscles pressing against the white fabric. Oh damn Lila, focus!

"Seriously, how can *that* not intrigue me?! It's like you say everything you think, as you think it… rather than choosing the right words."

8

I thought on that, probably for too long, but hey, it's my head. Maybe he was right. But then again, I wasn't saying these thoughts aloud so maybe not.

"That's quite insulting to be honest and also…. You're a lawyer!" There, I'd figured it out.

"Riiiight… is that supposed to be an insult? Lawyers work hard and make a lot of money and people respect them. But no, I'm not. And that was a pretty short sentence for you, Lila." He used my name?

"Oh, and how is that fair? I don't even know your name, Mr Intrigue." Okay, pretty lame but can't take it back now.

"It's Adam Drake actually. Intrigue is only my middle name and kind of a secret okay?" He was quite sweet, or humouring me. Not sure which but I'll take it.

"Okay Adam I. Drake, but can I go now?" He smiled and stepped towards me, oozing sexy masculinity.

"Are you sure you don't want to talk some more? I have a while 'til my next appointment and I haven't laughed this much in years…"

I stepped back – it was a little intrusive, stepping that close to me but also, he smelled really good and like I said, he's *hot*.

"What if you decide to axe murder me with…"

"-what's in my pants?!? Trust me, I don't carry *that* kind of weapon." His grin was a little dirty which made me smile, as it looked so out of place on his innocent, angelic face.

He stepped closer again and brushed a few hairs away from my eyes. I blinked at him, wondering what he meant by that. The gesture, not the pants comment. That was pretty obvious when you think about it. Which I mustn't… damn…

"What do you want from me?" I whispered. He smiled and stepped back.

"Who says I want anything? Just enjoying your unique perspective on, well, stairs and my murderous desires and the stashing of said weapons."

I grimaced and moved away again, now backed up against the wall of the lift.

"Oh no, you're a psychiatrist, aren't you?" He laughed out loud, throwing his head back a little, his lush brown hair shuffling with the movement. He met my eyes again, his still smiling then looked around to set the lift back in motion.

"Thankfully no, because I think you'd probably be in a bit of a fix if I were." He turned his back and watched the lift move down through the numbers. For just 10 stories it was a slow journey, not counting the few minutes we'd been stationary. I stepped forward again bravely, almost beside him.

"Um thanks for rescuing me from the evil stairs. This hasn't been the most terrifying lift journey I've ever had… which is nice."

He turned to look at me. "Even being trapped with potential axe murderers with secret weapons?" His smile didn't reach his eyes this time. In fact, he looked as if he had suddenly switched off and I'd lost any connection I'd had with him. I was surprised to feel a deep disappointment, which actually made my stomach hurt a little.

The doors swept open and I stepped out, blinking in the ultra bright light of the modern lobby. I turned to thank him again but he'd moved further back and was leaning against the side wall of the lift, arms folded, not looking at me. He looked impossibly young and alone and I realised I had no idea of his age. I walked back into the lift. Am I mental?

"Are you okay?" I asked, reaching a hand out to him. He shied away, only briefly meeting my eyes.

"You're free to go, Miss Lila. Thank you for visiting and entertaining me for a little while." He looked at the buttons of the lift, dismissing me. I felt a wave of panic. Suddenly I didn't want to feel like I'd never see him again.

"You seem so sad. Why don't you take a break with me?" I don't know why I asked him that. No man who looked like him would say yes to me and besides he had an appointment anyway so could only say no. Maybe that's why I was brave enough to ask. He sucked in a breath and looked at me, eyes filled with longing, or at least that's what I'm calling it because honestly when will I ever have the chance to imagine that again?

"I wish I could, but I have to stay. I did enjoy meeting you though." He stepped away from the wall and reached for the 'up' button. My hand covered his (hey, who took control of my hand?) and I stepped closer to him.

"Thank you for rescuing me, Mr Drake. You were very sweet." I stood on tiptoes and kissed his cheek lightly. Yes, you read it right, I kissed his cheek. And it was smooth and warm and I wanted to jump him but I thought that might be frowned upon so I turned and walked away on shaky legs. When I chanced a glance back before I walked out the lobby door, he was standing still with his hand against his cheek as if he treasured it. Yeah, so probably he was trying to wipe my crazy germs away but I'm going with the treasuring thing.

Chapter Two

So by now you'll have figured out that I do kind of have some kind of inner monologue going on but then doesn't everyone? I just choose to include mine as otherwise you'd never understand where the hell my words come from when I speak out loud. Actually, it doesn't always help but I'm hoping one day it will so it'll all have been worth it. Also, while I've not actually been diagnosed with any kind of attention deficit disorder I have to have one. I mean seriously, I can't hold a normal conversation without going off on some weird tangent or getting attracted by something shiny and what did he mean by saying he enjoyed meeting me? Does that mean he likes me? Should I go back? How would I go up those stairs again? What if he's forgotten me already? Oh. Damn. As I was saying.... Nope, sorry it's gone…

Today was totally weird, and I say that as I stir a cup of coffee to take to bed. Yes, I drink coffee in bed. I'd say sue me but I think I may have said that recently so don't want to be repetitive. Besides, there's nothing wrong with drinking coffee in bed. I don't really sleep anyway! Well, some judgemental people say that's why, but I'm sure it's just a coincidence...

Okay so I'm sitting in bed and still thinking about how weird it was meeting Adam Drake. I wasn't sure men who looked like him even existed. I mean I really should be concentrating on the TV but I've seen this episode of *Grimm* so I totally know what's going to happen. Oh, no I haven't. Damn it, rewind....

When I woke the next morning, he was still on my mind but more like a dream version of a man. I mean he wasn't really that amazing surely. Nobody is. He was kind of moody; he laughed at my expense and he lives in a damn tower. That would never work for me. Oh well, to be fair, he probably just works there and lives somewhere else but still that building is scary. Not in the conventional sense or to normal people, but to me. How could something I fear so much contain someone I want to see again so badly? I stretched, relishing the feel of the cool cotton sheets and groaned at the thought of getting out of them and ready for work.

I got to work, more or less, on time. I don't know why my boss gets narky about that – I mean I do a good job and I'm not too disruptive so it should be fine if I'm a few minutes late sometimes. Or most times. I sat at my desk, switched on my computer then wandered to the coffee shop by the cafeteria. It's no *Starbucks* but the coffees are fussy and fancy and I likey. My closest friend, Michelle, was waiting to buy a drink too.

"So, Michelle. As a receptionist, if a random person came to the building unexpectedly and didn't have an appointment and had a panic attack, would you be mean to them?" She stared at me a moment as she mentally replayed my words at a human speed. Luckily, she's totally used to me.

"Depends…. Is he cute?" And there you have it. No use at all. Still I love her most days. Except when she's on one of her crazy diets; then she's no fun and also when she drinks espressos instead of lattes because that means she gets cranky so that's also no fun.

"No, he's a girl." I said and she just stared at me, and then flipped her luscious curly blonde hair back in her trademark move.

"Why can't she have the panic attack somewhere else then?" Okay maybe I was too hard on that receptionist yesterday. I walked back to my desk mostly with her. At least until we got to reception and she had to stop. She made me promise to buy a bottle of wine on the way home so she could pop round and help me drink it. I'm sure she felt she was doing me a favour there, bless her. I don't even really like wine, so it was a pretty selfish suggestion when you think about it.

After checking my emails and finding no inspiration there I stopped by to see my editor, Colm Starkey. He glared up at me. And not because I'm taller but he was sitting down and I'm standing. I sat down but then he just glared across at me so I just can't win.

"You're late again. You arrive late then you disappear to the coffee shop for 20 minutes, Lila. What am I supposed to do with you?" I tried a smile but I don't think it worked because he carried on glaring across at me.

"I'm artistic, Colm. You know that. I can't be bound by the constraints of time." He tried to hide a smirk I'm sure but all I heard was some muttering about 'autistic you mean' which I chose to ignore because I suddenly had a great idea.

"Ooh ooh… there's this new building, well actually it's been there a while, but there's a company at the top of it and it's really secretive, and I should investigate it." Yeah, I forgot to breathe again but how cool if I could investigate Adam Drake… talk about a good reason to stalk him. And by stalk, what I actually mean is… okay yeah, I mean stalk. Can you blame me?

"As I've explained almost every day since you started working here, Lila. You are not a reporter. You are not an investigator. You are writing a psychic predictions column and it'll probably be late as usual. And you can't investigate the offices of Drake Solutions. There's no mystery there." He waved a hand to dismiss me. Apparently, I wasn't done though. Go figure.

"What does he do then?! Because don't go thinking he's a lawyer or shrink. Those would just be silly, random guesses." He gaped at me as if to ask if I was still there which of course I was.

"Seriously? Google it if you're bothered, but I can promise you he just runs an import/export business and he does very well from it. I looked into it when he first moved in there about two months ago. There's no story there. No smuggling, no drugs, no human trafficking. Just art and other valuable arty stuff – nothing newsworthy." He picked up his phone and pointedly started dialling. I debated staying to talk over his call but saw he was dialling security. Really? He was going to do that again?

"They can't throw me out, Colm. I have a staff pass and a contract." I marched out with my head held high. Probably too high as I tripped over a chair leg but still I only stumbled a little.

Yeah so, I have my own column in a real newspaper and no, it's not as cool as a Carrie Bradshaw style column. But let's be serious here for at least a minute. Probably less, knowing me. I don't live in New York. I live in a small town in Wiltshire, England, and also to write a column like hers, I'd have to have a life. Oh, and lots of yummy men to sleep with. Sadly, that life doesn't exist in England and especially not in Wiltshire, which sounds pretty dull, but it isn't I swear. Mostly. The town I live in is like a mini, mini London but mostly seems like London about 20 years ago. It's a little outdated and is heavily populated but some areas are smarter and more modern. Like the area where Adam Drake's building is. Oh wait, I'm supposed to be writing my predictions column. After some rummaging on my messy desk I find my keyboard and rest my hands on the home keys.

It probably sounds lame but I totally believe in fate and star signs and psychic stuff but I don't really do any of it properly. I generally just write what feels right and do my best to make it sound mystical and mysterious. Friends of mine have said it totally came true for them so I must be doing something right. Today, like yesterday, I can't feel anything so I'll just make it up. As long as it's nice and generic it'll be fine. That honestly feels like a total cop out but I just couldn't focus on it again.

I wondered what Adam Drake was doing while I was faking my column. Probably some high-powered businessy stuff. I also wondered what he was wearing – he looked so yummy in that shirt and tie. I debated going out to stare at his building but it was a whole 10-minute bus ride away and besides, it was a bit too stalker-like, even for me. And what if I arrived just in time to see him climbing into a sporty car with a beautiful woman, or even worse, that vicious receptionist? Ugh... that would probably be the most awful thing I could experience. Well, that or going there and being forced to actually use the stairs to come back down. I shuddered at the thought.

Speaking of stairs, I had such freaky dreams last night. I was in a big glass building and stuck at the top of a scary staircase. I know what you're thinking – could yesterday's events have triggered it? But the weird thing is I regularly have horrible dreams about being in buildings or worse, on open walkways where the only way down from a great height is a flight of stairs without proper railings or with huge gaps between steps which have to be jumped across... Bet it doesn't sound as scary as a serial killer dream but trust me they are horrifying. And sometimes there *is* a serial killer chasing me and my only way out is down those damn steps. Try not to wake up screaming from one of those dreams; I dare you.

Crap, my column. It's lunchtime and I've barely written a single whole prediction. Poor Taurus – it doesn't even make any sense so I'll have to rewrite it or they would be apparently looking for glass buildings and shiny men with sad eyes?!? Jeez... Oh well maybe I'll think better with food in my stomach. Michelle was working different hours this week so I was eating alone. Sometimes a good thing. Sometimes not. *Not,* for example, being today when my mind is too preoccupied to focus on my book. *Not,* definitely being today when the dreaded mutant decided to join me for lunch.

"Hi Lila. Mind if I join you?" He asked, sitting down with his lunch as he spoke. Bit hard to say no now but I really tried.

"Yes, I mind. Go away." He smiled.

"You don't mean that." He unwrapped his Panini (not as rude as it sounds I promise) and tucked in with a smirk.

"Reading another one of your lame vampire books?" He asked, one eyebrow arched, disappearing into his floppy dark hair. Oh yuck, he thought he was so hot. Admittedly so did I a while back, but a few months of seeing him and I really saw him... up himself, arrogant and selfish. He still kept sniffing around me though. I'd be flattered if it wasn't so creepy.

"Not that you know how, but reading is good for the mind and for the soul and go away you're putting me off my food." One breath well spent I decided as I picked up my eBook again and pointedly gazed at it. I could hear him crunching something in his sandwich and it grossed me out.

"Okay, Nick. What. Do. You. Want?" Might as well get it over with so he could go away. He smiled a bit smugly, although I suppose I could be biased, then wiped his face with his serviette and balled up the paper from his food. Yuck, I forgot how quickly he could inhale his food.

"Look I don't normally do this but I thought I would take you out tonight and remind you of what a good time we always have together. You look really cool with the goth hair and I thought it might be hot." I gagged a little and switched off my eBook to give him my full attention.

"Why the hell would I want a mercy date from you? You think I can't get a date? I can get dates, I get them all the time and to be honest you are a pig. I mean look at you, where the hell is your lunch already? It's been 5 minutes, Nick. You're gross and disgusting and yeah okay you're fairly hot to look at and you're good in bed mostly but honestly you just completely repulse me." I was proud of my vaguely coherent put down and decided to get out while the going was good. He reached out and grabbed my arm.

"Come on, if you remember how good I was in bed, you probably think about it a lot. Remember how much fun we had? We can have that again. I've never…" I cut him off there. I didn't want to hear any more and would rather go out for a walk than put up with him.

"I have to go, Nick. People to go, places to…. Oh, forget it." As I walked away I unfortunately heard the real reason for his renewed interest.

"Come on. I've never done it with a goth before."
Git.

I pictured him choking on his lunch but that just grossed me out and besides, he'd eaten it already. I stalked out of the building and marched down the street with purpose. Well actually, without any purpose. Where the hell was I going?

I had 25 minutes left of my lunch and couldn't go back in without bumping back into Nick again. A voice in my mind reminded me that it was just 10 minutes by bus to Drake's office. A quick glance at the bus timetable pointed out the very logical fact I'd failed to consider. The buses were 15 minutes apart and the next one wasn't for another 10 minutes so I wouldn't make it there and back without being late again. Probably not the best idea after Colm's little moan this morning. With the decision made for me, I slumped on the bench at the bus stop and wished I'd driven my car in that day. Of course, it was sitting on my drive with a dead battery but otherwise it would have been a great idea. I leaned back against the faux glass shelter and closed my eyes with a sigh. Why was I so caught up in Adam Drake and what he was doing right now? I only met him for a few minutes and since then he'd occupied my every thought. I even didn't feel my usual urge to slap Nick because I wasn't really concentrating on him at all. Which I think made my put downs pretty impressive in their own right, when you think about it.

Someone sat beside me on the bench and I kept my eyes closed so they wouldn't feel the need to converse with me. A man sighed and I groaned.

"I swear if that's you, Nick, I'm going to punch you in the…"

"Axe?" A male voice asked, in horror. My eyes flew open and I turned to face Adam Drake. At a bus stop; sitting right beside me. What the hell?

"Mr Drake? What's wrong? Did your big expensive sports car break down?" He just stared at me. I'd forgotten how he does that. He just stares and waits for me to beg the ground to open and swallow me. Which it never does, of course – that would be too easy!

A grin curved across his face and he pointedly leaned back with his eyes closed as if mocking me. Yeah it worked. Consider me fully mocked. He stayed silent and I took the opportunity for a full-on stare. He really was incredibly beautiful, with smooth, lightly tanned skin, full lips and brown hair you just want to run your hands through… and again I had that urge to jump him but I decided to be sensible and hold back. He was wearing another lovely grey suit and white shirt, this time with a dark red tie.

"Oh, please tell me you didn't happen to come here just to say 'axe' then ignore me and walk away?" He grinned again but didn't move or open his eyes.

"So, what are we doing here, Miss Lila? Are we waiting for the bus to take you to my building? Or are we waiting for something more mundane like say… your lunchtime to run out?" I gasped and looked at him. How did he know I was on lunch? Did he see my argument with Nick? Oh crap, did he see me checking the timetables for stalker possibilities?

Embarrassing…

He sat up suddenly and turned to look me in the eye.

"You don't have to think about me so hard you know. I *am* right here." He smoothed his lovely hair back as if it was bothering him but it just looked cute.

"I'm not thinking about you. I don't even know you. I'm thinking about someone else." He looked down the street to where a certain arrogant looking git was standing watching us, and then turned in the seat to face me.

"Nick, I presume? Shall I leave you alone so you can see your boyfriend?" I laughed when I saw how annoyed Nick looked.

22

"Oh, that's hilarious, look at his face. Annoying, stuck up, snotty, arrogant, selfish..."

"Do you plan on finishing this sentence *ever*?" Adam interjected with an easy laugh. He reached over and smoothed my hair like he did yesterday. Seriously, did my hair need that much smoothing? It was a fairly tidy shoulder length cut and I did use my GHD straighteners this morning so I was pretty sure it wasn't sticking up. I caught his hand before it fell.

"What did you do that for?" He blinked as if he didn't understand the question. "I uh... wanted to." Hmmm that's straight to the point. I was suddenly tempted to lick his hand and say, 'I'd wanted to' do that but that might have been a bit too weird even for me. At least this early in our relationship. Well, probably...

"So, is he a jealous boyfriend? Will I get my face rearranged by him in a minute?" Adam asked casually. I stared at him.

"You'd probably still look hot no matter what arrangement your face was in. Oh, except upside down... then again maybe you could pull that look off too..." He laughed and stood up.

"Come with me." I stood with him and we walked back towards the newspaper. How did he know? He took my hand as we walked and I'm sure we looked like a couple and it made me feel a little light-headed and at the same time smug when I saw the gutted, annoyed look on Nick's face. As we reached the door, Adam kissed my hand softly like a gentleman out of one of those old films. It was really romantic.

"I'll meet you here at 5pm." He started to give my hand back, seemingly reluctant to let go.

"Why?" I asked, confused.

"Isn't that when you finish? It's when most jobs in office type environments finish." I snatched my hand back from him.

"Why?" I asked again.

"Well, it has a lot to do with each company's contracted office hours. Some start and finish earlier but I took a risk that this isn't one of them." I glared at him and grabbed the door.

"Well, if you're going to be a smart-ass…"

"I'll still meet you at five and if you're working later I'll just wait." He laughed breezily as he walked away. He stopped beside Nick briefly and said something. I wasn't sure what it was but Nick actually paled and took a step back. He warily watched Adam leave and then walked towards me.

"If you were into total psychos you should have just said so in the first place." Then he shoved me away from the door and stalked past. I was confused but also almost late back from lunch and I'd already decided after this morning's chat that may not be a good idea, so I ignored him.

Chapter Three

t 5.10pm, when I decided I'd made him wait
enough, I headed out. I actually finished at
4.45pm so it was a long wait, but I stayed and
kept Michelle company even though she kept telling me
to get lost because she was busy. We finished with me
saying I was meeting someone so I wouldn't be home
early tonight or I might be but would probably forget the
wine anyway so maybe she should 'bite me' (a favourite
phrase of mine). We both laughed as I left.

There was a sleek black car parked outside. Not a
limo or a sports car but something that looked expensive,
masculine and dangerous. Don't expect me to know what
it was though. Seriously I barely know anything about
my own car. Apart from the fact that it's also black
(when it's clean that is) and it currently has dead battery
which, it turns out, doesn't fix itself no matter how long

you leave it sitting there. The passenger window wound down and Adam leaned over from the driver's side to look at me.

"You coming?" I grinned.

"No, it's just the way I'm standing." Oh, my god, did I really just say that? He laughed though so I got in. He was still dressed in the grey suit he wore earlier when I saw him. I liked it – I'd say he smouldered in it but that sounds worse than my attempt at a chat-up line, so I won't. I'm still thinking it though…

He pressed the button to close the tinted window on my side and started the engine. I fastened my seat belt and he peeled out into the traffic with a jolt of speed before slowing down to a crawl in the rush hour queues.

"Feel better, Speedy Gonzales?" I asked, knowing he had been showing off. He grinned and fiddled with the dials on his radio 'til a rock song filled the car. It wasn't too loud to speak but I liked it. A thought occurred to me.

"What did you say to Nick earlier?" He glanced at me then turned his eyes back to the road as he negotiated a lane change, which really didn't need that level of concentration at about 5mph. "Nothing much." He mumbled. I grabbed his arm. It was tight and muscular, but I didn't let it distract me. Not much anyway.

"He was pretty freaked out and even madder at me than before. And he was already pretty damn mad at me to start with, but mostly cos he's a jerk and I reminded him of that. Weird really, because surely other girls have told him that too…" He pulled his arm free and turned down a side street which was free of traffic.

26

"I just told him to stay away from you or I'd punch his lights out." He said casually. I thought about it. Nick looked pretty freaked for a threat to be punched out but then he was a wuss so maybe it made sense.

"That's all you said? He looked terrified." Adam laughed as he steered out onto a country lane and floored it. "Guess I really sold it then." We rushed along at a fast pace while I realised I had no idea where we were going.

"Where are we going? And why would he be terrified at the thought of you punching him? I thought all men relished the thought of fisticuffs over a girl?" Adam laughed again and turned the music up louder. I took it to mean 'shut up' so settled back and listened to the classic rock music as we dashed along darkened lanes and around poorly lit corners. It occurred to me to tell him to slow down but he wouldn't hear me anyway. Eventually I turned the music off when a song finished and leaned forward to try and see his face. With the dark roads and no headlights to reflect on his face, he was just a shadow and I felt a shiver as I finally considered the fact that I was in a car out in the middle of nowhere with a man I knew nothing about. I should so know better! He might not be an axe murderer but he could still be a psycho... Had I made a terrible mistake? Oh hell...

"Stop! Stop the car right now." I shouted, making him jump. He looked at me with a frown, confused.

"What for?" I tried the door handle but it was locked. I gasped and looked back at him, panic coming over me pretty quickly now. That's how you go from normal to freaking out in a few seconds.

"Please let me out. Adam, please!" He slowed down and smoothly pulled into a lay-by I hadn't seen coming. He turned to face me and switched on the interior light.

"My god, Lila, what's wrong? You look like you've seen a ghost." He reached out to brush my hair aside but I pulled back.

"Who the hell are you? Where are we and what are you going to do to me?" My breaths were little gasps as I realised how stupid I'd been. I'd trusted him just because he was hot, smartly dressed and seemed nice but then that's how they get you isn't it, the psychos? They look all yummy then trick you into a dark corner and pull out knives and dental instruments. He smiled softly. Uh-oh...

"I'm Adam, remember? And I'm just taking you to my house. I wanted to make you dinner. What happened? Why are you suddenly so afraid?" Staring into his calm rational face I felt crazy and irrational. It wasn't like he was an evil flight of stairs. He was a cute guy taking me on a date. I couldn't stop the trembles I felt from my panic attack and I covered my face with my hands. He gently pulled them away and held them in his warm grip.

"Please don't fear me, Lila. I would never do anything to hurt you. I just can't stop thinking about you and it's making me a little less coherent than usual. I'm really a highly intelligent businessman in real life." He leaned forward and placed a soft kiss on my forehead, before brushing my hair back soothingly. I relaxed and leaned back in the car seat. Panic drifted away as if it had never existed and in its absence, I felt a bit silly. Not unusual for me but still embarrassing.

"I'm so sorry, Adam. I don't know what the hell got into me. I just had a sudden panic that you might still be an axe murderer or something." He grinned showing lots of teeth.

"You mean with the weapon I stash in my pants? Haven't we already had this conversation?" He messed with the stereo until something soothing started playing... something classical and forgettable but relaxing nonetheless. I didn't worry as he switched off the interior light and moved back out onto the road. He drove slower and took corners with more care.

"Sorry if my driving scared you. You were right earlier. I was showing off a bit. I just love these twisty roads and wanted to have some fun with it." He took my hand and drove one-handed the rest of the way. I'm not sure it was safer but it felt nice and kept me relaxed.

After maybe a half hour drive in total, he pulled up at a set of ornate, tall, dark metal gates and pressed a button on a keypad, which he suddenly held in his hand. I hadn't noticed it before now. The gates shuddered open and we drove up a long gravel drive to a house. Well he would probably call it a house but I call it WOW how huge is this place? I mean seriously, it's like a manor house, and really well maintained and suits his apparent wealth. It's kind of gothic looking but not in a scary way, just really beautifully designed with lots of curves and angles and really ornate windows. It was up lit with lights on the ground and looked cosy and welcoming.

"Just how rich are you?" I asked, only noting as I spoke just how rude it was to ask.

"I'm comfortable. My business does pretty well." I shared a smug smile with him.

"The import/export business you mean?" He nodded briskly, helping me out of the car and leading me to the front door. A man opened it. He didn't look like a butler but he acted as if he was welcoming royalty into the house. He was respectful and polite. He called me Miss Lila, but then that's how Adam introduced me.

"It's just Lila, really." I protested as he disappeared into a room along the large, opulent corridor. Adam helped my coat from my shoulders while I tried to not drop my handbag, then he spirited it away somewhere and reappeared beside me. Taking my hand, he led me along the hall, around and under the large, curving staircase and into a big, well lit kitchen full of huge stainless steel appliances. He rolled up his sleeves as he directed me to a seat at the breakfast bar area.

"Now. What can I serve you, Miss Lila? I make a mean beans on toast, cheese on toast or um… soup, wait for it… with toast!" He finished with a big grin. I laughed and pretended to consider the options he'd presented. It was cute that he couldn't cook much – I guess the butler guy normally did the kitchen stuff for him.

"Well cheese on toast sounds amazing. Can I help?" He waved me away.

"Don't worry, I promise I won't burn it. Coffee? Beer? Wine?" He gestured towards the opposite side of the kitchen to the coffee machine and fridge. I stood up and walked over to the coffee machine, which was already hissing over a full carafe of coffee. The smell of the percolating coffee was delicious and I took in a deep, appreciative breath.

"You're not used to doing the kitchen work, are you?" I reached for two coffee cups and poured our drinks. Adam swooped over with sugar and milk and delivered a generous dollop of each to his before sipping it. I did the same. I could smell bread becoming toast behind him. We stared at each other while we sipped our coffee and said nothing. At some point, Adam dumped his cup on the counter with a curse and rushed over to rescue the burning toast and finish the 'cooking'.

Later as we sat at the breakfast bar, digesting our slightly burned cheese on toast and on our second cups of coffee, I realised how perfect our simple dinner had been. I'm not one for fussy foods and posh ingredients and cheese on pretty much anything is a favourite of mine.

"So, been cooking long?" I asked with a smile as I took a sip of coffee.

"Well, let's just say I don't usually burn it and leave it at that eh? I don't normally have such a distracting guest." He waggled his eyebrows at me and I giggled.

"There's more to you than I think, isn't there? I mean, you're not just a normal businessman, and you're way to young to have all this fortune from your business. Who are you?" His eyebrows drew together as he put his coffee down and leaned back, hands flat on the table in front of him.

"That's probably a longer story than we have time for tonight. What do you want from me?" He asked. It wasn't quite the same question I'd asked him then but I had asked it of him before. I had no idea what to say so unfortunately the truth came out.

"I want dazzling passion and excitement and I want it with you." I shook my head and looked down. "How do you make me do that?" He tilted his head, although his grin made it look funny rather than quizzical. "Make me tell the truth? I should have said something flirty and breezy and you would have been impressed at how cool I was. At least in an ideal world. Instead I was really sappy and practically threw myself at you." I dipped my head in embarrassment and caught sight of my watch. It was almost 7pm already. Should I just make my excuses and go home before I made things even worse? How would I get home? He lifted my chin with two fingers and looked into my eyes, fixing that brilliant blue gaze on me.

"All I ever want from you is the truth, Lila. You don't need to hide anything, fabricate truths or miss out on what you want. If you want dazzling passion, I'll take you to my bed right now and give you just that, all night. If you want to go home, of course I'll take you home, but I prefer the first option, just so you know. I know we only met yesterday but you've been on my mind ever since and I can't seem to think of anything or anyone else. How are you doing that to me?"

I was still shuddering inside at the 'take me to his bed' part of his sentence and didn't really answer or if I did, embarrassingly it was probably a moan or a grunt. Either one mortifying beyond belief.

"Why me?" I eventually asked, standing up and walking to the coffee machine for more, although honestly it was really just an excuse to put some distance between us. Giving myself a chance to cool back down. After pouring another cup, I turned to listen to his answer and I was shocked to find him right there in front of me as I moved; our bodies almost touching and the heat from him reaching out towards me. I put a hand on his chest to try and put breathing space between us.

"What are you?" I asked. He stepped back with a look of dismay. "I'm a man. A man completely taken with a beautiful woman. I just want to kiss you." I looked up into his gorgeous blue eyes and didn't stop him as he stepped closer again; placing his hand on my left cheek before he lowered his full lips to mine. They were scorching hot and he took possession of my mouth in a surge of intensity. His tongue massaged mine and I moaned as I lost myself in his passion. He really wasn't kidding about that. I was betting that a visit to his bed would leave me in either a daze or a coma. At that moment in time, I really didn't mind which. A polite cough interrupted us and we stepped apart with embarrassment.

"Adam, I've made up the guest room as requested. I'm going to turn in now unless there's anything more you need?" Adam thanked him and said goodnight. The butler guy looked at him sharply. "Are you sure, Adam?" He seemed to be hinting at something but whatever it was, Adam waved him away and said everything was fine. The butler guy shook his head then disappeared as silently as he'd appeared. We stared at each other, panting slightly, cheeks flushed as we took in what he'd said.

"Guest room?" I asked in surprise. He dipped his head as if embarrassed. "Unless you want to share with me?" He said shyly. I shook my head and turned to gulp some coffee. I needed to wake up my senses before I made a wrong decision.

"I'm not staying in your room *or* your guest room, Mr. Presumptuous! You need to take me home. I'm not some strumpet who sleeps over on the first date. I've got morals." To be honest, when I think about it I don't have that many, but yeah, I had to at least argue at his controlling behaviour. He's just planning a sleepover without even talking it through? I tried to hide how much I wanted to stay. I mean it's the principle of the thing, right?

"It's getting late and the roads back are not safe in this weather." I marched to the window to argue and was stunned to see a thick carpet of snow on the ground. It had been cold when we'd left but this was ridiculous. It was late January so in UK weather systems it was totally possible but still it threw me.

"SNOW? When the hell did it start to snow??!" He laughed as he joined me at the window. "It was already snowing when we arrived here. Didn't you notice?" I stared at him. Could I really be that wrapped up in him that I'd miss the fact that it was *snowing*? Yeah, obviously, I could.

"Well then, I guess I'll be needing that guest room please." I mumbled shyly. Lucky for me he had a big house. He gave me a tour then. There was an actual 'drawing room', although it was really nothing more than a nice polite looking sitting room. There was a library full of books older than me. "Anything from this century?" I joked as we left the room. There was a formal dining room, an office, and a room with a massive TV and several sofas aligned towards it and lots of other technology. Then he led me upstairs to a corridor with many doors. He pointed to a door at the end of the hall.

"That's my room. If you need anything at all during the night, wake me. Please don't feel you can't." I smiled shyly and followed him into the next room he gestured to. It was a beautifully decorated bedroom, which just made me want to moan at how 'me' it was. Pale grey floral patterned walls with heavy, dark red curtains at the window and over the four-poster bed which dominated the room. There was a large dark wooden wardrobe on one side of the room and a door to what I guessed would be an en-suite bathroom. It had a lovely large claw-footed bathtub and a separate shower cubicle as well as, obviously, a toilet and sink. It was grey marble with, again, dark red curtains and shower curtain.

"Wow. This is just the guest room?" He grinned as he opened the wardrobe and showed me extra bedding, pillows and even clothing. "This is your room, Lila. For tonight at the very least."

Chapter Four

He loitered in the room for a few minutes but seemed at a loss so said goodnight and left somewhat reluctantly it seemed. When the door closed, I looked around me and smiled. I could totally get used to this. What a heavenly place. And there was a gorgeous angel just down the hall. I looked at the clothing in the wardrobe. There was a white nightgown of some kind of silky cotton and a bathrobe. I grabbed both and headed into the bathroom. No sense in not giving that bathtub a try out. There were bottles of heavenly designer scents so I set the water running, adding a healthy dollop of bubbles.

It was so quiet in the house and I felt oddly at home. I finished my lovely soak in the bath and dried off, putting on the nightgown and bathrobe. Now this is probably going to sound weird but I always carry spare underwear in my handbag. It's not a one-night-stand kind of thing. You just never know when something will go wrong, like a scary flight of stairs or an attack of the womanly curses so I always carry a clean pair. I didn't want to wear them now though or what would I wear to work tomorrow? In the end, feeling deliciously naughty, I went without. The nightgown was floor length and I was alone so what harm would it do? Also, I couldn't work out why I kept thinking of what I was wearing as a *nightgown* but it just looked like one. No other word seemed formal enough.

As I stepped back into the bedroom the first thing I noticed was a mug of steaming coffee by the bedside. Who knew I liked coffee in bed? As I reached for it with a gasp of delight, a quiet laugh sounded from behind me. Adam, dressed in a white t-shirt and grey pyjama trousers, was sitting on the padded window seat with a book in his hands. He looked so fresh and young and beautiful. I told my hands to stay firmly wrapped around the mug I was holding and tried to forget I was (yikes) naked beneath the nightgown. And there I go again… nightgown?

His eyebrows quirked at me as if he could read my mind and I sat hurriedly on the bed, carefully pulling my legs up to one side and placing the long skirt over me as prudishly as possible. He closed the book and set it aside, then leaned forward with his elbows on his knees.

"Nice bath?" He asked such an innocent question but my cheeks burned as if he'd asked me something intimate. Could he tell I wasn't wearing underwear? Then again, there wasn't any here in the wardrobe so maybe he was just assuming. It was probably all part of his evil plan to seduce me.

"Where did you go?" He asked, standing up to walk over and sit on the bed beside me. I looked at him with bewilderment.

"You disappear into your mind sometimes and I just have to wait for you to come back to me. What did you decide when you left me just then?" His mouth smiled but his eyes looked worried.

I tried not to stare at his lips but they entranced me and I zoned again, this time coming back to find those lips on mine. His hands were on my cheeks, gently turning my face to his. Our breath mingled as our lips caressed each other and I honestly wanted to just give in and let him think I was easy because he was drowning me with his intensity. He pulled back and that's when I realised he'd taken my coffee away first and had placed it by the bed. I mean, thank god he did or I'd have been scalded by it. I don't recall him doing that but to be fair my mind was on other things. I was glad he'd pulled back now because I needed to think. Was I going to do this? Sleep with a guy I'd just met? Because it honestly felt like that's exactly what I was about to do.

"Whoa a minute. Let me think." I held up my hands and he leaned back, lying flat on his back on the bed with his arms tucked behind his head, his muscles straining against his tight T-shirt.

"Okay I really can't think when you're looking like that!" I mumbled under my breath. "Like what?" He asked with a grin, though how he heard me was just typical of my luck... And he so knew how hot he looked like that – he had to, right?

"Forget it. Look, Adam I need to ask you something and I need a straight, simple answer. Can you do that?" The grin faltered briefly then slipped back across his face.

"Sure…" He replied cautiously. I leaned on the bed alongside him, lying on my stomach, hands under my chin.

"Do you actually like me as a person? Or is it just sex you're looking for?" I blinked at how openly I'd just asked that question, but then I thought what the hell… time to hear the truth.

His eyes seemed to almost change colour in the light but I think I was just freaking out waiting for his answer. He cleared his throat.

"Firstly Lila, you utter a sentence with the word 'sex' in it anywhere and any normal guy is going to forget the rest of it but I see where you're going with this. So here comes the truth." I almost grinned but was too worried about what was coming next. I suddenly didn't want to know. What if he just wanted one night with me? He sat up on his elbows and looked deeply into my eyes.

"I really, really want to have sex with you right now. All night." I felt my heart drop, while his words affected me differently in other places. "And again tomorrow and the day after and the day after and so on forever." He finished with a smile. "I don't think you get it, Lila. I don't just invite girls to my home. There's something about you that I can't get out of my head and even though I know you're going to learn all my dirty secrets, I'm not afraid of that because I just want you in my life. Now and always."

I rolled over, away from him and fell back on the bed in shock. Isn't this what I'd always wanted? A hot sexy

40

specimen of a man who wanted me for how hot he thought I was? And who wanted me forever? I mean forever wasn't really possible in real life but we could still have a long life together and was I really thinking this about a man I met yesterday? He slowly leaned over me and looked into my eyes.

"Does that help at all?" His smile was so hopeful I wanted to cry. I also wanted to jump him. I didn't cry.

I leaned up and kissed him and he pressed against me as he took control of the kiss and deepened it. I moaned softly into his mouth and trembled as I felt his hands creep down my face and to my neck. His lips moved to trace a path down my throat and my insides quivered with every touch. He breathed against my skin.

"I want you so much, Lila. Do you want me?" His eyes bored into me as he lifted his face to mine. I didn't think. I just responded.

"Yes." I breathed. His lips descended on mine once more as he began to run his hands down to my hips. As his fingers traced over my hips, they obviously felt what was missing. Something I'd somehow forgotten myself. A delighted grin met mine as he pulled at the nightgown and it started to rise up my legs… past my ankles… up to my knees, then halfway up my thighs. His hand slipped under the hem and he stroked me, making me shudder at his touch. His warm fingers moved between my legs as his lips traced down my throat.

I pulled at his shirt, desperate to feel his warm skin against mine and he helped me lift it over his head. I ran my hands greedily over his muscular chest and traced his nipples with my fingertips. He shivered at my touch then dove on me again, lips at mine, hand between my legs.

41

Together we wriggled me out of the nightgown so I lay naked beneath him and he pulled back for a few moments to just stare at my body, like he was drinking in every detail.

I imagined that his eyes did that weird colour change thing again and he clamped his lips tightly for a moment as if biting back something he wanted to say.

"What?" I asked as I reached for him again. He hissed a little and pulled back, his body trembling as he tried to catch his breath. "Adam, what's wrong?" I pressed against him and tried to pull him back down but he stayed still as if afraid to move. His eyes seemed to fill with something dark and I wondered what could be hurting him so much. I tried to look down at myself – did something gross him out? No I looked fine. Well as fine as I could look. A little desperate perhaps?

"Please Adam, you're scaring me." He laughed bitterly.

"Well, it had to happen sometime." He pushed away from me and stood up; walking a few paces away to catch his breath, sweat glistening on his skin. He had turned from me so I couldn't see his face. His shoulders drooped though and he just looked so sad. While I looked like some kind of whore, draped across the bed, naked and panting and damp with cooling sweat.

"Seriously? This is how you're going to leave me?" I sat up and glared at him, folding an arm over my chest in a too-late attempt at modesty.

"Better than the alternative." He snapped, striding from the room and slamming the door. Unbelievable! Get me all hot and bothered, throwing my morals out of the window then leave me hanging. I snatched up the stupid nightgown to put it on and noticed it was torn almost in half. What the hell? I pulled on the matching dressing gown instead and marched out of the room after him. I headed for his bedroom having heard him slam the door. When I tried to open the door, I discovered it was locked. I banged on the door.

"Adam? Let me in and tell me what the hell is going on! You owe me that much at least!" Abruptly the lock snapped open but the door stayed closed. I took a breath, then walked into his room.

Chapter Five

The room was dimly lit and I could see him standing at the window, the moonlight tracing his outline like a halo.

"Just like an angel…" I muttered almost silently. His shoulders shook as he breathed a heavy sigh.

"Hardly." He said sharply, turning to face me. His profile lit up briefly then his face was in shadow but I'd caught the shine of wetness on his face. Tears? I walked closer to him to see his face.

"How did you hear me? I could barely hear myself."

"I'm no angel, Lila. If that's what you're looking for in me, you should leave this room right now and not come back." He pointed towards the door but I pushed his hand aside, stepping closer.

"I'm not looking for an angel, Adam. I want you and whatever your deep dark secrets are; whatever has you so sad. I get it; you're messed up or something. Well fine, you've listened to me ramble on when my inner monologue escapes. I'm clumsy; I'm socially inept; I'm average looking and for some reason you seem to find me attractive. I don't understand it but I don't want to let this pass me by. No man has ever made me feel the way you do. Okay sometimes I don't have a clue what I'm doing because you seem to overwrite my thoughts but maybe that's how it's meant to be... with the right guy?" He laughed harshly and grabbed at my arms, his fingers biting into my flesh uncomfortably.

"The right guy? Please. I couldn't be further from being the right guy. There's nothing good about me and to be honest my hunger for you was something I should never have allowed even for a minute. It's just leading me down a dangerous path. Dangerous for us both." He shook me lightly with those last words and the light caught his face. I gasped. He looked different somehow... or was it just the light? Were the angles of his face different? Were his lips fuller? I strained to see his face and he pulled me around so he was bathed in the light, letting go as I pulled back in shock. His irises were a softly glowing red and his lips were tightly pressed together but his mouth was different somehow. His cheeks looked sharper - almost gaunt.

"What's going on? Talk to me please. I don't understand what's happening, Adam?" He opened his mouth to speak and I fainted in his arms.

Chapter Six

I woke in his bed, with nobody beside me. It was light outside, suggesting I'd slept through the night, and I was alone in a strange bed in a strange room. A darkly masculine room with a lingering scent of Adam's cologne on the bedding. I stretched, luxuriating in the plush comfort of his bed.

A flashback from the night before shook me and I sat up with a whimper. I'd dreamed that Adam was a vampire! Or at least he had fangs. I felt briefly pleased I hadn't had the dream about the stairs but then went back to oh god, is Adam a vampire? He couldn't be though; because of course I'd watched him eat food. I'd seen him out in sunlight and he didn't burst into flames, dissolve into ash or sparkle like diamonds. Perhaps the vampire fiction I have access to isn't helping me that much. There was a knock on the door and I pulled the blanket up hurriedly as the butler guy from last night bustled into the room. He brought coffee and hot buttered toast. He placed it beside me almost unceremoniously then marched out with a sharp door closing which verged on a slam. Stuck up, moody… oh wow I'm hungry.

After polishing off the food and coffee I headed off to the guest room to find my clothes and other belongings. I didn't see Adam anywhere and it was after 6am so I figured I needed to get back to town for work. I didn't want to be late again and imagined awkward conversations with Adam before he'd take me back. I asked the butler guy if I could call a taxi but he just said something about Adam bringing the car back around so I waited outside on the snow-covered doorstep. Back around from where? The sleek black car pulled up outside and the passenger door popped open. I cautiously leaned in to see Adam sitting stony faced in the driving seat.

"Get in." He barked at me. Oh hell no.

"Seriously? You don't get to snap at me! What the hell was up with you last night?" I refused to get in the car and he got out and tried to help (manhandle) me inside. I mean, he would have only had to try a tiny bit harder and I'd be seat belted and on my way. The man is strooooong. My arms hurt and pushing up my sleeves I saw bruises on my upper arms, where he had grabbed me last night. His eyes darkened at the sight.

"Seriously Adam. I need some answers. Did I dream last night?" He grinned briefly, looking more like he had up until that weird moment last night.

"Yep. All just a dream. Let's go to work, Lila." He started to walk away and so I dropped my bag on the floor and very childishly sat on the snowy step with my arms folded. Big mistake because snow equals wet and cold.

"I know this may look like I'm being a brat or having a tantrum or something but seriously, Adam, please, I just need to know what happened last night. I mean at first it was sooo good and I've got to say you really know what you're doing…. But then you went all weird on me and you even kind of looked different if that's possible. Please explain. I just want to understand." He came over to crouch beside me and stroked my hair back lightly.

"I think you know what happened last night but if you can't tell me what it was, I think we should just leave it at that. Probably better for everyone, to be honest." His face was sad and his eyes seemed older and wearier. Did he really think challenging me would work?

"You think I'll just say okay because I'm too scared to say what I think aren't you? You don't know me at all or you'd know that pretty much anything I think finds its way out of my mouth." I glared at him. He just stared at me, blue eyes boring into mine, challenging me.

"Fine. Are you a fucking *vampire*?" I snapped. His eyes widened but I'm not sure if that was the question or the language. Seriously I really do try not to swear, but I was so damn angry with him. His mouth worked for a moment then he laughed a little shakily.

"Wow. You really do come out with just anything, don't you?"

I continued glaring.

"Okay. Yes. You're right. I'm a vampire." The way he said it was almost as if he was humouring me or something, but I just knew it was actually the truth.

"And why did you weird out on me last night? Did I do something to turn you off? I mean you seemed pretty um… up for it?" I was getting to the root of my own fears now. Had I scared him away with my average body? He *was* way too hot for me after all. Oh no… was it that? "Is it that I'm not… attractive enough for you? I know I need to tone up quite a bit." His face was a picture. He laughed despite himself and rubbed a hand across his face.

"What the hell are you on, Lila? No, it was nothing to do with you… or any part of you. You were perfect. It's just… It was… Well … I just wanted so much to bite you… that's what it was. Honestly, I've never said that to someone before. You make me speak the truth. What's up with that?" I was still trembling at the 'him wanting to bite me' part. Here I am, an obsessive fan of vampire fiction, and here's an amazingly hot man who appears to be a vampire who wants my body *and* my blood? Screw work. I'm calling in sick.

Chapter Seven

I made him go back inside with me so we could talk. We both called in sick to work. Well he basically called and told his 'staff' to reschedule his meetings for the day. That must be cool. In the meantime, I did my best to convince Colm I was ill. He hung up halfway through what I was saying so I think it worked. It was still rude though.

We sat in the 'drawing room' and stared at each other a little warily. He was on a sofa and I was in some kind of recliner. It was kind of awkward to talk now he knew I knew what he was, and I knew the guy was either a vampire or just crazy. To be fair, either way he was probably still my type.

"So... vampires?" I started... He smiled.

"Yeah for real. Doesn't that scare you?"

I shrugged.

"I've seen the *Twilight* movies, *Dracula*, *True Blood*, *Moonlight* and *Vampire Diaries*, oh and *Buffy* and *Angel*. I kind of love vampire shows and books."

"That's not really an answer." He muttered looking a bit confused. "Why do you like vampire stuff so much?" He asked with a frown.

I knew he wouldn't like my answer but hey it was honesty time. "It's sexy... romantic... hot..." He grimaced.

"A monster who has to drink human blood to survive is sexy? What's wrong with you?"

"Back at ya, pal. At least I'm not actually a vampire! No, wait, that's a lame comeback. Give me a minute and I can come back with something better.... Um... something about your face..." I pointed as I spoke and he laughed.

"How do you do that? Make me laugh when everything has just gone to crap?"

I shrugged again. "Has it though? Gone to crap, I mean? You've basically outed yourself to a woman who actually finds what you are really hot and isn't scared of you... ooh ooh *and* who will watch endless vampire movies and shows with you. I'm basically your perfect woman." I moved over to sit beside him on the sofa. The next part of our conversation went something like this:

Me: "Have you ever killed anyone?"
Him: "Yes."
Me: "Did you mean to kill them?"
Him: "No."
Me: "How often do you have to drink blood?"

Him: "Pretty much daily unless I get excited then I burn it up faster and need more."

Me: "So if we have sex you'll need to drink my blood too?"

Him: "Don't say that. It sounds so…"

Me: "-hot? Sexy?"

Him: "I was going to say gross and exploitative."

Me: "Are you immortal? Will you live forever?"

Him: "Immortal, yes, in the sense that I won't age or die naturally, but I can be killed."

Me: "Stake through the heart?"

Him: "Bad."

Me: "Sunlight?"

Him: "Really, Lila? We were just outside!"

Me: "Ahem…Holy water?"

Him: "Burns like acid. Just kidding, it's just water, but drinking it would be disrespectful, of course."

Me: "Decapitation?"

Him: "Hurts like hell."

Me: "Seriously?"

Him: "Only kills us if the head is immediately taken as far away as possible."

Me: "Like a metre?"

Him: "How is that as far away as possible?!"

Me: "Okay… Like a mile?"

Him: "That could work…"

Me: "What? Your head would walk back to your body??!"

Him: "Not walk, really. Doesn't have legs, does it?"

Me: "(frustrated sound)" I mean seriously how would you spell a frustrated scream/growl/moan??

We sat together quietly for a while absorbing our weird conversation. I was fixated on the whole blood drinking thing I'm embarrassed to say, but as a vampire-obsessed freak, why wouldn't I be?

"So…. Um I'm totally okay with you drinking my blood." I blurted, then blushed. What a stupid thing to say to a vampire! But sadly, it was kind of true. He turned to glare at me.

"That's actually not the most sensible thing to say in my company or that of any vampire. You really should be more careful who you offer your blood to."

"Oh, my god, are there others?"

"Well duh, obviously, there are others! You think I turned myself into a vampire?!?!" His incredulity was hysterical and I couldn't help laughing until he grabbed my shoulders.

"Is this the part where I awkwardly pull my head to the side to expose my neck for you to bite? Oh, and does it hurt or will it make me come like it does in some books…"

He smothered my words with a kiss. It was probably a wise decision. The kiss heated up so fast it was like lighting that magician paper stuff – you know, the stuff that burns up in seconds – whatever that's called. Oh wow, he kisses like a god. Oh wait, not a god, a *vampire*.

After a while I managed to coax him into some light touching, but mostly just over my top. It was a tantalising reminder of the night before but not enough for me. I wanted more. And there you have it, I'm a slut. But he was so hot and he was making me so hot. I pressed against him and put my lips to his ear.

"Please take me upstairs. I want you so much." He moaned against my collarbone as he pressed his face against me.

"I can't. I need to feed soon and I can't take the risk." My heart thumped in my chest. In a good way.

"But I want you to. Can't you show me what it feels like to be fed on?" He smiled as he pulled back.

"Are you asking a hungry vampire to bite you, Lila? That's a bit risky. What if I can't stop myself and drink you dry?!" He said it with a kind of 'mwahaha' voice though so I didn't worry... much. I just wanted his teeth in me so badly. It made me feel like something worse than a slut. What's worse than a slut? I mean is it worse to want him to bite me than to sleep with him so soon? And what if I did both? What kind of whore was I then? I realised he was watching me.

"I'm doing it again aren't I?" I muttered, blushing. He lifted my chin and kissed me.

"Let's go upstairs." He led me up to his room and sat me down on the bed. "Are you sure you want to risk going any further with me? You could have a normal guy."

"Like Nick you mean? He's a complete tw- uh git."

"And you were going to say?"

I blushed. "He's a twat." I said quietly. He laughed and lifted his t-shirt over his head. I only noticed then that he wasn't even dressed in his work suit but a t-shirt and running trousers, trainers, etc. It suited him. He looked so athletic it just looked like truth. He must have been planning to hit the gym before work or something. Oh... now I'm picturing him working up a sweat in the gym...

Chapter Eight

He crouched before me, then grabbed my hands and placed them on his naked torso and I greedily ran them over it. His eyes flickered a little and I looked into them more closely. The colours swirled in a beautiful kaleidoscope pattern.

"My god, your eyes are amazing." I breathed, moving my hands up to his face. "Show me your teeth. Do they get longer like in the movies?" He grinned for me and I watched, as his canines seemed to stretch out although not so much to look like extreme movie or TV vampire fangs. Just like much more pronounced canines with four normal teeth in between. "Huh… I think I've actually seen cocker spaniels with bigger fangs." I laughed. He growled as he stood and yanked me up from the bed and tight against him.

"You'd mock a vampire's fangs? That's like taunting a stripper for the size of his... well, no actually it's worse!"

I gulped.

He looked angry and those teeth suddenly looked so much longer and sharper. His cheeks were normal though, not gaunt like last night. He showed me his swirling colour changing eyes again and gripped my face in both his hands.

"Are you really sure? It's a big deal, you know. And you might hate it."

I shuddered, suddenly feeling like he was just dangling the idea in front of me and was never going to do anything about it.

"Oh, for god's sake just bite me and let me find out." Adam grinned and pushed me suddenly backwards. I fell heavily onto the bed and he dropped on me instantly. His hands ripped at my clothing, freeing my neck for him. It was so exciting, like suddenly being in a vampire movie, only real, and so much hotter. Adam gave off so much body heat it just overwhelmed me.

He kissed me hard and I could feel his sharper teeth with my tongue. I moaned into his mouth and he pulled back to look at me. His hands were in my hair and I just stared back into his swirling eyes as he gazed at me hungrily.

"Please... now..."

He grinned and dropped his face to my neck, covering it in light feathery kisses. I ran my hands down his body and to his ass. I slapped him once and he laughed against my neck. I felt him focus his attention on the right side of my throat, just below my ear and he licked at my skin, sending shivers down me. I gripped his back and giggled breathlessly, my heart pounding. There was a hot vampire at my throat! He kissed and nipped at my skin and I felt gooseflesh travel down my arms at his touch. Then I felt his mouth open and his teeth brushed against my neck. At last. I gasped and he paused.

"If you stop now, Adam, I swear I'll kill you." I barked. With a laugh, I felt him sink his teeth sharply into my neck. I was surprised to feel a sharp sting and the sensation of him literally sucking blood out of me, but then I started to feel a wave of something else, washing over me... a delicious lethargy... and more. My insides quivered and I felt as if he was sucking at other parts of me (I'm trying not to be rude here but that's just how it felt).

It made me feel so good that I pulled at our clothes to try and get naked and get him inside me. I wanted to feel Adam making love to me while he fed. He stopped abruptly, his teeth gliding out of my skin and his tongue swirling over my neck.

"So, what do you think?" He asked with a wry grin, licking blood from his bottom lip. He looked beautiful just then - almost glowing with health.

"Adam, I need you inside me now please." I gasped, pulling at his clothes. He laughed.

"Don't worry, that feeling will wear off any second now. It's just the effects of the feeding. We have to make it feel good or people wouldn't let us do it." I pulled at his trousers again with frustration.

"Please now. I want you now." He grinned and slowly counted backward. "5…4…3…2…1…."

Amazingly, just like that my intensity waned a little and I suddenly felt a wave of shame. I was begging him to do me like some cheap… hang on. My mind suddenly clear, something occurred to me and hey a subject change at this juncture, probably not a bad thing.

"Do your teeth stay inside the skin while you feed? Normally in movies they bite then the teeth are out."

"Vampire bites are um… magical, for want of a better word. As soon as our teeth are pulled out the wound closes instantly and disappears. I have to bite and drink then withdraw. That's why you don't hear stories of people with vampire bites."

"So then why did you lick my neck after? I thought maybe that was how you close the wound."

He blinked at me.

"Um there was blood on your neck? And I'm a vampire… I don't like to waste any."

I laughed at his tone, he was mimicking me, and I knew it.

"I still want you though. Please can we have sex now?"

He whipped his trousers off in record time then began pulling at my clothes. In a repeat of the night before, I was suddenly squirming beneath him, naked, with his hand between my legs.

"Barely a need for any foreplay. You're so ready." He laughed, as he twirled his fingers inside me. I shuddered and pulled him closer to grind myself against him. The friction was delicious and I almost came just from that.

"Please. Take me now." He dropped his shorts and was on top of me, crushing me with his muscles as he pressed me to the bed. My arms were above my head in his grip and his leg nudged mine apart.

"You asked for it." He laughed, his face open and excited.

He shoved hard inside me and I nearly lost it then and there. When he started moving inside me I pulled him tight against me with my legs and moved with him. He kissed me and I could taste my blood on his tongue. He picked up the pace and moved harder and faster while I gripped at him with my legs and pulled him against me frantically. Our breathing got louder and our moans longer and then I felt myself erupt and screamed out his name. He came just after and we just lay there, panting and laughing breathlessly. He leaned up to look at me, the look on his face quizzical.

"If you're going to ask if that was good for me? Just take this as my answer... When can we do that again?" I whispered triumphantly.

He grinned. "I was so hoping you'd say that."

Chapter Nine

So okay I've met a lovely man and yes he's a vampire but that happens all the time on TV and movies and in books and goes well. Actually, now that I think about it, normally it goes really badly but then this is real life so it won't be the same. But if he gets to live forever and he says he wants to be with me for that long does that mean I have to be one too? And was that a problem? I mean, wouldn't that be the perfect answer? Live forever, do what I want… okay, I'd have to drink blood but maybe I can get used to that. I mean people do that even when they're not real vampires, don't they? Don't get me wrong, I've never tried it but there are those people in America that I saw on some real life type show and there are probably people here too who practice vampire stuff. Like it's real. Well, I guess they don't know it is. Or maybe they do. Okay, I need to stop thinking now.

Adam ended up having to go in to work later that day. Some big important client meeting that couldn't be cancelled after all. At least I sent my man off to his meeting well fed and satisfied! I hope…

I chose to stay lounging and snoozing on his huge, comfy bed. I suppose I have to go home sometime but since I'm pulling a sickie from work, it's probably for the best that I'm not wandering around the shops and stuff. That's how they caught me last time. Typical - the one time Colm went shopping during office hours and there I was. In a store trying out an exercise machine I was never going to buy, while I was apparently in bed with flu. Damn him. I got a written warning for that too! Like it was *my* fault he chose to go shopping that day.

I actually can't believe Adam just went off to work like that after what we did. It was such a huge deal for me; but then again, maybe not so much for him. As a vampire, he'd obviously done that before. Oh no, what if it was just average for him and he's been with lots of girls where it was much better? Or what if he has a whole network of girls he does this with?! What if I'm just another number and he'll come to me every second Tuesday or… no wait, I go to the movies with Michelle every second Tuesday so that won't even work! I made another of those frustrated sounds I can't spell and decided a wander around the library would calm me down.

When I got up off the bed my legs shook a little and I realised I felt wiped out. Wow, was that the sex or the blood drinking? Or both? And thank the heavens I remembered to dress myself after he left. What if the butler guy had walked in? Does he know about Adam? I suppose he must or he would walk in on stuff. And, yikes, what if he'd walked in on us? Adam was right. I think too much. Or did he say I was mental? I can't really remember but I'm still going to go through his books. I wondered if he has any sexy vampire stories. On second thought, probably not. They'd just be books about his life. Hmmmmm.... No stop right there. I can't write well enough to write novels so there's no point in me entertaining fantasies of writing about vampires like him. After all, I can barely manage to finish my stupid column each week!

The library was as big as I remembered and was only the third door I tried. Honestly, I thought my sense of direction was better than that. The butler guy sure looked pissed off when I accidentally disturbed him doing paperwork in the office. Mind you I did throw the door open with a flourish so that it crashed into the wall. He probably peed a bit too from shock. And to be honest, that did actually make me feel a little better.

The books were as old and archaic as I remembered and I spent ages just trying to read the titles of them, realising most of them weren't even in English. I supposed that was normal. After all a vampire has forever to learn languages and, come to think about it, maybe Adam wasn't English at all. He might have been Bulgarian or Spanish or Latin. Is Latin a type of person or just an old language? I should have paid more attention at school; mind you they didn't teach us Latin so it wouldn't have been much use anyway. Phew, that's a relief...

I finally settled on a book which looked vaguely English although much more wordy, like Shakespearean

English. It appeared to be some kind of reference book about vampires so I settled down on the light blue, ornate-looking chaise longue to read it. I don't really know what a chaise longue is for but it turns out it isn't for comfort or at least this one doesn't seem to be. It just isn't that padded really. I thought it would be all romantic to be draped across it like some kind of beautiful maiden from olden times but they must have had no feeling in their limbs if they did that. Also, they didn't have black hair with flashes of red down the sides. Or maybe some of them did but those certainly aren't the ones who were painted or photographed on these things all the time.

I wriggled about a bit trying to get comfortable then gave up and sat on the floor, with my back to it. That was so much better. I wondered if they ended up doing this too back then. Eventually I actually focused on the book. It was really old. The pages were kind of crinkly and had thin tissuey pages between the ones with text and the ones with pictures. A picture of a starving vampire horrified and entranced me. His cheeks were gaunt and pointed, his eyes a vibrant glowing red and fangs horrifically long. Adam had looked a little like that last night. His cheeks were a little less pointy but his eyes were red like that. How many days did he have to go without blood to look like this? How many days could a vampire survive without blood? And what about animal blood? I never asked about that. They do it in some movies and on TV so maybe there's something to it.

I'd just reached a section which appeared to be about different types of vampires when my mobile phone rang. The creepy laugh of the joker scared the crap out of me, making the book fall into my lap and fall closed, losing my place. Seriously why did I keep that ringtone? I dug it out of my bag and looked at the screen. It was Michelle... on her work number. Uh-oh.

I put on a sick sounding voice. Mind you I'd said I had a migraine so would I really sound sick? It was too late though.

"Yeees?"

"Don't give me that crap. I know you had a hot date last night with that rich guy. Are you at his place?"

Her tone went a little dirty which would have offended me if she had been wrong. Actually no, it still offended me. How dare she assume that? Even though she's right.

"I'm at a friend's house and I'm not well. Why are you disturbing me and risking prolonging my illness?" Ha!

"Yeah right. You missed out on something weird here today, that's all. Well, it's kind of scary actually."

"Go on." Damn my voice sounded normal there. She wouldn't miss that.

"Turns out Nick got beaten up sometime last night. He was in the hospital but he's checked himself out already. He won't say who did it but he's seriously scared."

"What? How do you know?" I felt a chill run down my spine as I pictured Nick hurting and scared.

"Oh, don't get so jealous. I've known him much longer than you. He called me. They did a real number on him too. Broken arm, broken collarbone, lots of bruises and cuts and when they found him he'd lost a lot of blood. They had to transfuse him. And yes, I know this proves you're right about the value of giving blood FYI."

I imagined Michelle making her signature hair toss at those words.

"My god. That's awful. And he really won't say who did it?! Why doesn't he want them arrested?" Another chill crept along my spine as an unwanted thought occurred to me.

"I don't know. I'm going to see him tonight so I'll see what else I can find out. Maybe I can convince him to go to the police."

"Yeah, let me know how it goes. How he is, I mean. He's a douche but he probably didn't deserve that!"

I was worried now. Had Adam gone after him? Had he left me sleeping and gone to attack Nick? Was that why Nick was so scared? Or had he used some kind of memory thing on him so he couldn't remember? It was too much. Was this the guy Adam was? The kind to go and brutalise people who hurt me? And if so, was that a deal breaker? Or was it flattering? I realised while I was thinking about all of this my stomach was rumbling like mad and I was starving. I headed for the kitchen desperate for something to eat.

"What?" The butler guy asked when he saw me in the doorway. "I suppose you want something to eat? Feeling a little drained perhaps?" His grin was smirky to say the least but I nodded. "Sit down." He barked, pointing at the breakfast bar.

I obediently sat and watched him as he moved around the kitchen as if he spent all his time there. Maybe he did. How would I know? A plate of bacon, eggs and toast was dumped loudly in front of me.

"You'll need to keep up your iron intake as well as vitamins if you're going to insist on being here with him. I'll have some steak prepared for you both for dinner tonight."

I tucked into the food, which was cooked to perfection, and wondered if I could get more info out of him. At least he seemed to know about Adam. Not that he was the most open or friendly of guys but you can't blame a girl for trying.

"So, he can eat normal food?"

The look on his face told me he thought I was a moron.

"Did you not see him eat last night? Does he not drink coffee with you? Yes, he can eat normal food, but he gets only minimal nutrition from it. Am I to be subjected to your endless questions now?" His smile was less smirky, almost amused in fact, but I chose not to give him the benefit of the doubt just yet.

"What should I call you?" I asked. Calling him 'the butler guy' in my head was fine but that kind of behaviour led to embarrassing slips later.

"I'm Nigel and no, I'm not a butler. I simply look after Adam. And apparently, you now it seems."

"Can I get a taxi back home from here? I need to get some things or stay there. What does Adam want me to do?"

"Leave? You can't leave here without him. He hasn't explained this? Well, he'll be home shortly so ask him to explain things for you because I'm busy and really shouldn't be the one telling you these things. Your evening meal will be ready at 6pm sharp so don't be late if you don't want cold food."

With that he marched out of the room. If I wasn't mistaken, he wasn't quite as mean as he tried to be but I don't know why he would try to be. That in itself was kind of mean. I made a decision to try and change his opinion of me. Although if I got yummy hot meals even when he didn't seem to like me, did it really matter?

Chapter Ten

finished everything on my plate, and after sitting daydreaming and mulling over Nigel's words for probably an hour or more, I got up and looked for a dishwasher but couldn't work out what all the big shiny machines were, so took my dishes to the sink to wash them. I was just draining them when I realised someone was behind me. I spun around, ready to face a disapproving not-butler who was probably going to tell me I was washing up wrong.

Adam grinned. "Making house, are we?" I dried my hands and mimicked his posture, leaning back against the sink, with my arms folded. Big mistake, I'm a bit messy when I wash up and I could already feel cool water soaking into my back. I groaned but thought there was no point in moving now. Adam quirked an eyebrow at me.

"You don't know how wonderful it is to find you here waiting for me. I had this awful feeling you'd be gone. Not that you could of course, but still it is nice to come home to you." He made to approach me but seeing my face he stepped back again.

"What?"

"What do you mean I can't leave? What did Nigel mean by I can't leave without you? Tell me, Adam. Am I trapped here? Am I some kind of a prisoner? And what the hell did you do to Nick?" He stared at me for a few moments and seemed to catch up enough to reply.

"Okay, first things first. You're not trapped but you need to be travelling with me physically to get back to your um… town. I suppose I can take you there now if that's what you want?"

I stared at him not really understanding his meaning and not being swayed by the reasonable tone he used.

"Back to my *um* town?! What does that even mean? Why do I get the feeling from your words, that I'm not even still in Wiltshire? And if I'm not, where the hell am I and is that why it's snowing?" He laughed.

"Damn girl. One question at a time would be appreciated. No, you are not still in Wiltshire. Or in England for that matter, but I can get you back there in twenty-five minutes or so. Oh, and yes, that's why it's snowing. Because we're in a small Scandinavian village which actually has no name because it's so incredibly small. It snows here quite often, and is very safe and quiet and what's that look?"

"I'm not even in *England*? Don't you think stealing me away from my home *country* was something we should have discussed? And what the hell? How did you even do it? We only drove down some twisty country lanes. This is a windup, isn't it?" I marched to the back door and threw it open, stepping outside. It was icily cold and I instantly wished I hadn't. My back was wet, remember? The snow was deep and crisp and... oh hell no, I'm not going to start singing. It just looked like a very tiny, very snowy UK village. No fancy buildings, no people in lederhosen or whatever the hell they wear in Scandinavian places. Mind you, it was definitely cold enough to be outside the UK. I mean Wiltshire gets seriously cold but this felt like 10 below or more.

"Come on, you're going to freeze out here." Adam pulled me back inside and hugged me close, warming me with his body heat. It made me want him a little bit but I was still mad at him so I didn't allow myself to go all weak at the knees, even though they totally wanted to do just that. As soon as I finished shivering I pushed him away.

"I want to go home, Adam. Now please."

"Why?" He asked as if it was a strange request. He folded his arms and leaned back against the back door after he closed it.

"Why? I don't belong here, I don't have my passport so I'm probably breaking the law, your house has really uncomfortable furniture and Nigel hates me! Oh, and someone beat up Nick really badly and I'm worried it was you but I don't want it to be because he's really scared. And can you wipe memories?"

Adam sighed heavily and dropped into a seat at the breakfast bar.

"Seriously, Lila. You have an amazing ability to exhaust even me. You *can* belong here if you want to. *I* want you here. You can collect your passport if it worries you but you're safe here and not likely to get arrested for not having it. I can replace the furniture if you show me what you don't like although it's all antique and fits the decor. Nigel hates you?" He laughed a little. "He doesn't hate you. He takes a little time to like anyone at the start but give him time and he'll warm to you. He's really a very nice person, just very protective of me. And what is this about Nick? Is he the tw- guy from the newspaper? Why would you think I'd attacked him? For god's sake, Lila! Give me some credit here...when am I supposed to have done that? I was here in a different country all night, wasn't I?"

I stared at him. I had been asleep but I guess I had no reason to assume he'd slip off in the night to beat someone up? I shook my head and sighed.

"Forget it. I knew you couldn't have done it really. I'm just being silly. Probably because I'm freaked out, away from home and can't even just grab a snack when I'm hungry." Which I suddenly realised I totally was again already – damn vampire bloodletting!

"Is that a hint that you'd like me to cook for you again?" He shot me a grin as he pulled me to my feet and dragged me towards the kitchen counter.

"What would madam like for dinner?"

I laughed then remembered that if he can only cook soup and toasted sandwiches that would get old fast. Surely in however many years he's been around he learned to cook something? And a takeaway was out of the question because we weren't even in England. What do people eat around here? What foods are common in... where were we again?

"You know what? I'll just ask Nigel to whip up dinner a little early for us. I can see the wheels spinning in your head again." He lifted me up to sit on the counter, then headed out of the room. I grimaced. Nigel wouldn't like that...I mean cooking for me, not sitting on the counter. Actually, he probably wouldn't like that either. I hopped down quickly. No sense in annoying the person who would be cooking my dinner. Damn, I looked up and he was standing there, frown on face, arms folded.

"Please don't remove your bottom from my kitchen counters on my account. I can work around you, not that it's particularly hygienic." I stared open-mouthed as Adam walked up behind him and nudged him.

"Come on Nige. You know I put her there – how the hell would she reach otherwise?!"

He had a point. I'd nearly snapped my ankles jumping down. No that's silly, because surely, they wouldn't break just for a few feet... I was doing it again. I could tell because I'd noticed that Adam had taken to watching me with that look that says, 'she's doing it again'. I scowled at him.

"I have questions you know." He laughed and led me by the hand to the breakfast bar to sit down together.

"I'd be surprised if you didn't. And to be fair, it's better to ask me than ask yourself in your head. Your knowledge all comes from True Blood and Twilight!"

I stared at him trying to work out if he'd watched those things too. Then I imagined watching them with him. How romantic. Actually, if we watched True Blood together, it could get all hot and steamy. Like the show.

Why did I feel the need to explain that to myself? Arghhhh….

"You have to stop me when I do that." I told him, dipping my head in shame. He planted a soft kiss on my lips, which was so sweet I could have cried. Not that I'm hormonal or anything but it was really sweet, you know? He leaned really close to look into my eyes.

"I love it when you do that. And don't worry, I have both the Twilight saga and True Blood on DVD so we can watch them together if you like." His grin was a little dirty then and it hit me.

"Shit! Oh crap… vampires can read minds, can't they?!" Oh noooo, all the things he'll have heard me going on about in my head. He was still grinning at me, watching me freak out.

"Well? You should tell me these things, damn you!" I groaned, imagining things I'd thought about the last few days, and wondered why yet again the ground refused to open up and swallow me.

"Yes, some vampires can read minds…"

"Shit! Well don't go thinking I want to do all that stuff when we watch…. What?" His face was unreadable but his shit-eating grin wasn't.

"Some can read minds, yes, but I am not one of them."

He ducked vampire-fast as I slapped at him.

"Wish I was though. Why Miss Lila, what were you fantasising about us doing while watching… I'm guessing True Blood since Twilight is so teenaged?"

I glared at him and jumped when a plate of steak, chips and vegetables was placed in front of me. It looked and smelled divine and shockingly I was so hungry again already (jeez I only ate about an hour or so ago!). I had a mouthful of food a second later when I thanked Nigel. He tried to hide a smile and left us to eat.

"He doesn't want to eat with us?" I asked, swallowing my food in a rush. Adam shook his head, mouth full. When he could speak, he said.

"He'll probably eat later. I think he likes you though." He nudged me with his shoulder as he tucked back into his food.

He likes me? Yikes, what's he like when he doesn't like someone then? I imagined plates of food flying across the room then started to think about what he'd cook and it grossed me out so I changed the subject. In my head at first then for real – see I'm learning...

"So how old are you? Real years and vampire years that is?" He shot me a look.

"How old are *you*?"

I grinned, shaking my head slowly. "Seriously? You're going to do the whole deflection of questions thing? With *me*?! Amateur..."

He rolled his eyes. "I was 29 when I was turned." He carried on eating but I could sense that damn grin was back.

"And?"

"I've been a vampire for 127 years." Wow. He was seriously old. I wondered if he still celebrated birthdays and which ones?

"Did you have a 150th birthday party?" He snorted and choked at the same time – quite impressive. I busied myself for a moment, worrying about how I didn't know the Heimlich but then I realised it probably wouldn't kill him and besides he was now laughing... at me.

"What?"

"Did I have a 150th birthday party?! Really? Would you?"

"Hell yeah! It's a serious milestone! Do you celebrate actual birthdays or the anniversaries of when you were turned?"

He looked serious for a moment.

"Both every year."

I stared at him, picturing lots of gift buying in my future and then watched him laugh at me again.

"I celebrated my actual birthdays for a while but it gets old after a while. The day I was turned isn't really something to celebrate."

And of course, that opened up a can of worms for me. Why not? Should I ask?

"Why not?"

He shook his head at me.

"We're not talking about that right now. Let's not kill the mood."

He finished his food and took his plate to the sink. I hurried to finish the last of mine and did the same. The mood kind of felt killed already – damn me and my mouth. And I thought I was learning…

I followed him into the library where we both sat on the chaise longue. FYI, if I thought it was uncomfortable alone, with someone else it's worse. Seriously, it's like sitting on an uneven floor with uneven, jagged walls to support you. I wriggled to try and get comfy and sighed heavily.

"Okay I get it. It's this chair, isn't it?" He pulled me across his lap a little and that was actually slightly better. I snuggled into his chest.

"It was." I snuggled some more until he made an oof sound. I think I elbowed him in the chest. Still he's a vampire so can't have really hurt him, right? We sat in comfortable silence for a while. And by that, I mean the room was quiet but of course my head was not. Like that would happen?

"Ugh.... Stop thinking for five minutes, will you?" He groaned. If he can't read minds, how can he-

"And before you ask, no, I can't read minds but I've known you more than five minutes so I know you never ever stop thinking! Also, I can tell when you're doing it because you're all tensed up."

I tested myself and realised he was right. Maybe that's why I always felt achy and tired.

"No way. I'd never noticed that. Would being a vampire fix me?!"

"Whoa. That's quite a topic change."

I shrugged against his chest, concentrating on relaxing. And that's actually much harder than it sounds you know.

"Um, I'm not sure anything would fix you to be honest. Have you tried not thinking?"

I laughed quietly.

"Some would say that's how I function on a daily basis."

"Your boss?"

"No, Colm is a bit of a nag, but he's fine really. I'm so glad it's Friday though so I don't have to worry about going back in tomorrow."

"Nervous of going back? Seeing Nick?" I could feel that Adam's body was tensed a little at this point but thought maybe my elbow was digging into somewhere

79

again. I checked I wasn't damaging anything I planned to use later. Oh gross, who thinks like that? I'm glad he couldn't see me blush.

"No, just don't want to leave yet." I sighed and felt myself start to relax. No thoughts, no thoughts….

He pulled me closer to him and kissed the top of my head.

"That's such a relief to hear."

I smiled.

"Glad I want to stay?" He shrugged.

"Just don't feel like driving right now and do you know how cold it is out there? It's like minus ten!"

I elbowed him deliberately that time and was satisfied when he grunted. I sat up with an innocent grin.

"It's still really early. What is there to do around here?"

And that's how I found myself curled up on a big squishy sofa in Adam's arms, watching True Blood on the oversized TV I'd seen when I first arrived. I mean, could it get any better than this? Wow, Eric's naked body looks even more amazing on the biiiig screen. I felt a little hot under the collar watching him and Sookie together while in Adam's arms but it didn't seem to bother him.

"So…" I cleared my throat, which was suddenly so dry. "Is there something like tru blood for real?" I didn't meet his eyes, I mean; I bet I was all flushed and stuff.

"Jeez Lila. You really know how to kill the mood."

I glanced at him surprised. His eyes were doing that colour-changy thing and his teeth looked a little longer. Oh, he wanted blood. He pulled me up so I was pressed against him and I realised it wasn't just my blood he wanted. Oh wow, I think everything just tingled.

"The only blood I vant is yourrrrrsss...." He intoned, like one of those old time vampires. I laughed and pretended to struggle and he moved like a flash to flatten me against the sofa beneath him. "I vant to driiink your bloooood." He continued, looking increasingly dismayed at my giggles.

"Seriously, nothing scares you, does it?" He asked in his normal voice.

"Oh, do the voice again." I begged. He held my arms up above my head and pressed his lips to my throat.

"You are miiine." He muttered, sounding more like Bill from True Blood this time. Yep, things tingled again. He grabbed my top with his teeth and pulled and it ripped away from my throat and halfway down the front in one swift move.

"Jeez Adam." I mocked his earlier phrase and tone. "You really know how to kill a T-shirt don't you?" He laughed against my skin, and then trailed kisses from my throat towards the centre of my chest. I think my breasts actually heaved with my breaths, like on those raunchy book covers, and I shuddered pleasantly then jumped when I felt his teeth on my bra.

"Don't you dare, Adam! It's expensive!" He laughed and lifted his head up to meet my eyes.

"It's *expensive*? I'm being all vampirey and sexy and you're worried about your bra?"

I laughed and tried to move my hands to swat him. Nothing – seriously, it's like he's made of rock.

"It's my best one, damn you!" With a shrug, Adam practically sat me up, undressed my top half and laid me back down, arms restrained, in a flash. And I mean that, like in the blink of an eye... well maybe a few blinks. It was freakishly fast, but so incredibly sexy too. Another few blinks and he was topless too. I ran my hands lightly over the contours of his chest and around his nipples, smiling as he sucked in a breath and his eyes swirled with every colour imaginable.

"I love the swirly eye thing. It's so beautiful." I was silenced a second later with his lips and then tongue as he kissed me thoroughly. When he stopped, I was gasping for breath, well... and other things.

He did that high-speed thing again and we were fully naked on the sofa. Again, I worried about my less than perfect figure. I mean my breasts are a little on the heavy side, which some guys like I know, but my waist isn't exactly tiny and my stomach isn't exactly flat. He didn't seem bothered though as he made a point of kissing me all over, occasionally grazing me with his teeth and making me shiver with anticipation. He released my hands while he was tending to me and I fisted my hands in his hair, pulling his face up to mine.

"Kiss me." I breathed, taking his lips as if I was in charge. Who was I kidding? He took over, using one hand between my legs again to drive me crazy while he kissed me, his tongue stroking against mine in a rhythm I wanted to feel elsewhere. I tried to take control but my hands were once more restrained while he foreplayed me into frustration.

"Dammit, Adam. Stop messing around." He laughed against my stomach as he was kissing his way back up.

"Messing around? Most women would love this much foreplay."

I groaned.

"And it's great really… but get on with it."

He laughed again, moving swiftly up to kiss me, slamming into me at the same time. He caught my gasp with his mouth and laughed breathlessly as he pulled back to watch me while he thrust in and out so tantalisingly. I struggled against his grip on my hands, wanting to touch him, but he kept his hands on mine, and his forearms against my arms, holding me down so effectively.

I growled at him as he quickened his pace and caught a wicked gleam in his multicoloured eyes a mere second before his face disappeared and I felt the sharp sting of his teeth in my shoulder. I came so hard I'm pretty sure I passed out but it must have been only for a split second as I clearly remember coming again and again as he kept on thrusting, and drinking and the waves of pleasure just rolled over me like-

I woke on the sofa, Adam draped over me like a warm, heavy blanket. His soft breaths against my chin told me he was asleep. I wanted so much to stretch but didn't want to wake him. I wondered if I'd been asleep long, I almost still felt tingles running through me but surely that was just my imagination. I listened to his soft sleeping breaths as I marvelled over how wonderful and perfect he and my potential new life were. How had I found perfection so easily? I fell back asleep with that thought…

Chapter Eleven

It had been a heavenly weekend – just Adam and I together, well okay, sometimes Nigel too but only because he cooked for us and scowled a bit less while he did it. None of my heroic attempts at humour over meals even got him to crack a smile... and at one point I even made Adam spit out his food so it must have been funny. There's just no pleasing some people. Anyway, aside from Nigel being a grump, the weekend was full of lounging together in bed (without Nigel of course) and a few nice walks out in the snow. The first walk was a little embarrassing as I fell into a thigh-high snowdrift and Adam had to use his freaky vamp strength to help me up. It wouldn't have taken as long if he hadn't been laughing so much either. Seriously it wasn't even that funny! He was a hero though, carrying me back to his place so I couldn't really complain... much... for long...

Of course, to go out in the snow in the first place, he needed to lend me clothes as all of my stuff was at my house. In England. Still freaky to think I was in some far off Scandinavian village, which was magically only about 20 minutes away from home.

Going home seemed way too weird and way too soon. I'd like to say Nigel tearfully waved goodbye but to be honest, I think he just looked a little relieved. Adam seemed a bit quiet driving me back but even my best effort to cheer him up had him snapping at me to not distract him while he was driving. I mean jeez it was only a hand on his thigh. Still he made a good point about how an accident on the road probably wouldn't kill him but of course I wasn't immortal like him. I behaved after that. Mostly.

I wanted him to stay, so badly, but he said he had to get back to the house as he had work to catch up on.

"Will I see you again?" I had this awful panicky feeling that his goodbye was forever. His face softened as he grabbed my face in both hands and leaned close to me. His eyes swirled a little with pastel colours.

"You think I'm finished with you already?" He tried to look all vampirey but I saw right through him. We kissed and then he left in a rush, while I stood on the doorstep like a fool, staring after him. His car peeled away with a squeal of tyres which sounded cool to me but probably only peed off my neighbours. Ah well, that'll teach them to be spying on me.

"I knew it!" A triumphant voice declared from the side of my garden. Well when I say garden, it's got sides but is mostly just a rough mess of weeds and there used to be a path but now it's just mess. Michelle stepped over some of the weeds with difficulty. She'd been sitting on my pathetic excuse for a bench. Silly really, since she knows where I hide my key. She'd even have been better off sitting on my car while it rotted on the drive. Really should get that fixed...

"Spying again, Michelle? Really?" I let us both in and closed the door. The air inside was cool which means the damned heating was on the fritz again. I walked to the kitchen and whacked the side of the boiler and the green heating light popped on. Better late than never. I put the kettle on then turned to face the music.

Michelle, having laughed at my question, had quickly made herself at home on the sofa and was flicking through a magazine she'd found on the seat.

"You've been with him all weekend, haven't you?" She lowered the magazine to look me in the eye. It was amazing how boring it seemed to look at eyes which didn't change colour but it seemed dramatic to feel that way since I'd only had a few days of Adam's incredible eyes.

"Would you believe me if I said no?" I sat down and slouched into my favourite recliner chair beside her. Shame washed over me briefly then I remembered that I shouldn't be ashamed of falling in love.

"Oh, my god, I think I love him, Michelle. What's happening to me? I've only just met him!" I leaned over with my head in my hands. It was like crashing after a drunken night out or an amazing holiday. What felt right and perfect all weekend suddenly seemed strangely like I'd been rushing into something without knowing enough to make the right choice. Was it just because he was a vampire, or was it that combined with the fact that I'd only just met him? Michelle laughed and reached over to put her hand on my shoulder.

"Girl, you must have it bad! He's hot though so I totally understand why."

I felt like crying. Was it just the excitement of meeting a hot guy who actually wanted me? Had I fallen too fast because of that?

"Michelle, he's so amazing, but am I just being a ho?"

"If he is as good in bed as he looks, you go for it! Why should you worry about moving fast with him? If it's right, it's right eh?" She suddenly seemed like the smartest person I know. I hugged her and cried a little. Yes, Adam was amazing and yes it was moving fast but it feels right so that should be okay. No point in holding back when everything was telling me he was the one.

I sat up and tried to shrug it off. Really, that's a stupid saying. It did nothing to make me feel better and from the way Michelle looked at me, it may have made me look like I had an itch somewhere unspeakable or something.

"Okay, we're going to get a takeaway and you're going to tell me everything. Don't spare the details, babe. Enquiring minds want to know!" She pulled out her phone and dialed our usual pizza place for our usual order.

Over slices of yummy pizza, I told her what I could without giving away anything which had to remain a secret. Try talking about a guy without mentioning what he is, what he eats, where he lives or how old he is! It's not easy. Mostly I focused on how amazing he was in bed and we giggled about that for hours before she headed off home. After she left I realised I hadn't asked about Nick and she hadn't even mentioned him. My guilt didn't keep me awake though.

Chapter Twelve

olm wasn't in when I arrived, which was strange but had probably happened before at some point. I settled at my desk after fetching a coffee and enduring the knowing look on Michelle's face. I poked my tongue out at her on the way past, which was childish, I'll grant you, but also felt good.

My desk was awash with notes and information for my next projects so I just let myself sink into them and put everything out of my mind; and by projects, I mean things I put together only to be rejected by Colm while not so kindly reminding me I'm not a reporter. Lunchtime came and went and I was still glued to my latest article. It was around 2pm when I realised Colm still wasn't in and went looking for him.

"Hi Karen, is Colm not in today?" I asked his assistant. She looked up at me and smiled.

"He called in sick." I stared at her wondering if she was joking. Colm was never sick.

"Really? I've never known him to not be in." She laughed.

"He's human, Lila. It had to happen eventually. Do you need anything else?" I accepted the dismissal for what it was and said my goodbyes. I went to see Michelle. Well, while the cat is away and all that...

"Hey. What's up with Colm?" I asked her. If anyone had gossip, it would be her. She looked at me as if I was insane.

"How the hell would I know? Seriously Lila, do you think I wander around sticking my nose in everyone's business?"

Why do people always ask those sorts of questions? The obvious answer is yes but I'm guessing that's not the one she wanted. I decided it was safer to change the subject.

"Heard from Nick lately?" She shook her head, concern filling her face.

"Nothing. It's so not like him. And he's not in today but I guess he has broken bones so it makes sense. I mean, how long does that stuff take to heal anyway?"

She had a point. I went back to finish my column so that at least tomorrow Colm wouldn't be able to snipe at me. Okay not about that, but probably about something else. There was always something with that guy.

When home time finally arrived, having dragged its heels like you wouldn't believe, I headed off with a hurried goodbye to Michelle. I didn't have plans with Adam but at least wanted to get home in case he called. As I walked down the road to the bus stop I had that weird feeling, you know, like someone out there was watching me. I kept looking back but there was nobody there. Eventually I was totally creeped out so I legged it and only slowed down when I reached the bus stop canopy. Unusually it was empty, which was just what I didn't want tonight. I peeked around the side of the canopy to see if anyone was following me. There was nobody there so I snorted at myself for being a wuss and sat down again. A quiet chuckle from out there in the darkness had me up and looking again.

Seriously this was freaky stuff. Was someone stalking me? Surely, they'd pick someone prettier, like Michelle. I wondered if Nick was following me. I was certain he'd done it before, because it wasn't the first time I'd felt like this recently. But then again, he was laid up with broken bones so it probably wasn't him after all. I took out my phone and scrolled through, searching anxiously for Adam's number. Was it silly to phone him? Was I just scaring myself?

I dialed his number and waited for it to start ringing. I imagined his reaction when his ringtone played and laughed despite myself. I wondered if he'd noticed yet that I'd snuck it away from him over the weekend and had changed it to the theme from True Blood. As it began to ring at his end and I imagined I could hear Jace Everett's 'Bad Things' playing, I suddenly realised with a gulp I actually *could* hear it playing. Out here in the dark. Holy crap, Adam was here somewhere. Where was he?

I leapt to my feet and darted around, looking for him and then finally using my brain and following the music I could hear. It stopped so I rang again and kept following it. I found him standing halfway down a dark alleyway just past the bus stop. He was glaring at his phone and trying to shut it up. Eventually he did something really creepy and crushed it to pieces in his hand. The music cut out sharply and I gasped. His head swung around to stare at me and in one of those faster than the eye moments; he was suddenly behind me, one arm around my middle, and the other hand over my mouth. I struggled against his solid grip (I really did) and he put his mouth really close to my ear and said…

"Shhh, it's okay - it's me, Adam." Yeah like *that* was going to stop me freaking out. I had eyes. I had common sense at last… I now knew he was following me or stalking me and that was seriously freaking me out. I elbowed him in the gut and heard him grunt.

"Shit, Lila! Calm down. It's just me!" He tightened his grip on me and then did something even freakier. He jumped. And I mean, really jumped. One second we were standing in the alley behind Starbucks, near the bus stop, and the next we were standing *on* Starbucks; as in on their *roof.* He let go of me at last and watched me dart away from him, panting and gasping for breath.

"What the fuck? Didn't you know it was me? I *was* trying to tell you."

He looked surprised, and a bit annoyed and how dare he? I wanted to hit him so badly. I suddenly realised I really wanted to say what was on my mind rather than puzzle it out silently.

"What kind of fucking freak are you?! Why the hell are you following me? Do you have any idea how scared I was? Why would you do that? Or maybe it was fun for you watching me shit-scared and phoning *you* for help.

Bloody hell, I'm such an idiot. I thought you cared about me." I dropped my bag on the floor and hugged myself to try and stop the shakes, which ran through me in waves. How had it gone so wrong? What kind of psycho was he? I loved him, goddamn it. Why did he have to be a freak? Why were they always freaks?

He blinked at me and opened his mouth a few times then closed it, as if he didn't know how to speak anymore. Join the club pal!

"*Me* following you?! Shit, Lila. I was trying to catch the person who *was* following you. I almost had him. He was behind Starbucks but then my damn phone started ringing…"

"Me calling you for help is a problem?"

"Music giving away my hiding place is a serious problem if I'm trying to track someone. He heard me, but then how could he not? I know I should have turned it off but ironically I wanted you to be able to reach me."

I was supposed to feel guilty?

"Don't lay a guilt trip on me. How the hell was I supposed to know you were stalking someone? Or me…" I was still a little unconvinced.

He stepped forward and grabbed my shoulders angrily.

"Do you want to tell me why you're being tracked by another vampire? What did you do, put a message out on the Internet asking for vampire lovers?"

I slapped him. I don't even know how I managed it. Or had the nerve. His rising anger made the air tight around us. He could so easily kill me where I stood. As that thought occurred to me, my knees gave out and I lost my balance, almost falling down. His tight grip was all that stopped me and his eyes lost all the anger as he gently helped me down to sit on a raised part of the roof. His arm slipped around me and he pulled me to him. My face was crushed against his broad chest. His heart was pounding. I still didn't understand how a vampire had a heart that was still beating but didn't think now was really the right time to ask.

"I'm so sorry I scared you, Lila. I was honestly trying to protect you. Why can't you just trust me? I was so worried when you told me about your friend that I didn't want you being alone. That's how I figured out it was a vampire."

"My…. Oh… you mean Nick? That was a vampire?!"

He chuckled a little and let me raise my head. He stared at me with a wry grin.

"Well you thought *I* did it…"

The man had a point. I grabbed his hand and held it tightly.

"I'm new to this stuff, Adam. Help me out here. What's going on?" He shrugged and stared at our entwined hands.

"I'm not sure. Your friend getting attacked made me think you might have a stalker, especially when I got to my office today to find it had been trashed. I don't honestly know if someone is after you or me but I didn't want to leave you unprotected just in case. Someone was definitely following you tonight though. I almost had him. I was *this* close. Unfortunately, he's also fast as hell."

"And I ruined it. I'm sorry, Adam. I was just so scared. I could feel him watching me." And now I felt guilty. Scared to angry, back to scared and now to guilt; what a rollercoaster!

He looked so sweet as he covered our hands with his other and then pulled them to help me up. He brushed the tears from my eyes, probably making me look like Alice Cooper but it was still such a romantic gesture that it made my stomach hurt.

"I'm glad you could sense him. It's actually very hard to detect a Tracker vampire. You must be extra sensitive."

I grinned a little weakly.

"Nobody has ever accused me of that before. I was different you know, before I met you."

He kissed me so softly my knees weakened again. Wow, that man had the most amazing mouth. His smirk told me he knew just how good he was. I tried to pull away and he gripped me tighter.

"Please don't doubt me again. All I want is for you to be safe, okay? No, I'm not going to let you get a word in right now. Just grab your bag and hold on tight." He handed me my bag then grabbed me in a tight hug and leapt off the building. I would have screamed if I'd had a chance but suddenly we were miraculously by his car and he was helping me in.

"We're going to yours to grab some stuff and then you're staying with me 'til we can find this stalker of yours, okay?"

He didn't really give me a chance to agree or disagree as he closed my door and walked around to his side. My head was spinning with questions but I decided to just ignore them for a while. He drove us to my house and I packed a bag with clothes and some essentials I can't possibly live without, like my Molton Brown toiletries. Well just some shampoo, a few bottles of bodywash and my pillow spray. Oh, and my body lotion… to go with each of the scents of bodywash I'd packed. He watched with a sardonic eyebrow raised while I packed. Well I've always wanted to say that but really, he just looked bemused. Surely, he likes me to smell good? I know it's a priority for me so surely for him too?

Chapter Thirteen

When we got to his house, I realised I'd still seen no change on the journey to let me know when he'd crossed from England to Scandinavia. I was so drained by then that I didn't even care that much. Okay, so I was a bit disappointed but still very tired – I guessed it was the aftermath of all that adrenaline and excitement. Adam helped me out of the car and handed my bag to Nigel who waited with a slightly less frowny face than normal. Maybe he was tired too.

Although it was only a little after 7pm at this point, Adam took me straight to his room and helped me change into my pyjamas. Okay that doesn't sound so sexy but they comfort me and besides, he must have seen worse in all his years on this planet. He pretty much put me to bed and tucked me in. Nigel appeared around that time with a tray for me. There was some delicious smelling soup, some hunks of warm crusty bread and a cup of cocoa, which smelled divine. He didn't even glare at me when he handed it to me so I figured I must be in a bad way.

"Aren't you hungry?" I asked Adam as I tucked in. Then I blushed. Did I really just say that to a vampire?! He laughed at my face and stood up.

"Eat up. I'll be right back okay?" He swept out of the room and closed the door. I could hear the drones of his voice and Nigel's from the hallway but couldn't make out the words. I finished the food and put the tray beside me as I tucked into the hot cocoa. It was just what I needed to feel warm and cosy and safe. I was lying down and almost asleep when Adam came back in. He undressed and carefully climbed in beside me.

"You feel better?" He asked as he rolled onto his side and rested on his elbow to look at me. His hand trailed down my face, brushing errant strands of hair aside and tracing over my lips. His eyes were doing that swirly thing but it was calmer than when he's really horny.

"Oh. Do you need…" I brushed my hair aside, revealing my neck and he laughed, brushing my hair back down lightly.

"Do I need to feed on my tired, frightened girlfriend? Uh no, I think I'll let you off just this once." His sarcasm was more of an afterthought so there was no bite to his response. Haha Bite. I must have that on the brain.

"I don't mind…. Wait… did you say girlfriend?" His eyes smiled with his mouth, which I thought was excellent teamwork. It also made me go a little fluttery in my stomach but I could tell he didn't want anything from me tonight so I pushed it back and focused on him.

"I'm not so tired or frightened now, Adam. I don't mind." A flicker of annoyance crossed his face.

"Really Lila, you're not a vending machine! I like to drink from you when we make love but mostly because it heightens the sensation for us both. I'm not the kind of man to feed on you when you're vulnerable."

I actually felt a little disappointed. I mean, it feels great when he bites me. Mind you, I had been pretty exhausted most of the day, which could be from blood loss I suppose, so perhaps I shouldn't keep encouraging him.

"Stop thinking." He muttered, caressing my cheek once more. He moved closer so that he was lying with his arm over me, and his face very near to mine.

"Just relax and get some sleep. You're safe here, I promise." He kissed my lips lightly, but as chastely as possible. I guess he knew it wouldn't take much from him to get me all hot and bothered. I extracted my arm from beneath his and took a turn caressing the side of his face. When I cupped his cheek, he turned his face to place a kiss in my palm. His eyes were swirlyer than before (and yes, it is a word... now) but he resolutely moved my hand down from his face and pulled me tighter against him. He rolled onto his back, so I was draped over his warm chest, his heart beating at a relaxed pace. It calmed me.

"Sleep." He commanded.

For once, I did what I was told.

Chapter Fourteen

I was worried about returning to work, bearing in mind I'd been hunted by a psycho vampire the night before. Why was a vampire after me? I mean besides the obvious, that I'm full of blood making me a handy snack, oh and I'm dating a vampire. Coincidence? I wasn't sure but it made me almost feel too afraid to leave Adam's house.

"If you're coming with, you'll probably want to get dressed." He stared at me while knotting his tie. He was facing a full-length mirror (you know, the ones that stand on the floor and look so cool and grown up) and from where I was I could see his gorgeous rear profile with a little glimpse of his face and front. He wagged his eyebrows at me.

"See anything you like?" I cocked my head to the side and made like I was still deciding. He laughed and carried on with the tie. Seriously if I had vampire speed,

I wouldn't do *anything* at normal, human speed. I pointed that out.

"So, you think I should dash around and do everything faster than the human eye? Yeah, that wouldn't get old fast." He shook his head at me.

"Honestly, I did that for a while when I was first created but it burns tons of energy which means I need to feed more. Since I have to feed once every day, it's already too often."

I shrugged.

"I don't mind it daily."

With a vampirey growl, he darted across the room really fast and was holding me down on the bed. For a split-second I felt panic rush through me before remembering that it was Adam and he wouldn't hurt me.

"You like it daily, do you?!" The double meaning was so clear I couldn't believe I'd said it. I mean not that it wasn't true at that moment but it sounded so whorey. And yes, don't bother looking it up – that's also totally a word now.

I blushed and his eyes swirled. Sending your blood in a rush to your face probably wasn't the best way to deter a vampire. He gave me a large fangy grin and I felt the lightest shudder run through me (the good kind that is).

"Breakfast time, is it?" I asked lightly. We grinned at each other and suddenly he was back over at the mirror straightening the tie with a mock scowl. Yes, I'd grabbed it in my excitement and scrunched it up. And yes, I'm enjoying the view for the second time. I'd be a fool not to.

I toyed with the idea of staying home from work. I mean seriously, I'm being stalked by a freaking vampire – who *wouldn't* take a day off? But I realised I'd just be sitting around Adam's house all day with cranky Nigel glaring at me through the walls so I got ready in a rush and he dropped me off at my office building with strict instructions to stay inside until he picked me up. Like that needed to be said! Surely nothing could encourage me to go outside without him. He watched me go inside before driving away. I felt so safe knowing he was watching over me. And a bit horny, but that's not really appropriate at work so I filled my mind with unsexy things like coffee and chocolate and okay that just gave me a great idea that was making me even hornier. Michelle was walking out of our coffee shop when I swiped my badge at the turnstile and hurried over to me.

"Another hot night with the Sex God?" I slapped at her and nearly knocked her coffee from her hand. That'll teach her to be so crude. She huffed and marched over to her desk with me following. It was okay because driving in with Adam meant being not even just on time but actually early to work. Must be how fast he drives. Best not to scare Colm by appearing at my desk just yet.

"Don't be so rude then, Michelle! It's not my fault you can't hold your drink." With a snarky grin, I headed off to the ground floor office area where I work (see how well I planned that so I don't need stairs or lifts?) And yes, it was a question I asked at the interview. I'm still not sure how meeting me at an interview could make someone hire me but I guess I didn't act like I was on crack that day.

When I got to my desk there was a note saying Colm wanted to see me. I groaned and decided to show up earlier than my usual time of 10 past 9. Start things off well and maybe he wouldn't yell at me today.

"You wanted to see me?" I appeared in his doorway as if by vampire speed and reflexes. Actually, not quite because I banged my shoulder on the doorframe and made a loud bang. Either way he was startled so it was still a win for me. He motioned to the seat opposite his own.

"I need you to work on something different in addition to your usual column - an investigative project. You ready for that?" The look on his face clearly said he didn't think so but he knew I'd say yes as I was always asking for something like this. I grinned and tried to look as responsible as possible.

"Sounds great, Colm. What will I be working on?" He actually looked a bit tired to me and I remembered he'd been off sick the day before. I should have asked him how he was, I realised. Not that he'd dignify it with an appropriate response I'm sure, so probably just as well I didn't waste my breath.

"As you probably know, one of our own was attacked last week." Oh no. Please not that, anything but that. "Um yes…" I trailed off as he was clearly waiting for a response.

"I'd like you to write an article on the circumstances of Nick's attack. Turns out it was one of several in the last month or so, something's definitely going on." I gaped at him.

"Not to talk myself out of what I've always asked for, but isn't this the sort of thing the crime beat guys would normally work on? They have more experience with stuff like this." I realised I was, in fact, totally trying to talk myself out of this opportunity. Was I mad? Or was I being sensible for the first time in my life?

Colm stared at me. "I'll admit I'm a little surprised to hear you say that, Lila. You've done nothing but beg me for a chance like this and now you're trying to turn me down? I mean, I know you have a bit of a history with Nick. Hell, everyone here knows that." (eek!) "Still this is an opportunity that could get you moved to a real department rather than staying stuck in fluffville over there with the other weirdos." The man doesn't mince his words eh? I took a deep breath.

"Of course, I'd like to do it, Colm. Just don't want the vultures over in crime beat tearing me a new one because of it." Wow that sounded fairly cool. He just scowled at me. I got up to leave, keen to leave on a slightly cool note, that is if I could manage not to trip again on my way out.

"Wait." I turned back to him in response. He was holding a thin file with some papers in it. "You'll want to start here. Be thorough, don't be afraid to ask questions and make sure you get some direct quotes from Nick and the other victims. The ones who survived, that is." He broke eye contact then and I left, holding the file.

I sat at my desk, head in hands. What the hell? I didn't have the first clue of what to do next. I had already flicked through the contents of the file. It was just a few brief news reports on other attacks. There had been six in total. The first two victims had died. Multiple broken bones, massive loss of blood. All creepy and vampirey sounding. Was I really going to take the risk of investigating vampire attacks while being stalked by one? Probably the very one I'd be investigating? Adam would kill me. Well, if the killer didn't first. I hyperventilated a bit. In the end, I decided to do some web research first to see what I could find out on the other killings. It wasn't stalling exactly – it was preparation. Honestly! The stories were so violent that I actually cringed when I realised there were photos to accompany some of them. Thankfully they were only vague grainy images of crime scenes and not actual bodies.

I debated calling Adam's mobile but remembered how badly that went last time. And besides, I'd seen him crush it – how long would he take to replace it? Probably not that long – he's rich after all. I decided I'd at least get a taxi to Nick's to talk to him. I rang him and he grudgingly agreed to see me. He probably thought he was doing me a favour, the complete tw- no I'm not going to resort to name-calling. Not unless he starts it anyway. I watched for the taxi to arrive and hurried outside and hopped in. I gave Nick's address and made sure I got a receipt when I paid. I was totally claiming travel expenses.

Nick had told me where his key was hidden so I could let myself in. I knocked first anyway; it seemed creepy otherwise, bearing in mind our past history. He shouted to me to use the F-ing key and I nearly yelled back but held my tongue. Well that doesn't really make sense. It's not like I poked out my tongue and gripped it with my fingers... although now that's what I'm doing to illustrate how stupid it is. I shook my head at myself and wiped my fingers on my coat. I headed into Nick's living room. I'd been at his place quite a lot before so knew my way around. When I saw him, I stopped and kind of forced my mouth closed.

He looked terrible. He was pale, with dark circles around his eyes and bruises pretty much everywhere. I tried not to stare but took in the sling across his shoulder holding one arm. The other had a small cast around the wrist, encasing his thumb. How the hell did he do anything like that? I can't believe I did this but...

"Shit Nick, you look awful. Can I do anything to help you?" Famous last words. Half an hour later after making him a drink and something to eat, and helping him eat said snack I was sitting facing him and racking my brain for good questions. How unlike me... and god help me he'd better not want the loo next.

Chapter Fifteen

"So this is the part where you act like a good little nosy reporter and ask me loads of dumb questions." He said somewhat smugly, seeing how at a loss I was. I sighed – here was the reason why we weren't still together.

"Oh, don't be a twat, Nick." Okay, so apparently, I *was* going to resort to name-calling. "Tell me what happened. Where were you? Did you hear someone following you? Did they speak? Would you recognise them if you saw them again?" He looked vaguely surprised – that'll teach him to tell *me* to ask questions.

"Oh. Um I was walking home from work and was approaching the alley at the bottom of my street when I heard footsteps behind me. I looked but there was nobody there so I just carried on walking but faster… you know?"

Unfortunately, I did know now, so nodded.

"I heard a laugh but again there was nobody there. I uh… I freaked, and I ran." He looked so embarrassed I almost felt sorry for him but knew it would only bite me on the ass later. There I go again with the word bite. I must be obsessed. Damn vampire obsession…

"He jumped me." His words shocked me out of my musings. I scribbled some notes so it looked like I knew what I was doing.

"And?"

"And he just started pounding at me, fists like rocks. I think I eventually passed out but before I did I heard him." I looked up from my notes, seeing terror in his eyes.

"You did lock the door, didn't you?" He asked suddenly. I went to say yes, then realised I had no idea. Feeling a little spooked I got up and checked. Yep, all locked up. He didn't seem that relieved but carried on anyway.

"He called me by my name and said he knew where I lived. He said he chose me because 'she knows me'. I don't know who he means. I know a lot of girls what with work and all." He wasn't bragging, just being honest. I felt like I wasn't breathing. I forced myself to ask more questions.

"What happened next?"

"Like I say, I must have passed out. I woke up in an ambulance. They were saying something about blood loss and how it was weird because I wasn't covered in it, or lying in any and it shouldn't have been possible. I was in so much pain, Lila. I thought I was going to die." His eyes were teary and he tried to rub his face against the pillow propped up behind him. He gasped in pain as he tried. I guess the collarbone thing must have hurt. I pretended not to notice and helped when he asked for help taking some painkillers.

"I'm really scared, Lila. He told me he knows where I live. What if he comes after me again? What did he do to me? And why?" He seemed like a weakened, shadowy version of the Nick I knew and mostly hated.

"I'm so sorry this happened to you, Nick. You went through so much. I um… I guess you know you weren't the first?" He looked at me in horror. Crap, he didn't know then. Lucky he knew tact wasn't a skill of mine.

"What?! He's done this before?!" I nodded, giving in to my worst judgement and showing him the newspaper clippings Colm had given me. I watched the little colour he had left drain from his face as he read. "Fuuuuck, some of these people died, Lila. Why is he doing this? What does he want?"

"You're sure it's a man?" I asked. I mean it's a fair point that a female vampire would be really strong and scary too. Not that he knows it's a vampire of course. He stared at me as he handed back the file.

"Of course it's a fucking man, Lila. Do I look like such a weakling that a girl could kick my ass? He broke my bones for god's sake." Okay, that was more like the Nick I knew. I made my apologies and left. I mean, what can you say to that? As I walked down his path I realised two things too late.

Firstly, I hadn't booked a taxi to get back and that meant walking back along the actual route where Nick's attack had taken place.

Secondly, there was someone watching me. I couldn't see them, but I could feel eyes watching me again. I felt like evil was oozing towards me from some hidden place nearby. Wow, Nick had really freaked me out. I pulled out my mobile and scrolled through for the taxi company number. As I made to press the button to call them I heard a noise behind me. I spun on my heel to stare back at Nick's house but there was nobody there. A quiet chuckle told me that I was in serious danger. In a moment of insane clarity, I rushed forward and let myself back into Nick's house while I frantically located and dialled Adam's number. Nick called out to me asking why I was back as I slid deadbolts I hadn't noticed earlier into their homes and backed away from the door. I waved at him to shush as I listened to the phone ring then Adam's voice, thank god, answering me.

"Adam? Adam he's here... he's going to get me." I babbled, my breath coming fast and fear overwhelming me. I choked back a sob of panic as Adam cursed over the phone and said he was on his way.

"I'm not at work!" I shouted as he was saying something about staying inside.

"WHAT?!" His incredulous yell could probably be heard from the couch, where Nick was sitting, staring at me and glancing from me to the window and back. He looked terrified, like a horse about to bolt; except he probably wouldn't be able to get up to bolt in the first place.

"I'm at Nick's house. I um... had to investigate his..."

"Just give me the address!" He snapped. Seconds later I was holding a phone echoing with a dial tone and my saviour was on his way. Nick yelled my name at me several times to get my attention.

"What the fuck is going on?" I stared at him through slightly cloudy eyes as I heard someone try the front door. It rattled in the frame as someone shook it vigorously. I stared at the front door, backing away almost to the wall, watching the dark shape against the frosted glass as he shook at the door again.

"Lila! What's going on?!" Nick was freaking out.

"He's here." I said quietly. "He was waiting outside for me."

Nick's face contorted in terror and he tried to get up from the sofa, crying out in pain and falling back. I hurried to his side, praying the front door wouldn't suddenly explode open and the angry vampire wouldn't dash through the door and kill us. Do they have to be invited in? I realised I had no idea. Had I invited Adam into my own home? I couldn't remember in my panic.

"Stay down, Nick. We'll be okay. Adam's on his way." I tried to sound calming but to be honest unless someone knows that a powerful vampire is on their way to help, they won't find that much comfort from those words.

"What the fuck is that freak coming here for? What can he do?" He stared at me in shock. And by that, I mean I think he was actually going into shock. The front door crashed open as if blown inwards by an explosion and I heard a shout, followed by another shout and further crashing. I huddled close to Nick and waited for my doom. *Our* doom actually, since he'd kill us both. Nobody appeared immediately and the waiting was terrible. Waiting to die horribly is incredibly unpleasant you know. It's not over in a second, but drags on for hours.

A dark shape filled the doorway and we both screamed. Adam's face caught the light as he staggered inside and I felt a rush of relief as I leapt off the sofa and ran over to him. To be fair it was only a few steps but I went fast. He caught me as I threw myself into his arms. I think I was crying and I know I was shaking all over. Adam hugged me tightly for a moment then moved me away to look at me.

"Are you hurt?" He asked frantically. I shook my head and took in his appearance. His clothes were in disarray and his grey suit jacket and white shirt were ripped near the throat, the tie gone altogether. There was blood on his face and throat where I guess he'd fought with the other vampire.

"Omigod are you hurt? Adam, you're bleeding." I babbled, running my fingers over his face. There were deep scratches under all that blood but they were healing fast. Adam pulled my hand away.

"I'm fine. What happened here?" I looked back at Nick who looked no less afraid than before.

"I was just outside and I could feel him watching me. He laughed. Like before." Nick's face tried to make an expression.

"Like before?! You've seen him?"

Adam placed me on the sofa as far from Nick as possible and crouched in front of Nick, who drew back a little.

"He's been following Lila, Nick. What do you know about him?"

I gasped. "You mean he isn't dead?"

Adam stared at me in surprise. "No of course not. Why would you think that?"

116

"I heard you fighting with him." Adam looked away briefly. "He's much stronger than I am, Lila. He's obviously much older and more powerful. I just about managed to hold him off." I shuddered. A vampire who was stronger than Adam? We were screwed.

"Where is he?" I whispered shakily.

"He ran. I'm so fucking lucky he ran. He went for my throat but I had just enough strength to hold him off." As I absorbed his words, I could see Adam looked drained and his cheeks had taken on that slightly sharp look. Oh hell, he'd burned up almost all of his energy just fending the vampire off. I looked at Nick then back at Adam. Nick was trembling, practically catatonic if appearances were not deceiving.

"Can you make him forget?" I asked quietly. Nick looked at me curiously.

"He's a shrink?"

Adam and I grinned involuntarily, reminded of the day we met. A mere week ago. It felt like forever ago already.

"No. I'm too weak right now to try and get into his mind." Adam said.

"But if you feed now?"

He half-nodded, eyes fixed on the floor. Nick watched from one of us to the other. Curiosity filled his eyes.

"You need to get some food? Now? Seriously? What we need to do is call the police." He said incredulously.

Adam stood up and walked out to the hallway. I followed, pulling the door closed. I unbuttoned the top few buttons of my blouse and pulled it aside, baring my neck. Adam's eyes swirled, but they were mostly showing just shades of red. I trembled, watching his fangs lengthen. They seemed longer and sharper than normal. I didn't question it but just let him move in and tilt his head to my throat. He nuzzled me briefly and placed a kiss against my skin then his teeth sank in and I groaned, shivers running down my spine.

Too late I remembered my usual reaction to Adam's feeding and tried to silence my moans as warmth began to build up in my most private areas. I writhed against Adam's hard body as he fed. I could hear quiet slurping sounds as he drank. I could feel the blood leaving my body, disappearing into the place where his warm mouth was pressed. I felt his throat working as he swallowed and realised he was drinking a lot more than normal. He must have been really exhausted. The usual feeling he gave me drained away before taking hold. My legs began to tremble and I felt my knees give way. Adam's strong arms held me up, but he stopped drinking suddenly. His warm, flushed face stared anxiously into mine as he licked my blood away from his upper lip. His eyes widened, pupils swirling with colour, and he pressed me against the wall to help me keep my balance.

"Fuck! Are you okay? Lila?" I fainted in his arms.

Chapter Sixteen

woke in Adam's bed as I had several times before. I felt so weak I could barely find the strength to lift myself up or turn over. I saw a shadowed figure sitting in a chair beside the bed and gasped in shock. The figure in the chair startled and almost fell to the floor.

"Miss Lila?" Nigel actually sounded human and dare I say, a little concerned. His cool hand came to rest on my forehead and he gently brushed my damp hair back.

"I'll bring Adam at once. Don't move." He was gone quickly. Not vampire quickly but faster than I imagined possible. I fell asleep again I think. When I woke again, Adam was sitting on the chair, much closer to the bed and his shaky hand was stroking my face.

"Lila. Come back to me please." He spoke softly, as if he was afraid to wake me, which was weird because it also sounded like he was trying to do just that. I blinked and focused on his gorgeous but frightened looking face.

"Hi." I whispered, finding my mouth dry. Adam helped me to sit up against his many pillows then helped me drink some water. Once hydrated, I found my mouth worked much better.

"What happened?" He moved his mouth but no sound came out, as if he didn't know what to say.

"I fucked up, Lila. God, I'm so sorry." I tried to lift my hand to my throat, where he'd fed so heavily, but couldn't lift it without a struggle. It was like dead weight.

"I took too much. I lost control. My god, I could have killed you." I wished I could lift an arm to soothe him. He looked so desolate and yes, there were actual tears in his eyes.

Nigel interrupted us then bringing food and drinks and he hovered a moment as if he didn't want to leave. "Is there anything else?" he asked.

Adam thanked him and said no. I gave him the best smile I could manage and whispered thank you.

"Doesn't he hate me anymore?" I whispered to Adam. He laughed sharply then moved to sit on the bed. He stared at me.

"Do *you* hate *me*?" He asked warily. "You have every right to." I stared at him.

"I'm just tired, Adam. I guess I just need time to recover. Right?" He looked away. That scared me. What was going on? Something bad...

"Am I dying?" I asked suddenly. He met my eyes and I saw so much pain there. Oh shit. I was dying.

"What is it, Adam? Tell me!" He stroked my cheek and kept staring right into my eyes.

"I'm sorry. I didn't mean to. I lost control." I gasped, tears springing to my eyes. He rubbed at his face.

"I mean, of course I can give you my blood to help you recover, but I didn't want to do it without your permission. It'll heal you."

"Adam! You don't tell someone they're dying and hold back the 'oh by the way I can save you' part! What the hell?! Oh. I get it. I'll be a vampire, like you. I guess… I…"

"No!" His word cut me off and surprised the hell out of me. He apparently wanted to be with me forever but wouldn't turn me? I was glad I was finding out now.

"You won't turn me? You don't want me forever?" I asked, tears leaking out of my eyes. Honestly, I must be tired, I don't normally cry this easily. I mean I often feel like I will, but then I don't.

He cried a little too.

"Don't be ridiculous, Lila. I love you. Of course, I want to be with you forever. I can't turn you though."

I tried to push him away and climb out of bed but all I succeeded in doing was falling weakly to the side and hitting my head sharply on the bedside table. Two cups of coffee sloshed over their sides and I cried out in pain. Adam's reflexes had just let us both down. He did catch me of course, but not before I gave myself a concussion. It felt like hell. I burst into tears properly this time, exhaustion and pain taking me from weepy to inconsolable in an instant.

"Please Lila. Listen to me. I can heal your pain and injuries and weakness with my blood but I can't turn you. *My* blood cannot turn you. It's not that I don't want to. I just don't have that ability. I'm not a Creator." His words shocked me into silence and I stared at him. Nausea washed over me.

"You're not a Creator? What the hell does that even mean? Oh god, please fix me, Adam. Please… it hurts." My vision swam and I swooned to the side again but he was ready for me this time. He moved to sit behind me, so I was resting my back against his front. He placed a kiss in my damp sweaty hair and if that's not love I don't know what is. He bit into his wrist, tearing the skin and instantly the wound welled with dark blood. He pressed his wrist to my mouth before I could protest and held it there. I couldn't do anything other than taste his blood.

It was tangy, as if tinged with every single spice in existence, at just the right balance. It was thick like honey and a single taste made me want more. I drew on the cut and kept swallowing his blood. I guess it was only fair. He drank me nearly dry so I guess it was okay to drink his blood in return. Even though it wouldn't make me immortal like him. As I drank his blood, and relished the dark heady taste, I realised something with such clarity I was shocked into stopping for a moment. I definitely wanted to be like him. Immortal, safe, strong. If all blood tasted like his, I'd happily drink it for eternity. I resumed drinking until he forcibly pulled his wrist away. I think I actually made a growl of some kind because he chuckled and kissed my head again. I stared at the wound as it closed up quickly in front of me. I felt a sudden rush of strength through me and my head tingled for a few moments before all pain miraculously disappeared. I wriggled around until I was facing Adam and was shocked to see him looking tired and gaunt again.

"Well, touché Lila. You certainly got your own back." He laughed breathlessly, leaning forward to kiss me hard. He released me quickly and pulled me toward him so I rested against his chest. I listened to his heart thumping sluggishly. It sounded too slow for his heart and freaked me out.

"I've weakened you too much, haven't I? Why didn't you stop me sooner? You need to feed, Adam."

He shrugged. "I'll get something in a moment. Let's just relax here a little bit." He seemed too lethargic for my liking and a moment later when I hopped out of bed and hurried out of the room, he didn't try to stop me, drifting into a light sleep.

I found Nigel sitting on the stairs. He looked shattered as he looked up at me. He met my eyes in surprise.

"Miss Lila? You look recovered." He seemed relieved.

"Yes, but Adam needs something to feed on now. What do we do?" I said in a panicked tone.

He hurried to his feet and ran to the bedroom. I followed swiftly but stopped in shock when I saw Nigel slash his own wrist with a penknife and press it to Adam's mouth. Adam latched on and fed for a few long moments before releasing him. I was stunned. Adam feeds on Nigel? What was freaking me out here? Was it the guy on guy thing or just that it was Nigel? And why didn't Nigel have the reaction I normally do? As Adam lay back down and closed his eyes, I helped Nigel to the bathroom and dressed the wound on his wrist.

Chapter Seventeen

“You've done that before.” I stated, as I bound a soft pad to the wound with lots of bandage tape. Nigel nodded.

"It's what I do. I'm his blood donor. It's a bit different from him feeding from you of course."

I laughed harshly. "No kidding. I mean... oh god...." I dipped my head in shame.

Nigel laughed suddenly, taking in my embarrassment and pulling his wrist away. Good timing on his part really, or it would have been the size of his upper arm with all the sticky bandage tape I was putting around it.

"Please don't think Adam has ever taken blood from me the same way he does with you. We don't have sexual relations." I backed away and sat on the edge of the bathtub in shock.

"You don't?" I was relieved but still slightly freaked out. Nigel lifted my chin with his fingers.

"I'm a different kind of human in that my blood is more nutritious to vampires. Less of my blood can satisfy them, making me the perfect companion. I chose Adam a long time ago because I could see he would treat me with respect and not keep me as a prisoner. My blood replenishes extremely quickly, meaning I could feed several vampires each day without losing too much blood or being weakened."

"Like a vending- oh god, forget I even said that. What's wrong with me?" Nigel laughed as I sighed.

"I can see what he means about you. You are fascinating! Honestly, I do get some benefits as well as being provided with a more than comfortable home and life. I move faster than normal humans, I heal faster and I have heightened senses. To hear when I'm needed." My face reddened as I realised the other things he must have heard too. His wry grin told me I was spot on too.

"I'm sorry, but I don't understand why you serve Adam like a butler. Is that part of the job too?" He chuckled as he sat beside me on the edge of the bath.

"I was training to be a manservant when my birthright was revealed to me. After a brief time with a cruel master, I was freed and chose to live with Adam. I asked to act in the role I was training for, as it would make me happy. He still, after all these years, tries to do his own chores and I waste hours telling him off and fixing the messes he makes when he tries. And don't get me started on him trying to cook!"

"After all these years... wait... people don't train as a manservant these days. How old are you? If you don't mind me asking, I mean."

He shrugged. "I was 104 on my last birthday. We don't age normally or die easily so there's another benefit for you."

I stared at him. Firstly, it was amazing when he was being nice to me, which made it hard to remember what a douche he had been at first. Secondly, I had a much deeper respect for him, knowing he had been looking after my Adam all this time. He seemed to sense my thoughts.

"I care about Adam deeply. Love him like a brother. I was worried at first that you would be trouble for him. I can see now that he probably loved you from that first moment at his office." I giggled, remembering our bizarre first meeting.

"Wait. I *am* trouble. He's in there recovering from me drinking him nearly to death... after he did the same to me..."

"As I say. If he didn't love you, you would have never ended up in this situation. He'd never have given you a second thought after that first meeting. As it was he wouldn't shut up about you that first night until I threatened to go to bed just to get away from him! He's never brought a female here in all the years I've known him. He sees something in you. Now if he can only find a Creator willing to help, I'm sure he would ask you to be with him forever." His last words were almost muttered as if not really for my ears.

"What's the business with Creators? If Adam isn't one, what is he?" Nigel stood up and helped me up, leading me into the bedroom where Adam looked up sheepishly halfway through my dinner.

"That's for Adam to explain, love. Now you settle in with him and I'll bring you something else to eat. Someone seems to have eaten yours…"

With a shake of his head, he left the room and I climbed on the bed to face Adam. He polished off the last of my soup and bread and grinned.

"Sorry. I was ravenous when I woke up and it was getting cold."

I laughed. "I hope you enjoyed it." He looked so well again and it made me feel all warm inside. Actually, that made yet another question come to mind. "Weird thing to ask but… well I guess you're used to it. Why didn't I have my usual reaction at Nick's when you fed on me? It started… but then it faded away." Adam patted the bed beside him and I climbed under the covers, leaning sideways against the headboard so I could sort of face him.

"That's my fault I'm afraid. I have to focus to give you that experience and I was just so drained I got caught up in feeding. I'm so, so sorry, Lila. Please forgive me." I smiled at him.

"Of course I forgive you. It's not like you did it on purpose, but FYI don't stiff me out of my good feelings next time yeah?"

He laughed with surprise and his eyes swirled a bit. Nigel's reappearance with another tray of food and drinks distracted us and after insisting Nigel stay with us, we all tucked into food and hot drinks and chatted about nothing important. It was nice that Nigel was so different with me now. It felt right sitting with them.

Nigel disappeared with the dishes and a goodnight when we'd finished and Adam and I settled down facing each other and dozed on and off for a while. Truth be told, I felt too wired to sleep so just kept trying and failing. It was bizarre; I felt like I'd had about 50 coffees or something. Actually, I'm not sure that would even be possible but still it was an extreme feeling. I amused myself by drinking in every perfectly sculpted feature on Adam's face, and watching him rest. His full lips curved into a smile while he seemed to sleep.

"Staring at me while I sleep?" He whispered, grin widening. I giggled and swatted him.

"How long have you been awake?" His soulful blue eyes opened and fixed on mine.

"The whole damn time." He growled. "I can't sleep because you're so edgy it's rubbing off on me!" His eyes went all swirly which did things to me and before I could think, I did what I've always wanted since I met him and I dived on him. He laughed as I landed half on him and half across the bed like a dying fly. Okay, so maybe a dying fly wouldn't look quite like that but forgive me, my mind is elsewhere. I pulled at his shirt and felt incredibly gratified when it tore under my hands. The surprise in his eyes was replaced with something so lustful I quivered. He swiftly rolled us so I was beneath him and pinned me down as he kissed me hard.

His tongue pressed and rubbed against mine and I moaned into his mouth as I responded. I flipped us back over, with strength I didn't know I had, and pressed his arms down, raining kisses on his face, neck and chest while he breathed in panting breaths. He strained against my arms and flipped us once more. His leg pressed between mine and I willingly opened up to him but all he did was press his thigh between my legs and move so it rubbed against me. I wrapped my thighs around his and squeezed as he tore away the T-shirt I'd been wearing (his this time so I was glad it was his wardrobe suffering this time).

His hands moved to my breasts, cupping, and teasing and squeezing while I wriggled about trying to regain control. It was no good though. He had full control now and forced me to endure yet more teasing and touching, while I begged him to take me. Well I used ruder words than that but I'm keeping it as clean as I can here. When he finally pushed my legs wider apart and slid inside me slowly and deeply, I felt myself clench around him and moaned aloud. Yes, this was what I'd wanted ever since I'd fed on his blood. The feel of him inside me drove me wild and I found I was moving frantically against him for my climax.

He laughed and used his hands to hold my hips still as he pulled out and slid back in over and over, maddeningly slowly 'til I screamed at him. The swift change from slow to fast and hard was delicious and I didn't care that he was still holding me down and not letting me move with him. He did all the work, creating such wonderful friction that I screamed as I came over and over and felt him come hard inside me. We lay still, panting and laughing, our sweat mingling as our bodies cooled. He stayed inside me for ages and I could feel that he was still hard.

Was that a normal vampire thing or was it from all the blood exchanging? Testing him, I wriggled beneath him and felt him shudder as he lifted his eyes to meet mine, wide and swirling with colour.

"Not satisfied yet?" I asked, moving against him again, drawing out a shuddery moan. He brought his lips to mine, kissing me over and over as I writhed against him again and again, trying to move for both of us. While it wasn't doing as much for me, it was driving him mad. I could see the heat rise in his eyes and they swirled dangerously as he looked at me.

"What are you playing at, Miss Lila?" He asked in a gruff voice. I gave an innocent grin and then made a startled cry as he pulled out and flipped me over, onto my knees.

He was back inside me swiftly and took me slowly and deeply from behind. My arms trembled beneath the onslaught and I whimpered over and over as he kept thrusting in, out and back in again. His fingers crept around to my throat and he pulled my head around to kiss me as he pounded into me. I gasped into his mouth and felt him laugh into mine. Releasing my face, he went back to holding me in place and kept on shoving into me. I came twice and he just kept going. My arms finally gave out and I collapsed, but he kept hold of my hips and kept thrusting harder and harder till I screamed again with climax and felt him finish.

I was relieved when we both flopped down on our backs side by side on the bed. I was exhausted in ways I'd never felt before. Not that it was a bad feeling, but I was surprised by the intensity of our second time – It literally nearly blew my mind. I mean I've never had a guy take me like that before. Nick's idea of 'lovemaking' was to lie me down and just go for his pleasure while I often faked mine. I'd never been with anyone before Nick and I had always been glad he'd not shared that information when we broke up. Quite good of him I supposed.

I wished for a moment that Adam had been my first. What a wanton introduction to womanhood that would have been. Adam was still panting beside me, and he placed one arm over his eyes. His hair looked as if I'd gripped it in my fists, which actually I may well have done at some point.

"Satisfied now?!" I gasped, turning my head to look sideways at him.

"Whoa, what came over me?" He breathed back. "I'm sorry, that was really intense." No shit. I didn't bother voicing that. Eventually our breathing slowed and we both fell into an exhausted sleep.

Chapter Eighteen

magine my horror the next morning to find out that in addition to Nigel, Nick was also under the same roof as us. Adam hadn't wanted to leave Nick behind for the other vampire so had put him in 'my' old guest room. I hoped he was in a doped up asleep all night or he couldn't have helped but hear us (sorry but I'll say it this once) fucking all night.

As I got out of bed and went for a shower I was rudely aware that I felt stiff and sore but it was a comforting feeling. I jumped as warm hands touched my shoulders and I nearly slipped. Strong hands spun me around to face a smirking Adam as he stepped in beside me and pulled me close for a kiss.

"Morning sexy." He muttered as he pulled away. I grinned then briefly panicked about morning breath. He didn't seem bothered by it though. His eyes slitted at me and I gulped as I remembered what that look seemed to mean normally. He rushed against me, pressing me against the cold, tiled wall. I gasped with shock as my back cooled suddenly. His lips were on me and he pressed his hard body against me. He took me hard and fast against the wall, allowing himself to come only when he felt me climax. I was so glad he was holding me up or I'd have melted to the tiled floor like goo. It took a few minutes for my legs to regain their strength and then they went all trembly again when Adam took it upon himself to wash me. There is something so sensual about a man shampooing your hair in the shower. His hands were firm and massaged my scalp as the ethereal scent of my Molton Brown shampoo filled the room. I was absolutely in heaven. I didn't ever want to leave.

Going back to work was too scary a concept after what had happened at Nick's yesterday. Not to mention I had to explain for my unexpected absence and provide some kind of research for Colm. In the end, Adam convinced me that staying at his place and calling in sick was the safest option. I called in to Colm explaining that I would work on the story from home. I told him I'd seen Nick and had a good story from him. At that point, he asked me where Nick was. I was surprised, as I had already forgotten Nick was in the house with me now. After promising Colm a story by the end of the week, I finished the call and found Adam in the kitchen. He was finishing some breakfast (and I don't mean Nigel) and pointed out a fresh cup of coffee, which he'd poured for me.

"Nigel's going to cook for you. Anything you want. His words, not mine." I smiled and sat down with my coffee. "You guys seem to have bonded at last." Adam finished. He took his plate to the sink and came back to sit down with the last of his own coffee.

"He explained who he is. What he does... I was a bit shocked when I saw him feed you I'm embarrassed to say." I muttered, ashamed of my reaction, especially now I was facing Adam. Adam nodded.

"He said. Don't feel bad for that. You didn't know what to expect. And I didn't want to tell you that Nigel, my friend for so many years, is also my happy meal. It still feels awkward sometimes. I don't think I'd still be here if not for Nigel. He keeps me grounded, human, you know?"

It sounded a bit bizarre to me – how does a superhuman donating blood make a vampire feel human? I nodded though and hoped Adam didn't see anything in my face disagreeing with him. He took his mug to the sink and came back to me, pulling me to my feet, while simultaneously plucking my coffee from my hand and depositing it on the table.

"Please, please stay inside, where it's safe. I don't think the Tracker can find you here, but just in case, please stay out of sight. You know that once I leave I'll be about twenty minutes away so Nigel and Nick's safety is also reliant on you not leaving the house and letting him track you." It angered me briefly that I was being made to stay indoors and having the pressure of their safety on me but I knew deep down he meant well. He cupped my cheeks.

"I know you hate being told what to do so I'm asking, Lila. Not telling. Asking. Hell, I can even beg if you like?" His grin made me smile back and I cupped his face in a reflection of his gesture.

"I promise to stay indoors like a good girl, Adam." His grin turned to a sly smirk and somehow, I just knew he was thinking of our behaviour the night before and how that was anything but good girl behaviour. I kissed him and felt him sigh as he pulled away from me.

"I wish I didn't have to go but I have a big contract on my desk which needs my personal attention. I'll be back as soon as I can but there's also a meeting at 3pm I have to attend too." He checked his watch then headed out to the hall. I ran after him.

"Adam, please be careful too. He knows you now. He's been to your office already. If he can track me, he can track you too. Be safe." He hugged me tightly then left quickly. I stood in the hallway for a few minutes after he left me, wondering what to do with my time. In the end, I poured some coffee and went looking for Nick. He probably had questions and for once I had answers. I think.

Chapter Nineteen

I found Nick, sitting up in the guest bed, reading a book with a faded cover, which looked like it came from Adam's library. I knocked and he nodded as if to say come in. To be fair, it really was just a nod but what else could it mean?

"I brought you some coffee." I said lamely as I walked in. He thanked me. That was weird. It was like Nick had been body snatched and there was a nice guy in his place. I didn't knock it and leaving the coffee beside him, I settled into the window seat.

"How are you feeling?" I didn't want to say anything about what had happened in case Adam had erased it all already. Nick looked up from the book and placed it down with a bookmark in his place. He looked at the coffee and I got up to pass it to him, as he didn't have much mobility in his arms. Wait. There was no cast or sling and he was in fact using his arms holding and putting down the book. Interesting. I watched him reach for the coffee and wrap his hands around it.

"Well I feel tons better than I did thanks. Whatever your boyfriend did seemed to really help." I was confused. Had Adam healed him with blood? He was in a cast and sling yesterday and looked like death. Today he looked like Nick, but nice. Only vampire blood could have done this, I was sure.

"Um. You look better? What did Adam do exactly?" Surely, he hasn't left him with knowledge of what he is?

"Oh uh... it's a little weird."

"Uh huh try me." Nick shrugged.

"He gave me something to drink. It tasted kinda sweet and spicy and everything just started to feel better."

"He gave you *something* to drink. Like what? GHB? A miracle cure?" I couldn't help but sound sarcastic. What did Nick think had happened?

"He told me it was an old-fashioned form of pain relief but it didn't taste like it. It wasn't bitter or nasty and seemed to start working instantly. I don't know where the cast and sling went. They were gone when I woke up this morning. He should totally market the stuff he gave me though – it's incredible. Holy shit... even my bruises on my arms are faded." He checked his chest by pulling his shirt open at the neck. "Jesus. I look almost back to normal."

"Yeah a normal twat." I marched out of the room. What the hell had Adam done? Did he think that Nick, a *reporter* no less, was going to just 'forget' that he'd cured him? He'd want to know what it was, where it came from, why the world didn't know about it... etc. etc...

And even if he wiped him now, others would notice he'd recovered way too fast. It was a minefield!

"Nigel?!" I shouted, heading down the corridor. As I reached the office I threw the door open expecting to see Nigel sitting at the desk. He wasn't there. I turned to leave the room and ran straight into him with a startled shriek. Nigel's hands steadied me then he took a few steps backward as if to put 'personal space' between us.

"Are you okay, Miss Lila?" He asked with apparent concern.

"Stop the 'Miss Lila' thing okay?! It's really pissing me off!" Actually, it wasn't but I was pissed about everything else so why not that too?

"I'm sorry. I'll stop if it bothers you." He sounded so damned reasonable I wanted to hit him.

"What the hell has Adam done to Nick? The guy thinks he's had some miracle cure and he's nearly healed and now he's going to want to know everything and he'll write about it because he's a reporter and that's what they do and he won't stop till he gets the truth and why didn't Adam think of that?" Nigel looked a bit dizzy.

"Hmmm yes, Adam warned me about the fifty word sentences."

"What?!" I shrieked. "This is serious!"

Nigel led me to a seat by the desk then perched on the edge of the desk to face me.

"Yes, Adam gave Nick his blood. He healed him so that he can protect himself or you if needed. It would have been selfish not to; to leave him suffering in that way. Adam isn't a selfish man."

"He's not a man at all. That's the point! Don't you think Nick is going to want to know what the hell he drank and why he's instantly better? He won't let it go, Nigel! Adam's just put himself in even more danger." I groaned the last sentence, the fight leaving me as I slumped in the seat. I suddenly felt old, and weak and... human... surely not...

"Nigel, does Adam's blood.... Or any vampire blood for that matter, make a human stronger or anything?" Nigel laughed.

"Of course, it imbues the human with a taste of vampire abilities. I thought you were well informed via vampire fiction? You're coming down from it now, that's all. It also heightens the libido although I unfortunately know you discovered that one last night too."

Oh gross, I wanted to die and get swallowed up by the ground. Of course, Nigel heard everything. I put my hands over my face.

"Oh god, oh god. I'm so sorry Nigel. I don't know what came over us."

"A blood exchange heightens all emotions, senses and abilities. You both felt like gods and acted like it. I'm sure it won't be the last time."

"Was it the first time? I mean..."

"You mean has Adam done that with lots of girls? The answer is no. He hasn't really taken much interest in any females since I've been here with him. To be honest I was beginning to think perhaps females weren't even his type."

I laughed; picturing someone not realising Adam was seriously straight. I mean I was walking proof of that.

"So, to get back to the point. Adam healed Nick with his blood. What has he told him? I don't want to put my foot in it or anything."

"It's a little late for that, Lila." Nick's voice sounded from the hallway. Nigel and I turned identically horrified faces to the doorway as Nick stepped inside.

"*You* talk about vampires like they're a real thing." He said, pointing at me. "And *you*." Pointing at Nigel. "You don't correct her or laugh in her face like you should, as any *sane* person should." He looked from one to the other of us. "One of you had better explain what the fuck is going on right now. I'm beginning to think I've had a breakdown and I'm in a loony bin." I briefly thought of going along with that but Nigel's face stopped me in my tracks. He gestured to me to do the talking. Coward.

"So, Adam is a vampire, the guy who attacked you is also a vampire and Adam gave you his blood to heal you. Oh, and he brought you here to somewhere in Scandinavia to keep you safe. Nigel is some kind of superhuman blood donor thing and I'm just a vampire wannabe…"

"Who spent the entire night screwing a supposed vampire." Nick finished with a smirk. I covered my face again. And then I looked up as I realised he hadn't laughed or argued with me.

"You knew." I accused, standing up and facing him. Nigel stood up too. Maybe he felt left out, I don't know. Nick's face was a little sly.

"Please. A man attacked me so violently that I passed out and I woke up with hardly any blood left when I clearly hadn't bled out everywhere. My psycho ex-girlfriend gets followed to my place by said attacker and calls her new boyfriend along who has an almighty scrap with the guy and comes in half dead. You then disappear into the hallway, where I hear what sounds like either a major snogging session or worse and you end up passed out while he looks like he's just been hit with a major dose of who knows what! He somehow carries us both out to his car in seconds and drives to a place where it's gone from dry to snowing heavily in the space of half an hour. Then he gives me some kind of spicy drink, which heals me completely? Trust me, I didn't want to believe my mind would go there at all but vampire did actually spring to mind." He dropped into a seated position on the floor as if he'd exhausted himself with his unwitting impression of me and I mirrored his pose. Nigel looked at us both and sighed heavily, dropping down to the floor also.

"We do have perfectly good chairs all over the house you know." He groaned. I laughed and patted his knee.

"This is totally a sitting on the floor moment, Nige. You know that. Besides that *thing* in the library does *not* count as a perfectly good chair!" He laughed and leaned back against the front of the desk.

"Everything you have both said is correct. I had believed Adam would help you forget what had happened, Nick, but he's lost a lot of blood in the last twenty-four hours so perhaps he wasn't able to. He will of course do so for you when he's back to full strength."

"Now wait a minute. Nobody is going to screw with my mind. I need my mind. I'm a writer." Nick said warily, leaning back as if that would protect him from being influenced. Foolish really but I could kind of see why he did it. Nigel did look pretty intense.

"Surely if he promises to keep it a secret, Nigel? Can we ask Adam to at least consider it?" Nigel glared at me.

"I'm sure Adam will do whatever you ask as usual, Lila, but please be reasonable. His safety is at risk with this secret. And with his safety goes yours and mine. And we do have a Tracker vampire out there right now which is of much greater importance than all of this. He won't stop until he finds you. He'll go after everyone you care about, he'll go through them all violently to get to you. If we don't get him first, you'll end up giving yourself up to him to save your friends. It's how they operate."

I stood up in a hurry, fists clenched.

"Why the hell does Adam *never ever* tell me the real story? So, everyone I know is in danger of being a vampire chew toy just because for some bizarre reason he wants to catch me? And then what will he do? Feed on me? Kill me? Why isn't anyone telling me what's actually fucking happening?" I marched from the room to the library, stopping only to use the hall phone to try and call Adam. Voicemail. Brilliant.

"When you get this you lying little sack of sh- actually, you know what, Adam? Call me if and when you're ready to actually be honest with me for once in your damned life." I slammed the phone down realising that made no sense at all. Oh well, that was his problem. I was so angry I was surprised I'd managed any message at all. I stalked off to the library. Time to find out the real story without waiting to be drip-fed the truth. I slammed the door hard, which kind of did that vacuumy-sucky thing some doors do which is so irritating because I just wanted it to slam... *loudly*. I tried again with no success and decided a third time would be pathetic. Besides it just pissed me off even more. Now where was that book I'd been looking at last time I was in here? It mentioned different types of vampires. Ah... this looks like it.

It wasn't. It wasn't even in English! I debated throwing it on the floor but it looked old and wasn't it some kind of sacrilege to throw books around? I wasn't sure but decided not to risk it. It wasn't the book's fault that Adam was a lying shit. I did risk kicking that horrible chaise longue thing but only succeeded in stubbing my toe, which really hurt. Why couldn't I even have a tantrum properly? In the end, I sank to the floor in the corner of the room, my back against some of the dusty old books on a low shelf. I sighed and pulled my knees up, wrapping my arms around them. Was this going to be my life now? Trapped in a vampire's house, hiding from other vampires and forced to spend my time with *Nick*?! Nigel was bad enough (yes, I've changed my mind about him again but I'm a girl, it's allowed) but Nick too? Jeez. I heard the phone ring and stayed where I was. It was probably a sales call or someone for Nigel. He had to have friends, right? I heard low mumbling in the hallway and Nigel briefly raised his voice although I took no notice of his words. I was so drained and fed up. I rested my forehead on my knees and closed my eyes.

Chapter Twenty

guess I fell asleep like that. The room was dark when I woke up. I was sleeping a lot lately but I guess that made sense if I kept losing blood to a vampire. I lifted my head and groaned, feeling the kink in my neck protesting. And that was nothing compared to the aches in the rest of my body. Take my advice and never fall asleep in such a scrunched up position. It does you no good at all. Actually, take my further advice and stay away from vampires. They seem all sexy and romantic until you have a psycho Tracker after you and can't ever go outside again and what if I needed to get women's supplies? It had just occurred to me I was stuck in a house full of men and would need certain supplies very soon.

I wriggled away from the shelf and sprawled out on my back on the thick carpet, stretching out with a sigh and staring at the ceiling. It was mostly dark so really, I was just staring into nothingness. It was peaceful for a while but then I heard the bang of the front door and raised voices in the hallway. I debated sitting up but couldn't be bothered. Adam threw open the door to the library and the crack of light which dashed across the room and hit me straight in the eyes, made me wince. I draped my arm over them to bring back the blessed darkness.

"Smooth." I muttered snidely. He crossed the room and dropped to crouch beside me.

"What the hell are you doing lying on the floor in the dark?" He grabbed my arms and unceremoniously dragged me to my feet using that annoying vampire strength and not much gentleness. I tried to pull away from him. I was pissed off at him remember? He stared me in the eyes, and I could suddenly see just how angry he was. A tingle of nerves crept across my spine. Why did I decide to intentionally rile up a vampire? Again? It had seemed like a good idea at the time...

"Come on." He snapped, dragging me from the room and depositing me in the kitchen where Nigel and Nick were sitting waiting at the dining table. It was like one of those ridiculous 'intervention' things Americans have. I mean I'm sure we probably have them here too but call them something less interesting like disciplinaries or arguments or something.

"We need to talk." Adam started, slamming a coffee in front of me, then grabbing one for himself. I was starting to feel freaked out by the whole situation. Where was my sweet sexy vampire who wanted to protect me? This one looked like he wanted to kill me.

"Okay." I muttered, wrapping my hands around the mug and daring to sneak a look up at him, before looking away.

"Why the hell do you look shit scared of me? For heaven's sake, Lila! We've been through this!" Even my fear annoyed him? Well that annoyed me a bit too.

"Stop acting like a complete psycho then! You're scaring me!"

Nick snorted and I saw Nigel look away with a smirk. Adam took a deep breath.

"I'm sorry. But why the hell would you be scared of me?" He finally looked a little calmer thankfully.

"Um because you're an angry vampire glaring and yelling at me? Why the hell wouldn't I?" Another sigh.

"A *really* angry vampire but I'm not the one who wants to kill you, remember? What the fuck was that message about earlier?" I had no idea what he was talking about at first. Then I remembered why I'd been so angry in the first place. It rushed back at me, giving me courage.

"Why didn't you bother to tell me the Tracker is going to hunt me down through my friends and family?" I meant to ask quietly but typically of me it ended up more of a yell. He looked a bit surprised, and exchanged a look with Nigel.

"Don't look at him as if to say, 'who is this crazy woman'! You knew this would scare me and piss me off so you kept it to yourself. You're keeping Nick and I safe here and that's great and all but what about the others I know and care about? I mean, there aren't many but I had a right to know and a right to try and keep them safe. Would I give myself up to a psycho vampire

147

threatening to hurt my friends? Eventually when I've stopped shitting myself with fear, yes, I would, because it's my decision, not yours, and you need to stop hiding stuff from me!"

Damn, I need to learn how to breathe between sentences. Actually, I don't think there were many sentences in that tirade… Three stunned male faces with identically dropped open mouths met my eyes when I looked up. It was hysterical but I wasn't going to laugh. Well I tried not to but it was hard. I might have sniggered for maybe a second. Then I pasted a scowl back on my face. I was still mad after all. And out of breath. I sucked in air and waited for Adam's excuses. Adam opened and closed his mouth a few times. I was a tough act to follow after all.

"I feel like I need to breathe for you, Lila. How do you even do that?!" He eventually asked with a tiny grin. He really was adorable but I had to stand my ground.

"Don't be cute, Adam. You know why I'm mad – don't I have a point?"

He nodded.

"I was going to tell you, really I was. I just wanted to try and find out more about this Tracker first. So, I made some calls; asked around a bit. Um, anyway, the news isn't good." He looked at Nigel then back at me again.   "And I know I should have wiped Nick's memory but he didn't actually seem to need it. He was actually pretty out of it 'til you sat him down for vampire 101 this morning." Nick made a kind of humph sound but stayed quiet.

"Actually, I think he probably guessed when you fed him some yummy red liquid which healed all his wounds overnight, Einstein." I hated when I was really angry and someone managed to completely deflate my anger with a few words. Unfortunately, Adam seemed to have a gift for it. "Go on. Tell me this not good news. He wants to kill me yes?"

Adam sighed.

"Not exactly no. His name is Stig and he's notorious for hunting down human females with potential gifts so he can sell them to Creators."

"Stig? Like Stig of the Dump? Seriously? Did his parents name him that or worse, did he choose... hang on, potential gifts? What does that mean?"

Nigel stood up and refilled his own coffee.

"I think it's time to explain the different types of vampires to her. It'll help to understand why he wants her."

I looked at Nigel in surprise. Different types of vampires? Sounded ominous. He sat back down and waited.

Adam ran his fingers through his hair, rumpling it up so he looked like he had bed hair. That made me a little warm but I forced myself to focus.

"Um. Okay there are different kinds of vampires. I'm known as a 'Traveller', which is a really lame name for what I can do, but it's a fairly rare gift. Probably forty-nine out of fifty vampires are just standard vampires. You know, they feed on people; they are strong and fast and violent. The other 1 in 50 develop special gifts when they are turned. Apparently, these gifts can be sensed in humans by a special type of vampire. They're called 'Prophets' and they can sense all kinds of things about humans and vampires. They usually team up with 'Creators' to help them find the most worthy humans to turn into vampires." I raised my eyebrows. This was way more complex than my usual vampire fare.

"But this one's teamed up with a Tracker?" He nodded; a little surprised I'd followed his explanation so easily.

"A Prophet has obviously sensed something in you and has sold this information to a Tracker. The Tracker in turn wants to hunt you down and sell you to the Creator. He'll then make you into a vampire and will own you with whatever gifts you'll develop. To be honest it's not unheard of for these kinds of collaborations but it's the first I've come across in fifty years or more. Nigel?" He looked across at Nigel who nodded.

"I've heard the stories but never been party to it actually happening. Do we know who the Prophet or Creator might be?"

"No. I only know it's Stig because it turns out there are only six known Trackers alive at the moment and we've now confirmed the locations of the others. I have no idea how many Creators are out there, you know how they like to hide out until they want to... um... procreate."

I shuddered at the word.

"Prophets are so rare I can't get a bead on any in existence at the moment. Basically, they *have* to hide, they're so in demand."

I shook my head and looked at Nick.

"As one of two normal people in the room (no offence) what can we do? I mean, I can't hide here forever, and neither can Nick. Can we bargain with him?"

Adam laughed harshly. "I don't think you understand Trackers yet. They become so fixated on their prey, it's like an obsession. He'll give every last second and ounce of strength to finding you. He'll crawl half dead across broken glass and wooden stakes to try and reach you. It's in his blood. It's practically what makes his heart beat. It's what he is. They are the most obsessive and dangerous vampires of all."

"Well these Prophets sound pretty kickass. Can't we try and find the one who sold me out and appeal to them?"

Nigel looked at Adam, who shrugged tiredly.

"You know we'll have to call reinforcements, don't you?" Adam sighed and rubbed his hand over his face. "You know how that's going to go though, Nige. It'll be a madhouse again."

Nigel grinned.

"It'll be nice to have a houseful again. And you've missed them, you know you have." Adam groaned but nodded.

I had no idea what this all meant. I was still kind of stuck on the whole potential gifts thing. What could it be? What other types of vampires are there?

"Adam, what else is there? Apart from Travellers, Trackers, Prophets and Creators? Oh, and basic ordinary vampires."

"I wouldn't call them that if I were you." Nigel chuckled, getting up and moving around the kitchen obviously preparing food. My stomach growled and I grimaced. Anyone with vampire-like hearing obviously heard that. A quick glance at the smirk on Nick's face told me it wasn't just Adam and Nigel who heard it.

"Okay I'm hungry, so sue me." I snapped. Adam leaned to whisper in my ear.

"Stop blushing – you're making me hungry too." He did his old mwahaha chuckle in my ear and made me giggle.

"Hey, no eating the human 'til she's been fed." Actually, that just sounded lame but it was too late to take back. I'd said it. Nick laughed and gave me a funny look.

A quick glance at Adam showed me the heat in his eyes and I realised my words could probably be taken another way. I blushed more, which just made him grin wickedly. I could see that he looked a little thin in the face though. He'd been out wasting energy again.

Nigel cleared his throat. "If you two lovebirds could stop making eyes at each other, perhaps Adam would like to explain about other vampire types?" His tone had no bite to it but it shook us out of our world just the same. Probably a good thing for the others in the room! He cleared his throat.

"Um… well there are Shapeshifters and Compulsors and Seekers and…. You know what. I've got a book in the library which explains it better. I'll just show you after dinner." He got up to help Nigel in the kitchen and I sat back down with Nick at the table after ditching my coffee cup.

He grinned at me. He seemed so different away from our normal life. More like the guy I'd fallen for a year or so ago.

"So…"

"Yeah great conversation opener, Lila. So...." I slapped his arm and laughed.

"Why aren't you so much of a dick now?" I asked before I could stop myself. He laughed though so I guess it didn't offend him. He shrugged.

"Maybe my priorities have changed? I don't know. Seems like there's a lot more going on around us than who slept with who and who thinks who is a twat." I pointed from me to him with a sly grin as he said the last part. He tried to scowl but seemed in too good a mood to carry it off.

"Pretty freaky stuff eh?" I asked lamely. He nodded seriously.

"I never imagined all this stuff could exist but I'm kind of glad. Life would be dull without it right? Jobs and rules seem kind of pointless when there's so much more important stuff going on." He had a point.

"Yeah that's true. I mean, I'm being tracked by a psycho torturing vampire nut job so why should I worry if Colm is going to get cranky if I'm late for work."

"You're not going to work." Adam interjected with a sheepish grin. I looked at him in surprise.

"What, ever?" He shook his head, which didn't really make any sense – did that mean yes never, or no, not forever, just not for now? I looked at Nick who nodded as if agreeing with Adam. Okay now I'm confused.

"What does that mean?" I asked Nick. "Well *I'm* quitting anyway." He commented evenly. "Much more going on in life than writing a crappy column for a crappy local paper. I want to know more about vampires, and what else is out there. I'm going to study this life,

153

and put my focus here. So, some politician is padding
out his expenses? I don't care. Vampires are *real*. *That*
is the only news I needed to hear."

"You're going to write about vampires?" I asked,
confused.

"No. Duh! I'm going to learn about them. I'm
going to find something to do with my life which leaves
me free to learn more about this other life going on
around us mere mortals." He seemed so enthused by his
idea I didn't have the heart to tell him he'd end up living
in a cardboard box or eaten by a vampire. Or both. I also
conveniently put Adam's comment about me not going
back to work out of my mind. It wasn't his decision
anyway, right?

Dinner found its way to the table then in Nigel and
Adam's capable hands and we all tucked in as if we'd
never eaten before. It was delicious and we all seemed so
comfortable with each other. Mind you among us we'd
all shared blood in some way so I guess it made sense. In
a creepy kind of way.

We all crowded around the book in the library later
and Adam talked me through the different types of
vampires. Nick listened so intently you'd think he had
slipped into a coma with his eyes open. I was surprised
he wasn't taking notes. Maybe he was recording it on his
phone I thought with a laugh.

Anyway, to break it down for you, it goes something
like this:

Creator

These vampires can create other vampires. They are rare and also have super speed, super strength and can fly. Along with the usual vampire killing methods Adam explained, they are also unable to go out in sunlight (the only vampires affected by this restriction).

Traveller

These vampires can create portals to travel great distances and can escort one person at a time. They are also rare and have super speed, super strength and can fly.

Shapeshifter

These vampires can take another form, (animal only that is) and are the source of werewolf myths. They are fairly common and their special skills include the skills of whichever animal they take the form of, hence why they often choose wolf form. In addition to the usual vampire weaknesses, they find moonlight empowers them and are more active during the full moon, tending to gather in packs for hunting parties.

Reader

These vampires can read minds/thoughts/intents, sometimes clearly but other times in random images. They cannot read certain types of vampires such as Prophets so can't do what they can by proxy. They are quite rare and have the usual super speed and strength but can't fly.

Seeker
This type of vampire can find any object by seeing its path taken to its destination but they need to touch something deeply connected with it to see it. They are extremely rare and also have super speed and strength.

Prophet
These vampires can see/dream the future or past including knowing what type of vampire a human would make (working with Creators to help choose the best 'children'). They are extremely rare and practically invulnerable with superior strength and speed.

Dreamwalker
They can enter the dreams of any being and interact with them from great distances (sometimes changing the outcome of the dream if particularly talented). They are uncommon and have super speed, strength, and the gift of flight.

Compulsor
They can influence the mind and actions – mostly with humans but the highly talented can also influence some vampires but not all types so it's risky to try and fail. They are quite common and have the usual flight, speed, and strength. While all vampires can influence to a small degree, a Compulsor could, for example, literally make someone choose to never eat again until they starve (ignoring instincts which would possibly override the

compulsion if laid by another type of vampire).
Compulsion laid by a Compulsor can only ever be
removed if the same Compulsor chooses to lift it. Close
proximity is required.

Tracker
As we already know, a Tracker will track its prey
forever until it finds it – often resorting to
capturing/torturing loved ones to flush out the object of
their obsession. It's said that they will literally die
trying. They are very rare and have the usual superior
strength and speed, flight, and are particularly twisted -
taking great pleasure in the pain of others especially if
they are the one inflicting said pain. They thrive on
messing with minds (using various psychic tricks) and
wearing down their prey before selling them on.

Standard Vampires
These most common vampires have superior
strength, speed and mild influencing skills coupled with
occasional flight skills. They are more susceptible to
sunlight than any other kind (except Trackers) with
prolonged exposure to sunlight leading to blistering,
burning and eventual combustion.

Wow. That makes interesting and terrifying reading.
I found myself wondering which type I might be. I knew
which ones I didn't want to be. For a start, I definitely do
not want to be a Tracker. It sounds like that warps the
mind completely. Or is it that all Trackers were mental to
start with? I wanted to ask but it was getting really late
and we were all shattered. And I could tell Adam needed

to feed but wouldn't talk about it in front of Nick (weird really considering he'd shared his blood with him). Nigel gestured to Adam who looked at me and gave me a quizzical look. I assumed they were debating whether he should go feed on Nigel or if I was happy to donate. I tried to discreetly gesture to my throat as if to say I'd do it. Well typically of me, all that did was get Nick's attention.

"Oh gross. Just say it out loud. Bite me pleeeeeease, Adam…." He did a falsetto, girly voice which sounded nothing like me but then he looked pretty startled when Adam suddenly turned towards him, with fangs at full length, and said okay. It was hilarious. He stepped back in shock then leaned back in to inspect Adam's fangs. It all got a bit awkward then and Adam and I quickly made our apologies and disappeared. In the bedroom, we laughed as we got ready for bed.

"He would have shit himself if you'd made to bite him!" I laughed. He grinned at me, showing his fangs like a vampire on TV would.

"Maybe I should have tried. He's so fascinated with vampires maybe he should try it!"

"I'm sure he'd prefer a girl vampire though even though you're such a hottie." I teased, climbing into the bed. I can't believe I was so comfortable getting into bed with this man, like we'd been together for ages. He slid between the sheets and turned to face me.

"Are we like an old married couple or what?" He joked, stroking my hair the way he seemed to like so much.

I grinned. "Less of the old… well for me anyway. You… not so much." He lunged at me then with a growl, which quickly shut me up and after a few hot kisses leading in a trail down to my throat, I felt the familiar sensation of teeth sliding into my skin and Adam was drinking my blood. He didn't forget to make it feel good this time. I hoped Nick didn't hear. Mostly…

Chapter Twenty-One

On the morning I woke up with a decision made which I hadn't even known I was considering, although obviously Adam's comment the night before had made me realise it. I was going to leave my job at the newspaper. I was off 'sick' more often than I was there lately and there was no way I could write a story about an attack by a creature which was actually hunting me. I had no idea when I'd be able to leave Adam's house again and that didn't leave room for a job. I tensely waited while Adam was in the shower. What would he say? Would he think I was expecting him to support me? And what about Nick? If he was planning on quitting too, how was he going to support himself?

The bathroom door opened, steam billowing out along with the gorgeous scent of the body wash Adam used. He stepped out, towel around waist, hair wet, skin glistening and pink from the hot water. I tried to ignore the impulses the sight woke up in me. This was so not the time. Adam had stopped moving and was staring at me. Damn, he could tell I was thinking again, or talking to myself, or whatever it is I do. A grin crept across his face and he made a point of glancing at his watch then back at me. I threw a pillow at him. Damn vampire reflexes. He caught it in a flash and flicked it back at me.

"As much as I'd love a naked pillow fight with you right now, I'm guessing there's something on your mind?" He approached me and sat down. I scooted a few inches away.

"Sorry, am I getting you wet?" He asked innocently. I grimaced, knowing he knew the answer to that double-edged question.

"Stop it, or I'll forget what I need to say." He made a show of wiping the grin from his face and leaned back. His chest flexed as he moved, toned and muscular, and I wanted to lick it.

"Adam!" I snapped, trying to keep my focus. He was innocence personified – the look on his face actually said who, me?

"I need to tell you something I've decided and I don't want you to think that it's because I'm going to expect anything in return or because I'm not willing to pay my way and..."

"You're quitting your job?" He interrupted with a smile. Ugh it sounded so pathetic, like I was going to join the millions of wasters who turned up each week for their free benefits from the government in return for pretending to job hunt. I almost talked myself out of it then steeled myself.

162

"Yes, but only because I don't have a future at the newspaper. If I go out or carry on working on this story I literally won't have a future at all. I'd like to find something else. I have savings." I added, as if that made me sound like less like a freeloader. Adam leaned forward placing a warm damp hand on my shoulder. He also used those amazing reflexes to catch his bath towel as it tried to fall open. What a gentleman. Damn vampire reflexes!

"Lila, I don't think for one minute you're planning to be a lady of leisure, but I've got to be honest here, this is a huge weight off my mind. I can't track the vampire and watch out for you while you go about your investigative role. It's too dangerous, so I'm just really glad to see you're protecting yourself like this. Oh and…" He waggled his eyebrows suggestively "You'll be here each night when I get home hungry and horny!" I slapped his arm but only gently because I liked the sound of that too.

"Oh, and I can help Nigel out here until I find something less dangerous to do! See… it'll work." He obviously realised I was trying to convince myself rather than him as he took that moment to distract me by ruffling his hair hard and showering me with water. I shrieked and leapt away from him. And somehow into him as he was suddenly also behind me. Damn vampire speed!

After Adam left for work, and I missed him so much more when he was in such a playful mood, I sat in the library trying to think about what to say to Colm. I'd have to work out some kind of notice. But how? What if he expected me to go back into the office now? Oh god, and what about Michelle? She's kind of my best friend.

163

How do I tell her I might not see her again? Nick walked in while I argued with myself.

"Yeah I know that look. It's definitely one of two things. Either you're plotting something devious, or the voices in your head are having one hell of an argument and you're caught in the middle!" I tried to kick him but he hopped over my foot. Actually, he looked completely well and healed and it annoyed me a bit. How does Nick just drift so easily into vampire life? Well, not vampire life exactly, as he's not one but oh my god I bet that's what he wants in the end! Focus, Lila.

"I'm just trying to work out how to tell Colm I'm not coming back. And don't be a smartarse, you know it doesn't suit you." Nick grinned and sat opposite me on the chaise longue while I was sitting on the floor as usual. He frowned and wriggled a bit to get comfortable.

"*See*?! I told Adam that thing was horrible but apparently, it's an 'antique'." And yes, I did those quote marks with my fingers when I said it. Bite me.

"I think all furniture from the dark ages was like sitting on a pile of rocks." Nick joked. "So, quitting the paper eh? I knew you idolised me but to copy me so blatantly, well, I guess I'm just a bit taken aback, you know?"

At that moment, I really wanted to punch him in the face.

"I'm not copying! I just can't go back out there for who knows how long. I'm like a prisoner..."

"You and me both, Lila. But you know what, without Adam we'd probably both be dead or worse... I know I thought he was a prick but I've changed my mind on account of him saving my life and all." That reminded me of something.

"What did he say to you that first day you met?" He frowned at me. And then realisation dawned and he grinned.

"Oh he told me to stay away from you or he'd *rip my throat out and drink my life's blood*. It freaked me out because coming from him it just seemed suddenly possible. I think he even did the red eyes thing a bit at the time. I wonder if that still stands…" He mused, tapping his fingers on his chin.

I give up. It's like talking to some kind of weirdo. Or another me. Although no, I'm pretty sure they're two different things. Probably.

"I'll tell you what, I'll remind him later for you." I said as I got up and walked from the room. Playing back what Nick had said I laughed involuntarily. Adam playing bad vampire again and didn't even get the wording quite right. I'm sure it's heart's blood… Anyway, my resignation went a bit like this:

Me: "Colm, I need to talk to you."

Colm: "If you're not about to say I've got a great story here ready to go to print, then don't bother. I don't have time for your shenanigans."

Me: "Please, I wish I was up to some kind of shenanigans. There are definitely no shenanigans. That's such an awesome word by the way, I need to find a reason to call shenanigans – that's a thing, right?"

Colm: (sigh) "I'm hanging up now. Write the story."

Me: "No wait. It's important."

165

Colm: (bigger sigh) "I doubt it. But I'll humour you on this occasion – you have one minute."

Me: "I can't write the story, Colm…"

Colm: "I knew it. I knew it was too much for you. You beg and beg for the chance to write an exposé and you just can't do it. Back to the psychic crap for you then."

Me: "No, I mean I quit."

Colm: (silence)

Me: "Colm? Did you hear me?"

Colm: "Your contract states two weeks notice. I expect you in the office in 20 minutes to work out your notice period."

Me: "I can't do that, Colm. Sue me if you have to but I can't come in." (Eeek why did I say that?) I palmed my forehead.

Colm: "Fine, in that case, you're using up your annual leave for the next two weeks. I want your resignation in writing by the end of the day."

Me: "I'm sorry."

Colm: (dial tone)

Me: "Screw you then."

Colm: (still dial tone)

Me: "And your crappy newspaper."

Colm: (still dial tone)

Oh crap… I've just quit my job. What was I thinking? Panic set in. I paced up and down in the 'drawing room'. I needed something to calm me down. Adam would do it but he's not here. Nigel. Where's Nigel? My eyes fell on my iPod, tucked in the side of the sofa. I'd been looking for it everywhere. I needed my favourite music to calm me down. I scrolled through and found the playlist I was looking for. *30 Seconds to Mars – A Beautiful Lie...*

Aaaaaaand... relax. Halfway through the first track, *Attack*, I was already singing along –they'd worked their magic once more. Halfway through *The Kill* I saw my mobile phone screen was lit up. I danced over to it and picked it up. Michelle. Reluctantly I pulled out my earphones and switched off my favourite song. It'll keep, I promised myself with a frown.

"What's going on?" She barked as soon as I pressed the answer button.

"With?" I decided to play it cool.

"Don't be fucking coy with me. Colm says you're not coming back and you've run away with Nick or something. What the fuck? I thought you were screwing that Adam guy?"

Okay she was a bit pissed at me. That'll teach me not to keep her in the loop.

"Okay firstly, I so did not run away with Nick. You know what a twat he is. And secondly, I'm not *screwing* that Adam guy. I'm in love with Adam and sort of practically living with him. Oh, and yeah I quit." A brainwave hit. "I'm moving out of the country with Adam." As soon as the words were out I realised my mistake. She would easily be able to find out Adam was still working 10 minutes down the road from her every day. Shit.

"Don't give me that rubbish. I know Nick's with you. He's gone and his house is all torn up. Is- are you both okay? Something's happened, hasn't it?"

Bless Michelle. She could be pissed off and worried about me at the same time and sound like it. I suddenly missed her so much.

"Sorry we disappeared. You're right. The guy came back for him and attacked us both. We're fine. We're safe. We're staying at Adam's place out of town."

"So, next time just tell me the truth eh? Moving overseas, please. You? You practically think the next village down the motorway is abroad for fuck's sake!" I bristled at that but she had a point and, ironically, she was also almost right!

"Look, just be careful when you're out and about. This guy's still on the loose and he's *nasty*. If you hear or sense anyone following you, get inside somewhere busy straight away. Oh, and if you hear a laugh or chuckle behind you, just run like hell."

"A laugh? What is it, a killer clown? What are you on?!" That wasn't fair. Although, actually it sounded pretty nutty so maybe it was. Nick walked into the room while I was talking to Michelle and had an armful of Adam's books and a notepad. He looked around then turned to leave. What the hell was he playing at?

"Those are Adam's. Put them away." I told him. He shook his head and headed into the kitchen to use the table there. I followed him. "What are you doing? You can't just borrow his stuff. It's not a... okay technically it *is* a library but still... Have a little respect."

"Um hello?" Shit, Michelle. Damn my attention span.

"Sorry about that. Look, I've got to go. Nick the prick is ransacking Adam's stuff and I'm about to kick his ass. Be safe." I disconnected the call and tucked my phone into my pocket.

"Nick, seriously, stop messing with Adam's stuff." I tried to take the books away as he piled them on the table but he just swiped them back and did it again.

"I'm just doing some research, Lila. Bugger off, will you?" He actually looked irritated – like I was the one in the wrong!

"What?!" I snatched the books back and headed into the hallway towards the library.

"Seriously, Lila! He said I could use his books, so will you pack it in?" He snatched the books back, making me stagger away and then he was gone. Prick. And where the hell is Nigel?

Nigel, I discovered, was holed up in the office, making calls. He jumped out of his skin when I threw the door open. I have to stop doing that. Why can't I open a door like a human? Especially as I actually am one!

"Are you okay?" Nigel asked, replacing the telephone receiver. I rubbed my arm where the door had bounced back and hit me. See... another perfectly good reason why I should open doors properly.

"No." I grumped, slumping into the chair directly opposite Nigel. "Whatcha doin'?" He piled up paperwork and tucked it into a desk drawer.

"Just calling in some favours. Have you eaten?" I shrugged. "I don't want food. I want to do something apart from lie around in this house waiting for Adam or certain death." Realising how that sounded, I groaned. "And I sound like the most ungrateful bitch ever! You're both trying to keep me alive and I'm moaning because

I'm bored." Nigel laughed and leaned forward with his face in his hands and stared at me.

"What do you want to do?" He asked reasonably.

"See Adam. Do something. Become a vampire." Oh no, that slipped out. My hand covered my mouth although it was far too late to stop the words coming out or stuff them back in. Nigel frowned.

"Didn't mean to tell me that did you, love?" His eyes were kind. It made me cry. He came around to crouch in front of me.

"I'm so confused, Nigel. Two weeks ago, I was a normal girl in a crap job with a crap boss and no sex life. Now I have no crap job or crap boss but I have an amazing man and so much sex. Why am I crying? Oh, cos someone else wants to gut me or tear my throat or turn me into a slave vampire and then probably kill me anyway because if I'm this annoying now how annoying would I be forever?" Nigel's hand patted my shoulder gently if a little awkwardly.

"Have you talked to Adam about this?" I didn't dare look at him. "Every conversation leads to sex so I get distracted. Or he drinks my blood which usually also ends up leading to that. And all of that would be a good thing except I don't feel like I know enough to know if I'll be able to stop myself or someone else getting hurt. I left my job but the Tracker already followed me from there so will know who I hang with and go after them." Nigel looked bemused and who can blame him – my inner monologue had escaped. We're all doomed.

A sweet coffee and a cake helped. Who knew Nigel baked? And when the hell did he have time to make these lemon drizzle things? They were seriously yummy and yes when I say *a cake* of course I mean two. He ate two as well so I guess it's not so piggish.

"I think things will improve for you very soon, Lila, you just have to be patient. We'll have some guests soon and that'll help to keep you occupied while you're stuck indoors."

"Guests?" I vaguely remembered some reference to others last night.

"Yes, some old allies of Adam's and mine. They're already travelling here and will arrive over the next few days."

"All vampires?" It made sense to ask now. Would I be expected to let them feed on me too? Would Nigel? Is blood sharing really blasé among vampires or is it a sin to drink someone's girlfriend or donor? What was the protocol and why is Nigel looking at me like I've grown another head?

"Come back to me Lila. Don't try and work things out alone. Ask me."

I can't believe this is the same guy who scowled and slammed things at me two weeks ago when I asked questions.

"Where will they- um how will- do they bring people...um..."

"They may or may not bring donors with them. They may simply bring chilled supplies with them. They won't expect to feed on either of us. Oh, or Nick. Although I do think he'll take a shine to one of Adam's friends when she arrives." He had a sneaky grin on his face and I decided what the hell I wouldn't ask, I'd wait and see. Can you see how I'm trying to change?

"Then I'll call shenanigans." I said with triumph. Nigel just tilted his head at me as if he was unsure what he was looking at. I chose to ignore it and I ate a third piece of cake.

Chapter Twenty-Two

Adam rang to say he'd be late home. It kind of
deflated me, which was weird because I
thought I was already pretty deflated. I'd
gone looking for my iPod to let *Mars* cheer me up again
only now I couldn't find it again. I tried accusing Nick of
moving it but he just ignored me. I was sure I'd left it in
the sitting room when I took Michelle's call but it was
nowhere to be found. That just made me cranky. I need
my music to keep me sane. Without it I'll go crazy, and
actually, now I think of it, nobody will probably notice.

After about half an hour of hunting around, under
chairs and between cushions I had to give up. I decided
to watch something on TV. I scoured the shelves of
DVDs to find something appropriate to watch. I needed
something that would take my mind off of everything
going on... oooh Twilight! He really does have it. Well
all five movies actually. I fantasised about a movie

marathon with him but realised it probably wasn't feasible with all that was going on. I curled up in front of the huge screen and settled in for the perfect vampire boy meets human girl movie. Around the time that Edward was explaining about his vampire nature to Bella I realised I wasn't alone any more. Sitting in the corner of the room was a girl. She was blonde, with pixyish short hair and the cutest heart-shaped face. Where the hell did she come from? I hit pause and she switched her gaze from the screen to me. Her eyes were a violet colour I noticed as she got up and came to join me on the sofa.

"Seriously, nobody gets scared at that part!" She joked. "Shane." She added, sticking out her hand. I guess she meant it was her name. I shook her hand then let her extract it. I mean it's not like I gripped it like a crazy person or anything but I guess she just had a 3 second limit.

"I see what he means." She laughed. I fought the urge to sit and puzzle over her words. "Sorry, just a bit surprised. You weren't there when I walked in were you?" She grinned and grabbed the remote control, unpausing the film. "Got here about 15 minutes ago and made a beeline for Edward's voice. I mean I know he's waaaay younger than me but a girl can dream, right?!" I glanced back at her. She looked about 25.

"How long have you been around then? Or is that rude, like asking a woman her age?" She quirked an eyebrow. "You *are* asking a woman her age, Lila." We both laughed. I liked her and relished suddenly having another female around. I had so many questions bubbling up inside but decided to switch that part of me off and just watch the film with someone I hoped would become

a new friend. At some point, Nigel must have dropped
some popcorn in because we were suddenly tucking into
it and giggling over Jacob's hair and the fateful baseball
game.

"Is that how it really is when vampires play
baseball?" I asked idly. "Please... do I look like I play
sports?" Good point. She was just so wee, like a delicate
flower. Oh crap.

"You're not one of the mindreading ones, are you?!"
With a laugh and a flick of her hand, showering me with
popcorn, she abruptly paused the DVD again. Turning to
me to give me her full attention, I went a bit shy. Was it
rude to ask these questions? And if she was a mindreader
I'd just asked her that without even meaning to.

"If you're planning on thinking your questions at me
you'll be disappointed. I wish I *could* read minds. I bet
yours would be like an episode of Jeremy Kyle... on
crack!" She was funny; I liked that. I stopped myself
just before I told her to bite me. After all, who knew
what vampire etiquette dictated if a person said that?

"Um. Do you mind if I ask more about your vampire
powers? I've only just learned about the different types
and I'm intrigued."

"Why don't you see if you can guess which type I
am?" Shane posed with a serious face, which just made
me crack up. She joined in though so I guess she didn't
mind being laughed at, which was lucky for me,
considering she could probably remove my head with one
hand.

"How the hell do I guess? Oooh... can you change shape?" "Like into a rectangle or hexagon?" This chick was hilarious!

"Animals or humans?" "Well I prefer animals for company and humans for blood and sometimes sex." I groaned. "God, it's like having a conversation with myself. A mindreader around the two of us would kill himself in, like, ten minutes."

"I bet five minutes."

"Oooh I'm in! What does the winner get?"

"Not covered in popcorn next time we watch a Stephenie Meyer film." Good deal. We shook on it.

"Do we even have a mindreader coming here?"

"Probably, Adam knows one or two. Oh, we'll have such fun trying to drive him insane."

"So, it's a him then?"

"It's usually a him. I don't know why. Readers and Creators are usually male. Prophets and Dreamwalkers are most often female. The others are kinda random." Oooh a clue...

"Are you a Prophet then? Oh, or a Dreamwalker? Or was that a red herring?"

"Okay, I'll let you have that. Yes, I'm a Dreamwalker. It's kind of lame, except when I can sneak into some hot guy's dream and... well, interact with him." She said 'interact' like it was a dirty word. By the look on her face when she said it, I believed her. It sounded like a cool power and kind of spiritual, which I liked. Of course, I guessed it could be intrusive if you didn't know if your dreams were safe.

"Have you ever done that to Adam?" She blinked. "No, why; do you want me to?" I inadvertently matched her surprised blink.

"Hell no! I mean that wouldn't be very nice, would it?" Honestly that was the understatement of the century. "Um, on that subject do we have to tell you not to do it to us or do we just invite you in if we do want you to?"

"It's not like a compulsion! If someone was injured or in a coma, it's extremely useful and could help them. I don't go jumping from dream to dream looking for action. Have you looked at me? I'm cute enough to get plenty of that. Well some, anyway." She switched the film back on and we watched the final scenes together. Somewhere around the time Edward took Bella to the prom, I heard the front door go and had to force myself to stay still and finish the movie. I mean I'd seen it like a dozen times. My heart sped up at the thought of seeing Adam though. I thought I saw a grin cross Shane's face but chose to ignore it. Well a little. I did flick some popcorn at her though, which just made her giggle. Thinking about it, that was a good thing too. Bear in mind, she could probably tear my throat out without missing a second of the film.

When the credits rolled, I 'casually' hopped up and headed through the house looking for Adam. I smelled his cologne a brief second before he wrapped his arms around me from behind. I leaned into him a second then turned around to face him.

"Aren't you meant to shout, 'honey I'm home' so I can run out here with your pipe and slippers?" He laughed and kissed me hello. Without turning he said hello to Shane. I didn't know she'd followed me but there she was. She was so petite, Adam looked a bit like a giant beside her. That's a total exaggeration but I think you're getting to know how my mind works now. It speaks first and thinks later and often dies of shame after the eventual 'thinking' part.

"Well Adam, you know you picked a Twilight fan, right?" She joked as she breezed past him and into the kitchen. I realised I could smell food and followed behind her with a chuckle. I glanced back at Adam and pointed to Shane.

"She's totally in love with Edward." I whispered. "I heard that." Shane remarked. No fair.

Dinner was a nice relaxed affair with Nigel being proved right. Nick couldn't take his eyes away from Shane and kept starting conversations with her just to hear her voice, or at least that's my opinion, but the guy was totally smitten which is the real point here. She seemed to enjoy the attention so maybe it wasn't all bad. I could just imagine it being Adam and I having to cover our ears tonight and that made me blush furiously. Adam, of course, didn't miss a trick.

"Feeling a little hot under the collar, are we?" He whispered so close into my ear that I could feel his lips touching me. Like that helped. The smirk on Shane's face told me she heard even that. Damn vampire hearing. I kicked at Adam under the table but only succeeded in somehow kicking the leg of the table and getting everyone's attention. That helped even less. I shrugged an apology at them.

"Sorry, had cramp in my foot." Yeah, I think I got away with that. Nope, on second thought, nobody seemed to be buying it.

"So, Halley and Eloise will be here tomorrow." Adam commented to Nigel, saving me from that moment where the ground doesn't do as it's told and open up to swallow me. I could see from Nigel's nod that he was familiar with both ladies Adam mentioned. Hmmm....

"Do you know any *male* vampires at all?" I asked. I mean, not that I'm jealous. It's just that any one of them could be an ex girlfriend. Or his Creator... when would he tell me more about that?

"Yes, I do, but they're probably not quite close enough to be here tomorrow. I'd have thought you'd like having some girls around to talk to anyway."

"I have Shane." I said quickly, then realised that sounded a bit odd. "I just mean I expected lots of male vampires. Don't know why. Too many vampire books I guess."

"Vampire chicks are kick-ass, don't worry." Shane said with a righteous look on her face. "I bet you'll be a scrappy little thing when you turn." All eyes settled on Shane who looked like she had just accidentally said a rude word in the middle of a speech.

"What?" She asked.

"*When* you turn?" Nick asked although Adam looked like he was thinking the same thing.

"Oh... shit, I'm sorry, is that not the plan?" Shane looked horrified and I felt sorry for her. Then me. Especially me. I thought this was settled!

"What do you mean '*when* you turn'?" I mocked Nick's tone of voice, but I was looking at Adam. Nick made a noise but didn't reply, seeing that this was about to be a tiff between me and Adam and knowing he was better out of it.

"Well-I. Um I just mean…"

"Forget it. Message received." I slammed my plate into the sink and walked out through the back door into the cold dusk night. Stupid really. Why the hell would I go outside in a very cold country instead of heading into a warm room with a satisfying door slam? Not the library, though. We already know that stupid door doesn't slam.

I shivered and swore at myself. How the hell could I slink back inside and face them now? Why did I even get upset? I was sure Adam hadn't changed his mind about me.

"I didn't mean I don't want you to be a vampire. Come on, Lila, we've had this conversation." Thank god Adam had followed me. We could have a quick row then I could storm *inside* and get warm again.

"I overreacted. I'm sorry." Where did that come from? It was absolutely freezing out there. I tried not to let on I was turning numb. Adam was as perceptive as I was stubborn and hooked his arm around me, leading me back inside.

"I'm sorry, I can't concentrate talking to you when you're jiggling like that." I didn't realise how much I was shivering but I guess it was bad.

"Changed your mind about frostbite, Lila?" Shane asked with a half-apologetic smile.

"Um… oh I can't think of a clever retort, I'm too cold." I sort of joked. Adam led me upstairs and set a hot bath running for me, dutifully measuring out my Molton Brown bath salts for me, turning the water a soothing sea green. I watched him as he did these things for me and wondered why I was so high maintenance and insecure. He was such a sweet guy and kind of a god to me. Wasn't it better to act like a mature sensible person? Particularly when I'm trying to encourage him to spend forever with me? Who wants to spend forever with a spoiled brat with impulse control problems? Adam sat me down on the bed and crouched in front of me, rubbing his hands up and down my arms to warm me up. To be honest I was much warmer already but it would be a bit silly to discourage him because it felt so nice.

"Why are you so good to me?" I murmured, reaching up to cup his cheek. His skin was warm and so smooth and yet I could feel the beginnings of stubble on his cheeks. That was sexy. His lips curved into a smile.

"Later on, you can be good to me if it makes you feel better." His eyebrows waggled mock-suggestively and kind of broke the mood a bit but that was okay. I went for my bath and bless him; he sat on a chair beside me the whole time, talking about this and that. Nothing of any real importance, just small talk to keep me company. Wow, I loved him. That thought just stopped me in my tracks. I am actually *in* love with him. Should I tell him? Is it too soon? Will it freak him out? I mean, he's sort of talking about forever so maybe not. I realised he was still talking.

"-gone somewhere again, haven't you? What do I have to do to keep your attention?" He had a wicked grin on his face and I had the urge to say something rude but something else came out instead.

"I love you." Ooops, cat so firmly out of the bag, that in fact the bag has burst into flames and burned away. There's just no putting it back. His face seemed to freeze-frame. Like time had stopped. His eyes swirled at me though so I knew time was still, well, time.

"I thought I'd be the first to say it you know." He commented, moving closer to crouch in front of me so his face was only a few inches from mine. His eyes actually looked a bit wet but maybe it was from all the steam in the room. "Really? With my brain to mouth issues?" He grinned and kissed my lips so, so softly.

"I know, right? Honestly, I've loved you since the moment you hyperventilated at the top of my stairs. I am so grateful my meeting was cancelled that afternoon or we might never have even met."

"I so wasn't hyperventilating. I was just breathing in really fast shallow breaths. Totally different." He laughed as he kissed me again and in a moment of bravery I pulled him into the bath with me. Needless to say, water went everywhere, but all we did was kiss and whisper to each other until the water started to cool.

Chapter Twenty-Three

$\mathcal{S}$hane was only the first of several vampires due to join us but I liked her and felt comfortable talking to her although she could be caustically sarcastic; a trait I admired, and sometimes it was like I had to almost fight Nick to get time with her. The guy was completely smitten. We ended up all sitting up really late chatting that first night. We filled Shane in on the Tracker situation. At the mention of his name she grimaced.

"Uh oh… you didn't say it was Stig, you know."

"You know him?" Adam traded a glance with me.

"*Of* him and it's not good. He's incredibly good looking and gives off a kind of magnetism, which draws his prey if he gets close enough. A bit awkward I gather, with male prey. Not that it happens often. He prefers tracking females. Oh, and he's particularly fond of torture, although heavy on the emotional torture rather than knives and other sharp objects." I didn't know whether to feel relief or throw up. On the one hand, he might not carve me up with sharpened spoons, but on the other hand he could take my already complex head and turn it against me. I'd end up carving *myself* up with sharpened spoons...

In the end a deck of cards appeared and somehow, we got deeply involved in a poker game, which took us way past 1am. I was losing so wasn't particularly gutted when we stopped. I mean, how is a person like me supposed to bluff? One look at me each time and everyone knew exactly what kind of hand I had. I noticed Adam was taking on a slightly gaunter appearance and decided to call it a night by playing the sleepy human card. He readily agreed to turn in with me and the other three stayed up playing, but a few moments after us we heard Nigel following up the stairs.

"Tired too, Nigel?" Adam asked as we headed towards our room. "Not really. Just didn't want to cramp the boy's style." He disappeared into his room with a chuckle and closed the door.

As we got ready for bed I asked about Shane.

"Hmmm... I've known her about 28 years and she's always been a good friend. Always ready to step in and help when needed. She's got a great soul."

"So, you slept with her?" Adam gaped at me. "I'm not accusing or anything – just curious. It's not like I'm jealous. Really, I'm not jealous." Adam shrugged, knowing I was a bit jealous.

"She's more like a little sister. A really little sister." He laughed, climbing into bed.

"She ever visited your dreams?" I didn't mean it like did he have sex dreams about her but I guess it could have been taken that way. He shrugged.

"Not to my knowledge. She doesn't intentionally intrude. She's helped out before when we've needed to reach someone. She can visit a person's dream from anywhere, so she doesn't need to be in the room with them. It helps if someone's gone missing or whatever."

"Does that happen a lot?"

"What, people going missing?" He turned to face me, so we were lying down face to face. I enjoyed the intimacy of it.

"Well just general situations where you need other vampires to help out?" He frowned then shook his head.

"Uh... not often no. For example, you're my first human girlfriend who had a Tracker fixated on her."

"First human girlfriend with a Tracker or *first human girlfriend*?" I raised an eyebrow.

"Well, I wasn't celibate before I was turned but yeah, since becoming what I am, I have only had relationships with vampires. And to be fair they've really been little more than a few nights here and there."

"All *female* vampires?"

His face was a picture. "You have to ask that question?"

I shrugged. "Hey, people experiment. You've had a fair bit of time to do that. You've never been with another guy?" A mental image popped into my mind and I shook it away quickly.

"Have you been with another female?"

I blushed.

"Of course not!" He mimicked my facial expression.

"Well, 'of course not' in answer to your question too!"

He scooted closer to me so his lips were millimetres from mine.

"Are you tired?" I felt tingles here and there. I don't think I need to elaborate.

"No, why? Are you?" I asked, my lips tickling his.

"No…"

"What's up then?" A grin, followed by the words, against my lips. "I want you."

I flopped onto my back with a sigh. "Oh man… if we must!" Adam laughed and covered me with his weight. "Oh, we must…" His lips took mine in a swift kiss, while his hands seemed to devour my pyjamas. I know what you're thinking. Why wear pyjamas in bed with a sexy vampire? Well I'll explain. There are other people in this house too. And what if there was a fire? Well apart from the one Adam's creating in me right now. I moaned into his mouth and then pushed him away with a gasp.

"What?" He asked with a frown. "Shane! She'll hear us. Vampire ears remember?"

"You say that like they're a visible thing like Vulcan ears! Of course, she'll hear us. You think it's the first time she's heard two people having sex? I'm sure even Nick heard us the other night you know."

"I don't care. No… that's not true. I do care. But I don't want her to think badly of me."

"What's bad about intimacy with the man you love?" His lips touched mine, and then trailed down my throat and across my collarbone. I quaked beneath his feathery touch and held back a groan.

Adam's hands moved about my now-naked body leaving a trail of tingles and tremors. When he kissed me again I returned it while trying to keep quiet. Eventually he sighed and pulled away from me.

"You're going to hold back just to try and hide what we're doing?" I nodded a little ashamedly. His annoyance turned to wickedness and I saw a determined look cross his face. Oh no...

In a swift move, he wriggled down and disappeared beneath the covers. Oh nooooo. He's evil, I thought as I frantically tried to stop him disappearing. Then I felt his breath on me. A shudder ran up my body. His lips and tongue went to work then and I tried everything from holding my breath to smothering my moans with my hands then a pillow but he knew what he was doing and actually made me scream as I climaxed suddenly. It was like an electric shock. He didn't come back up to face me straight away and as I started to wonder about the delay I suddenly felt his arm wrap around my right leg. His breath touched the skin on my inner thigh a second before his teeth sank in and I writhed and moaned as he drank my blood while using his fingers between my legs. Oh, my god. I forgot about Shane, Nick, the Tracker, life, my name, *everything!*

I lay still, breathing heavily and feeling the need to stretch my muscles out as Adam crawled up the length of my body to pop his head up from under the covers. His hair was ruffled and adorable and his mouth held a smug grin, which made me laugh. The playful version of Adam was the stuff of dreams. I mean seriously, the guy was intent on making me scream just so Shane and Nick would know exactly what we were doing. I blushed as I thought about that. Oh well hopefully they were busy with themselves. I couldn't hear anything from them.

"Can you hear them?" I asked quietly. Adam laughed. "You don't want them to hear you but you want *me* to spy on them?" I swatted at him and with a mock growl he went all vampy, pinning my hands down and giving me swirly eyes and fangs. I rolled my eyes at him. Am I supposed to be scared?

"How is it, when I'm being perfectly normal, human even, you're afraid of me and yet when I show you my vampire features you feel perfectly safe?" He dipped his head to graze his teeth along my shoulder, up to my neck, then ear, then down across my throat. He nipped once or twice and laughed, hot breath caressing my skin, when I shuddered. When he kissed me, I felt his fangs retract and he was just Adam again. He kept me pinned down though. I nipped at his bottom lip and drew a moan from him.

"Is that all you've got, big scary vampire man?" I batted my eyes at him and then shrieked as he went back to nipping my throat, this time with human teeth. He kept teasing me for ages before he pushed inside me and began to move. I moved with him, enjoying the sensation of being completely dominated by him. He owned me. I know that's not very pc or feminist of me but I don't really care about being either of those things. I care about being his. I slept well with Adam wrapped around me that night, feeling perfectly safe.

Chapter Twenty-Four

The new arrivals the next day changed things a bit – the whole dynamic shifted. There were three, two females, one male. The females were the ones Adam mentioned, Halley and Eloise, and both had an air of superiority around me, which made me want to slap them. I was pretty sure slapping a vampire would only reward me with a quick death though so I held my tongue and resisted the urge. Truly though, anyone who knows me knows that won't last.

The male was more interesting. I knew my bet with Shane had started as within seconds of arriving, he looked strained and confused and made excuses to disappear off with Adam alone to talk. I exchanged a look with Shane who winked. Oh yes, this was our mindreader. His name was Tatum and he looked cute and young and at the same time there was an age in his eyes that went far beyond whatever age he looked. I know that probably doesn't make sense but I guessed he'd seen (or heard) some pretty bad things over the years. Poor guy, he didn't know what he was in for, in this house. I grinned then wondered if he could still hear me.

"Yes, I can." He moaned loudly from the room next door where he'd been quietly getting the update from Adam. Whoops. Still it's not my fault he can hear my thoughts, is it? Can't he just *not* listen?

"NO." He shouted. He stalked out of the room into the hallway, right up to me. "Don't you think if I could switch it off I would? Seriously, being in a house with this many people is hell for me. You can't help but think. You can't help but think of the exact things you *don't* want the mindreader to pick up on. Oh, I killed someone last night, best not think of that. Too late. You had deviant sex last night with Adam? Yeah, let's not think about that either. Everything that pops into your mind, before you quell it, I've heard it. Now maybe you people will understand why I live alone, isolated from every other living being, and damn it, I told you, Adam, coming here was a bad idea." He headed for the front door, Adam running behind him.

They murmured between them and I just knew that Adam as apologising for me like it was my fault I had to think. He must have known bringing a mindreader into *this* house would be a nightmare. Poor Tatum. It had just been a hypothetical to me; I'd never realised what hell it could be for someone with that gift… or curse.

"Definitely a curse." Tatum muttered walking back over to me.

"I'm sorry." I said. After all, what else was there to say?

"Nothing else, you're right. I know you didn't mean any harm and to be fair, Adam did warn me about your um… overthinking." Nicer way to put it than I could come up with. He grinned at that. "I haven't been around people for a few years, so you'll have to forgive me if I struggle at first. I need to remember to focus my energy into blocking you all out. It's exhausting but I'll give it a try, for Adam. I owe him."

Forcing my mind to be as quiet as possible, I held out my hand. "Nice to meet you, Tatum. Sorry I'm such a mind-fuck. I'll try to work on it I promise." He smiled; looking so young and unburdened then cringed again. Yeah, it wasn't me this time. Phew. Oh… whoops, that was. He accepted my apologetic grin.

"Apparently, Shane is planning a Stephenie Meyer movie with you tonight? Something about popcorn…" I laughed, then realised I was thinking about the bet. The smile disappeared and I dipped my eyes. "Don't worry, it's not the first time people have bet on how quickly they can drive me nuts. And it's definitely not a first for Shane." He patted my shoulder and walked away. Wow, I was lucky he was such a nice guy and not an arse like those two Shapeshifter bitches. He barked out a laugh as he headed upstairs to whatever room Adam had assigned to him. Whoops, I was really going to have to watch myself from now on. He laughed again but this time it sounded a little incredulous to me. And that's just rude.

Shane eyed me when I went into the kitchen and mouthed the word 'popcorn' to me. "Yeah, I got the message, thanks so much for letting Tatum read *that* in your mind." She laughed. "He's used to it – I like to think of the most bizarre, kinky, freaky things when I know he's around. He's so easy to weird out. Watch." She closed her eyes, a sly grin on her face and looked gratified a moment later when there was a crash upstairs like something was dropped on the floor and Tatum's voice yelled "SHANE!" in a disgusted tone. We both laughed, although I wondered what the hell he'd just seen in her mind. Scratch that, I probably didn't want to know after all. This would be fun though. "Lila." Adam admonished behind me. Maybe not. I followed him out into the hall and across to the library. He quietly closed the door behind me.

"I don't know who you're trying to get privacy from by doing that. Everyone in this house is either a vampire or donor or probably jazzed up on vampire blood. We might as well yell to each other in the garden." Adam wiped a smile away but not before I'd seen it.

He made for the chaise then rethought it and led me to window seat I'd not spotted before at the back of the room. Man, how did I miss that this whole time?! We sat, facing each other.

"I just wanted to ask you to take it easy on Tatum. He's had a rough time of it and has been in seclusion for many years. It's the only way he can keep sane and believe me; you don't want to see an insane vampire. He's a really great guy and I want him to like you. I know this is asking a lot, but please don't think too much. If you have something weird on your mind, don't dwell on it... just say it. And as I say that I'm wondering what I'm about to let myself in for. Hell..." He actually shuddered. I swatted his arm. "I'll try. I can't promise not to think, but I'll try and voice things before they play on my mind too much. I guess it's easier for Tatum if he's not the only one hearing them? Like he's not a secret keeper or something?"

"I think some people think really loudly too. I'm not saying you do!" He added quickly, holding his hands up as if threatened with a gun. "Shane, for example, loves to mess with his mind. She's not cruel but she gets a kick out of it, causing mischief. Because she's a Dreamwalker, she can send him images rather than vague thoughts. It means she can really freak him out. She means it as a joke but he gets quite offended by some of it as I'm sure you can imagine."

"He managed to pick out of my head in seconds what we did last night and I wasn't even actually thinking about it at that moment. How?"

"He can not only hear what you're thinking about at the moment but also what you're trying to suppress. It's extremely confusing for him. Just try not to suppress stuff and it'll help him a lot."

"Okay, so you look really sexy in that shirt. Makes me want to rip it off you and bite you. And I'm not even a vampire." He just stared at me; open-mouthed and I heard a laugh from the kitchen. Shane. Of course, she could hear us.

"Oh, and on the subject of the Shapeshifters – they don't like me. Why? Have I offended them? Am I not good enough for them because I'm human? I can't see them wanting to help us if they have such contempt for me." Well listen to that, I sounded quite eloquent when I actually spoke my thoughts. After a lifetime of doing it

the wrong way around! A knock on the door interrupted
my thoughts. Poor Tatum. I'm really trying here, dude.

Halley popped her blonde curly head in the door.
She was alone. Adam greeted her and she stepped into
the room, stealth and grace in every step. Me, I'd have
tripped in the doorway. I've done it before and I'll do it
again I'm sure. Probably before the week is out. I
wondered if I'd get that graceful as a vampire. Oh shit.
Sorry Tatum. I forced my mind blank with a sigh.

"It takes practice." Adam soothed as he patted my
shoulder.

"I bet he hates me."

Halley grinned. "Tatum?" She asked, and I nodded.

"Hey, it's tough to keep your mind clear around a
Reader. Trust me, I still struggle." She seemed nice,
which confused me. She read my expression.

"Sorry if you thought I didn't like you. And I didn't
mean to overhear your conversation but I was literally
just in the hall." I was speechless for a second. It
freaked me out, purely because it was so rare.

"Oh. But you didn't, did you?" I was emboldened
by Adam's hand still on my shoulder. He squeezed
slightly. Comfort or a warning?

"I wasn't sure what to make of things but even just a
few minutes around you two and it's clear you're crazy
about each other. I'm cool with that. El might take a
little longer to warm up to you for obvious reasons, but
I'm in. Oh, and I hear we're watching a movie later? I
also hear there's popcorn!" She giggled as she left the
room and I turned to face a bemused Adam. Yeah, he's
probably the only one who doesn't know about the bet
now. I shrugged sheepishly.

"Never mind." He muttered, pulling me in for a hug. Something occurred to me.

"Why will Eloise take longer to like me? What are the 'obvious reasons' Halley mentioned?" Adam's cheeks pinked slightly. Oh.

"You and her?" Incredibly succinct for me. Oh, my god, if he'd been with a hot vampire Shapeshifter, what the hell did he see in me? My body was average... my face too. My hair was cool but only because I had changed it completely. He seemed so into me when we were having sex or messing around but was that just because she'd finished with him or something? Horrible images of them together forced their way into my mind; deviant positions and activities with her as some kind of pvc-clad dominatrix. Uh oh. A door slammed upstairs and rapid running feet headed down the stairs and through the hall. The front door slammed and the house fell dead silent.

"I think you literally just mind-fucked Tatum." Adam commented dryly, his cheeks back to normal. I groaned.

"Do I have to go say sorry?" He nodded, but he looked relieved we'd been interrupted.

"This isn't over, Adam. I need to know and you'll tell me. Or maybe I'll just ask Tatum." I gave him a smug grin as I opened the door and headed out into the hall.

Several pairs of eyes met mine as I saw Shane, Nick, Halley and Eloise standing in the hall. "I know. My bad. I'm on it." I said briskly, heading out the door. I could see footprints in the snow left over from the night before and new fresh ones leading away from the door. They

195

were deep and spaced well apart (from running I guessed) and headed around the side of the house towards a dense wooded area that I was thinking must also be Adam's land. Not that he'd told me but there wasn't a fence stopping me going in. I shivered, realising too late I should have grabbed a coat. A hand touched my shoulder suddenly and I turned to face Nick. He handed me my coat.

"As the only other human here, I remembered you'd be cold." He said simply, turning and walking away again. I shouted my thanks after him as I gratefully slipped the coat on and zipped it up high. It was a quilted type of coat and very warm. I headed after the running footprints. I heard a groan a few feet ahead and slowed to a stop.

"Oh no, not you, please go away." Tatum said, his voice strained. I couldn't see him but obviously, he could hear me approaching. In more ways than one. Damn.

"Yes, *damn*. You're going to be the death of me, Lila. What the hell was that back there?" He appeared as if by magic, between two trees.

"As if by *magic*?! Seriously. What the hell is wrong with you?" I was silent. Too afraid to speak or think. It was exhausting.

"I'm sorry, Tatum. I'm so sorry. I can't switch it off, it's like there's a crazy person in my head and the more I try not to think the more it wakes it up and now I find out that Adam probably had some kind of affair or relationship with Eloise and that really freaks me out. I can't compete with her. I mean, look at her! I'm wondering, yet again, why he's with me. What he sees in me and- why are you smirking? That's really not helpful." Twat.

His grin widened. "It's just such a relief to hear you actually speak rather than think. Why do you hold everything in like that?" He walked towards me looking like an angel, the sun catching strands of his blond hair, making them shine like gold. His grin gave birth to a fully-grown smile. Oh shit.

"An angel eh? Well, that's a first for me. The first descriptor you thought is more commonly used to describe me." I shrugged, focusing on keeping my mind blank. I took deep breaths and concentrated on them, eyes closed.

"Yes, Lila, that's actually working but you're going to end up hyperventilating doing that." Tatum's hand dropped on my shoulder and I jumped a little. I sighed, dropping my shoulders and opening my eyes again.

"I don't mean to be such a freak, you know. It's just been years of having to hide my thoughts and emotions and concerns and it's just so hard to stop now especially with so much going on." He squeezed my shoulder lightly then let go.

"It takes great concentration. Just like it does for me to block it out. I'd almost succeeded upstairs until you started picturing Adam and El doing those *things* together. Those are images I can never *ever* unsee. Ugh. It's horrifying."

I sniggered. "Tell me about it." My smile disappeared fast.

"Were they?" I asked. Tatum shrugged. "I think it was unrequited on El's part. Adam never showed any interest that I saw." My heart felt relief and I smiled at him.

"You're not so bad when you're not running away from me." I commented.

"You're not so bad when you're not filling my mind with pretty much everything you *ever* think of." We both laughed.

"Are you ready to come back in yet?" I asked him. He frowned.

"They're probably all thinking about my childish little outburst. I can't listen to that right now. I might just walk for a while." He turned away. He looked so lost, like a child. I slipped my hand into his, stopping him in surprise.

"Can I walk with you?" I asked. He nodded after a moment.

"Only if you stop thinking of me as a lost little boy or an angel." I giggled, and then let him lead me into the woods. We tried walking in silence but I think that was hurting him, because naturally I couldn't keep my mind silent. So eventually I suggested we play I-spy. It meant my mind was focussed on something other than my own thoughts and really seemed to help, even though Tatum kept winning of course.

Chapter Twenty-Five

I was nervous about any more vampires arriving. Not because I was afraid of vampires of course, but because once again we seemed to have a fairly good balance. I looked around at the people surrounding me at the dinner table. I felt really close to Tatum already (a smug grin appeared on his face when I thought that so I poked my tongue out; FYI I'm allowed to act childish because I'm the youngest one here by a hell of a lot in most cases). Shane was a lot of fun and I was really liking Halley now she'd decided I wasn't a threat to Adam. Eloise was still a little distant but I could see why if I'd snagged the man she wanted. I'd be the same in her place. A look from Tatum told me I was thinking too much so I looked down and focused on my dinner and tried to mundane up my thoughts.

Mmmm steak. We eat a lot of steak in this household. It was cooked to perfection for me, slightly charred on the outside and a little pink on the inside. Probably not bloody enough for the vampires at the table though. Tatum sniggered and I met his eyes. He showed me his fangs as if to show me he'd heard my thought and his eyes went a bit pinker and swirled. I laughed and everyone stared at us.

"What?"

"Vampire fangs at the dinner table, Tatum? Really?" Shane giggled.

"Bite me." He joked and we all ended up laughing. It was nice to see Tatum relaxed, at least for now. Adam's hand found my thigh and I looked up into his eyes. 'Thank you' he mouthed. I wasn't sure what he was thanking me for but I accepted it, leaning in to him for a kiss.

"Making out at the table, Adam and Lila? Really?" Halley giggled, mirroring Shane's comment to Tatum. We glanced at each other then turned to her and said, "Bite me" in perfect unison. We all laughed again and I was relieved that nobody with fangs took it as an invitation to actually bite me. Tatum laughed so hard when I thought that, he almost choked on a mouthful of food. I didn't dare meet his eyes.

Later, as we all settled into the massive TV room to watch the next Stephenie Meyer instalment, I realised with horror that several very large bowls of popcorn were dotted around the room. I looked down at the shirt I was wearing; my favourite *30 Seconds to Mars* T-shirt. Hell no! I excused myself with a gulp and headed upstairs to change. I heard laughter in the room as I reached the stairs so guessed Tatum had just told everyone what I was doing.

Having a mindreader in the house was going to really let people into my demented psyche – was Adam ready for that? And for that matter, was I?

I laughed to myself as I pulled on one of Adam's T-shirts. I walked back into the room with a grin and saw Adam's face when he recognised his T-shirt. I shrugged and dropped back down on the sofa between him and Tatum. Tatum's smirk confirmed that he'd told them all. I deliberately poked him in the ribs with my elbow as I sat down, making him laugh out loud. Shane pressed play on the remote control and the opening credits came up.

Seriously, if you'd told me a month ago, I'd be sitting in the most opulent TV room I'd ever seen, surrounded by vampires watching a Twilight movie, I would have laughed in your face. It should be ridiculous. Instead it felt perfect though. Even Eloise seemed relaxed and laughed with the rest of us at the funny parts of the film. I was surprised nobody had doused me with popcorn yet but perhaps they'd wisely chosen not to waste it. There was a shit-eating grin on Tatum's face for most of the movie which left me a little apprehensive but I soon lost myself in the film, relaxing into Adam's side, his arm around me. As we reached the penultimate scenes, with Bella and Alice rushing to Volterra to save Edward, I found myself suddenly covered in popcorn although nobody seemed to have moved.

It was like a scene from Carrie. Damn vampire speed! I laughed in shock and flicked popcorn at both Adam and Tatum. Shane was across the room from me meaning one of these two was the culprit. I stood up and shook my clothes (well mine and Adam's) and covered both guys with popcorn. Everyone was laughing and it was the perfect end to the day. We didn't really focus on the final scenes with Edward and Bella as popcorn was tossed back and forth around the room. Nigel tried to look disapproving the whole time but I saw him throwing some back at Halley with a grin so I knew he was enjoying himself too. I ended up sitting down in Adam's lap after he'd had to stand up to shake his clothes clear and there ended up being more popcorn on the sofa than anywhere else. When the film finished, people started disappearing to their rooms, starting with Halley and Eloise who had travelled the furthest. Shane and Nick disappeared soon after but somehow, I didn't think it was for sleep in their case.

Nigel glanced around the room with a groan and declared he'd sort out the mess in the morning, before heading off to bed himself. Adam and Tatum said they wanted a beer so headed into the kitchen to grab them. I had been feeling so guilty looking around the room because I didn't want Nigel to have to deal with it in the morning. I grabbed the wastepaper bin and started scooping handfuls of popcorn from the sofas into the bin. I'd done two sofas when Adam and Tatum reappeared. Not with beers after all but dustpans and brushes.

Without a word, they helped me clean up the mess. During the cleanup, I spotted two large empty bowls either side of the sofa I'd been sitting on. Proving to me without a shadow of a doubt that not just one but both of them had dumped the popcorn on me at a prearranged moment. I held them up like incriminating evidence and watched them both grin, glancing at each other like co-conspirators. Once the cleanup was done, Tatum said goodnight and Adam took the cleanup tools back to wherever the hell he'd found them. I stared at the tidy room and smiled in satisfaction.

"Lila?" Tatum was back, his hand on my arm. "I just wanted to say thank you." I looked at him in surprise.

"For what? Am I thinking less now?" He laughed quietly, crushing my pride a little.

"Not at all, but I'm slowly getting used to it. I meant for Adam."

"I don't understand." He stepped closer.

"I've never seen him this happy or relaxed. You're good for him, believe it or not!"

"Even though I've put him at risk and he's had to call in reinforcements?"

"Trust me. He's got something to live for now. I've always worried that he'd give up. I'm not so worried anymore." It made me want to cry. I blinked back tears.

"He was that lonely?"

"He was that full of emptiness. I could hear it in his thoughts. There was nothing in life for him. He'd hang out with us, and he'd fight with us, but he really didn't care if he lived or died. His business kept him busy but not fulfilled. I always worried I'd get a call from Nigel saying he'd ended it. That kind of emptiness can just kill a person. Even a vampire." He hugged me tightly. "Look after him." He muttered in my ear. He was gone a second later and Adam appeared in the hallway.

"Ready for bed?" He asked with a lascivious grin. "Shower first." I declared, reaching up to my hair. Yep, I was still wearing popcorn.

"No wonder you've been looking at me like I'm good enough to eat. How long has there been popcorn in my hair?" I ran up the stairs laughing as I heard him follow.

Chapter Twenty-Six

he next day brought no new arrivals, although an early morning call had woken Adam and he'd left the house early. It wasn't a work day but I guess he'd been called in anyway. I decided to reach out to Michelle and see how she was. It had been several days since I'd heard from her. I knew better than to call her before 11am on a Saturday so made myself busy sorting out some laundry first and took it down to the utility area. It was really more of a posh laundry room and after a few minutes I finally found my way around the big fancy machines and set a wash on. I'd grabbed Adam's stuff too so the machine was full. Nigel walked in as I sat and watched the machine start up.

"You don't need to do this, Lila. I can handle it." I stared at him. "I've had to do my own washing for quite a few years now. I don't expect you to do it, Nigel, but thank you. Besides I'll bet with a houseful you're busy enough. Why are you up so early?" He sat beside me on the leather sofa, which totally wasn't out of place in this room.

"Adam woke me before he left. He's gone to pick up some supplies. He'll be back later today. He wanted me to let you know when you got up rather than waking you so early." "That was sweet but he didn't have to wake you instead. It doesn't seem fair."

"I like to wake early and anyway, he always lets me know where he is. It's a vampire/donor thing." It still didn't seem fair but I wasn't one to argue with the rules. I'm not sure since when but that's beside the point.

"Is everyone else still asleep?" I asked as I packed away the detergent boxes and stood up to leave the room. Nigel followed me.

"I think they are all still in their rooms. Thank you for clearing up last night. I came down prepared to have a mess on my hands and there was nothing left."

"It was fun last night, but not fair for you to have to deal with the cleanup. Adam and Tatum helped too – I think it was the least they could do after starting it all!"

"It was certainly fun – I've never participated in a food fight, but I found it quite refreshing." He laughed, and again I was struck again by how different he was from when I first arrived.

"Well with this crowd, I can't promise it'll be the last time!" We headed to the kitchen and I helped Nigel prepare breakfast. Vampire sense of smell brought hungry bodies to the table so by the time we were ready to serve, the table was full. Everyone tucked into the full English breakfast with ferocity and the atmosphere, although quiet except for eating sounds, was comfortable and relaxed.

I realised I liked having others around like this. It felt more like a big family. Tatum met my eyes with a smile that said he agreed. I think he was being honest when he said he was getting used to me. It didn't seem to pain him like before. If he'd been a bad person I'd have had a field day with tormenting him with hideous thoughts and images but because he was so sweet and adorable I didn't want to do anything that would cause him pain. He was still staring at me and gave me a sharp look when I thought the words 'sweet and adorable'. I just returned a smug grin and carried on tucking into my food.

After breakfast and clearing up, I busied myself sorting out the laundry into the dryer and then checked the time. It was almost 11am so I risked calling Michelle.

"Hello?"

"Michelle? You're awake? Thank god, I thought you'd kill me over the phone if I woke you."

"Hello to you too, Lila. I've been awake for a while thanks." The way she said it made me think she'd not been alone.

"Okay what's his name?" She laughed and I heard rustling, which I assumed was her getting out of bed or something.

"How do you know I'm not alone?"

"Because, yuck that's gross and I don't need to know. Why wouldn't you tell me you're seeing someone... or is it a one nighter? Not that that's something to be ashamed of or anything."

"Okay Lila aaaand breathe! Yes, I've been seeing someone. I mean it's only been a few days but he's amazing, and sexy, and funny and well, I'd have told you if you hadn't disappeared into oblivion on me."

"There are these things… they're called phones and if you dial a number you can reach another person and talk to them. It's quite ground-breaking…. Oh, and we're *on* one right now." She laughed and must have walked around her room as I caught a burst of what sounded like the shower.

"Oh, my god, he's there in the shower right, now isn't he?"

"What the hell… have you got super hearing?" I thought on that for a moment, surely not any more. It had been days since Adam had fed me his blood. Wow, so much had happened since I last saw Michelle…

"You deliberately went past the shower so I'd hear him and you know it. What's his name, what does he do and… you know… what does he *do*?" We both laughed. This wasn't a first time conversation for us. We'd both tried out a few relationships but they'd never gone anywhere. How weird that I was now living with a failed one and the new perfect one at the same time. I wondered if that was a bad sign?

"Well he's really hot, and has dark hair and eyes and his name's St…"

"*Stig*? You're seeing someone called Stig? Listen carefully, Michelle. He's dangerous. He's the one after…"

"Stig? What the hell? You think the best I can do is that guy from the dump in the book? Sorry to say this, Lila. Maybe it really is time for you to get that help

Colm kept mentioning. You know, when he kept giving you flyers and sending you emails about that mental health place…"

"That was just rude of him! And oh, I'm sorry. Tell me all about him." Phew!

"Well don't interrupt this time. His name is Steve Michaels and he works down the road from us. Something to do with banking or loans or something. I mean that could come in handy, right? He's amazing in bed; the word, Lila, is stamina. I-oh… he's just turned off the shower. I don't want him to hear us. I'll call you later. Hiiii…."

I ended the call on the breathy 'hi' she gave to her lover. I didn't need to hear even that much. My heart was still racing from the fear that she'd ended up dating the Tracker. Maybe that would be too obvious though. But then Adam and Nigel did say he'd get me through my friends. I suddenly realised being at Adam's was isolating me so much I had no idea what was going on out there. Stig could be insinuating his way into friends' lives and I'd never know.

Hell, I didn't even know what he looked like. Oh no, what if he was torturing and killing them and I didn't know they were dead? I got trapped in some horrible mental scenes just then, Colm and others from the paper, lying in bloody shapes on the ground, agony on their faces, life fading from their eyes. A man standing with blood on his face and evil in his eyes, fangs at full length and bloody, knowing I was next. There was an incredible rush of air and I felt someone grab me hard as I staggered back from the force.

"For god's sake, stop thinking like that. Stop please!" Tatum shouted, his hands on my shoulders, gripping me painfully tightly. His face was contorted and he looked shell-shocked. I felt awful and that made me just burst into tears in front of him. His face softened and he pulled me in for a hug.

"I'm sorry, I'm sorry." He kept saying that, which made me feel worse, because I was the one who was hurting him. I tried saying it back but it was just gibberish. He kept holding me tightly and trying to soothe me. I hiccupped, trying to get back to normal. What was that? I don't normally cry easily. Tatum's warmth soothed me and soon I was pushing him back and trying to compose myself.

"Shit, I'm so sorry, Tatum. I'm so sorry you had to see that." I wiped my face with shaky hands.

"What, the flood of tears or the terrifying scenes of blood and carnage?" He muttered dryly. I tried to laugh but another hiccup came out.

"Both." I turned to walk away but he followed. I grabbed my coat and gloves. "I'll go out for a while. It'll clear my head and give you some peace." He stopped me.

"You don't have to do that, Lila. I know you couldn't help it." I zipped up my coat and reached for the door handle, pulling open the door and staring in dismay at the falling snow. Damn this place.

"I can't promise I can stop right now, Tatum. Please just relax, I won't go far. I need to let out all the crazy."

"Holy shit, how long would that take?!" he joked, following me outside. He grabbed my hand as he shut the door.

"What are you doing?" I asked, looking at him.

"Walking with you." He stated simply, leading me away from the house. It kind of defeated the object since he was the one I was trying to give some peace to, but it gave me comfort so I selfishly kept him with me.

We'd walked for probably a mile or so and I could no longer feel my toes so felt it might be time to turn back. Tatum just turned me around and started walking back. It was refreshing hanging with someone who knew what I wanted practically before I did.

"Imagine the type of lover a Reader can be." He commented with a dirty grin. I laughed. We were still holding hands and it felt quite comfortable. I was never really a handholding type but it made me feel safer and I guess I'd started it the last time we'd walked together. We'd played I-spy for a while but it got boring picking 's' for snow, or 't' for tree. We tried getting clever with it, like snowdrift, snowflake, etc. but it still got old fast. Keeping my mind quiet was getting easier though. Apart from now when it was suddenly occurring to me that this was probably the calm before the storm. At some point Stig would find me. Of course he would – that's what Trackers do. How would I defend myself against him?

Chapter Twenty-Seven

"You can't." Tatum said, stopping suddenly and moving a step ahead to face me. I was getting used to him answering questions I hadn't asked yet so didn't get annoyed.

"Not at all?" I asked, my heart thudding heavily as I finally, truly, realised that meeting Stig would mean dying by his hand, or worse.

Tatum shook his head. "I'm not going to do an Edward and start ripping trees from the ground and stuff just to make my point. That's not cool or necessary, but that's the kind of strength you'd be fighting against." I looked at Tatum. He didn't look so strong, but vampire strength had surprised me before. He shot me a devious look.

"Oh really?! Okay. Let's put it to the test. I'm going to grab you. All you have to do is simply break free. That's it." Well, it didn't sound so hard. I grinned. "Bring it."

With a vampire growl, Tatum lunged, hands locking around my upper arms tightly. They were bruisingly tight and while I tried to hide the discomfort I felt, I know I thought about how painful it was.

"I'm sorry. But this is my point. I'm actually being gentle here. I could literally crush your bones with just a little more force." I struggled against him, realising very quickly it was not only completely fruitless but also would leave awful bruises. I stopped fighting against him and took a deep breath.

"Seriously? It's going to be over that easily?" He released me, rubbing my arms a little as if to ease the burn left by the grip of his fingers.

"He's not going to get close enough, Lila. We'll make damn sure of that. But you do need to understand what you're up against. If he's as old as Adam thinks, he'll certainly be stronger than me. Trackers also have an added strength borne of their madness."

"What if I run?" Fruitless, I guessed. "Try." Tatum said with a shrug. "Do you think I'd have a chance?"

"No, I mean, try now. Run from *me*." I stared at him. More humiliation was about to follow. That much was obvious. And who can run in snow anyhow?

I suddenly spun and ran as fast as I could but Tatum was immediately in front of me reaching towards me. I screamed and ran in another direction. But no matter which way I ran, he was always there first. This went on for a few minutes then I was shattered. I fell to my knees in the snow.

"He's going to kill me." I gasped in short breaths as panic set in. "He's going to catch me and torture me and kill me. Oh nooo…" Tatum dropped to his knees in front of me. "We're not going to let him, Lila. I promise. We're all here to protect you."

"You just said he'll be stronger than you, maybe all of you."

"Not all of us *together*. That's how we'll beat him. He won't be ready to fight so many of us. We could probably take him down with just the few already here." I sucked in a shaky breath and tried to quiet my mind, which was just rushing with images of me being hunted, tortured and ripped to shreds. Tatum's hands circled my face.

"Please stop. You're torturing yourself."

"And you…"

"Trust me, I've seen worse. Even from *your* brain. You can fight this fear if you'll just believe in us. Trust that we'll protect you."

"I can't. I don't think I realised just how hopeless this is. All I'm doing is sharing the danger with others I care about."

"Fuck, Lila. I'm sorry; I didn't mean to scare you. I was trying to help."

"Help? By pointing out I'm as helpless as a mouse being hunted by a psychotic lion on steroids?" I tried to stand up but the snow had soaked into my legs, carrying numbness with it.

"By making sure you know not to go off alone." He said sternly. I stared at him. How did he, oh…

"Yeah, I've picked up several stray thoughts about somehow getting back to your home town and keeping

Stig away from Adam and everyone else. You really think that would help? If anything happens to you, Adam will die, just as sure as if Stig killed him at the same time as you. He lives for you. You still don't see it though, do you? After everything I said last night?"

I stared at Tatum and tried again to get up but snow is incredibly unhelpful when you're practically sitting in it. Finally, with a sigh, Tatum hopped effortlessly to his feet and helped me up. I shivered, feeling the cold seeping down my legs from the middle of my thighs. Tatum didn't seem affected so I tried to keep the fact hidden. We were starting to walk back anyway.

"I just wanted to find a way to bring an end to all of this. Keep everyone safe."

"That's not the answer, Lila. I hope that's the lesson you learned today from me. I wasn't trying to terrify you but I do want to keep you realistic. If a Tracker gets within a few metres of his prey, there's usually no saving them, especially with the added danger of his magnetism. That's why we're keeping you out…" He stopped short and looked around him.

His eyes turned red and swirly and his fangs descended. He looked so terrifying in that moment I stepped back. His hands snapped out and grabbed me in a tight grip once more, holding me in place. His nostrils flared as if trying to pick up a scent. With a rush of movement, he suddenly scooped me into his arms and was running. So fast. Faster than I'd ever seen anything move, despite the thick snow on the ground. Everything around me was a blur. It was really dizzying and made me feel sick.

216

"Do not… throw up… on me." He panted, the effort clear in his voice as he ran from whatever he'd heard out there. I saw the house approach fast, then we were suddenly inside and I was dumped lightly onto the ground.

"**Trouble**!" Tatum yelled, locking the front door super-fast and coming back to help me to my feet, so fast I'd barely had a chance to move.

Footsteps sounded but with vampire speed I almost heard them after everyone had arrived, apart from Nick and Nigel although they were pretty close behind.

"What's going on? She's drenched." Nigel sputtered, stepping over and helping me out of my coat. I went with it – too frightened to argue.

"**Quiet**!" Tatum shouted. I guessed belatedly he was telling us to stop thinking. A glare made me stop that too.

"There's a Tracker on the grounds." He breathed, leaning towards the front door as if to listen. He turned to the Shapeshifters. "Ladies?" He reached for the front door again and with a rush of air and some pretty scary growls, there were suddenly two huge light grey wolves standing in the hallway beside piles of clothing. They were gorgeous, but I smothered any other thoughts as I watched Tatum pull open the door for them to rush outside. He closed and locked it again. There was obviously some pre-arranged plan in place for such emergencies I realised as I watched them work.

"Where's Adam? When's he due back?" Nigel was trying to lead me upstairs to, I assume, get me to change into dry clothes. I was shuddering uncontrollably but I think it was mostly fear. He stopped to reply to Tatum.

217

"I'm not sure. He said he had supplies to pick up on his way back. I'll try his mobile."

"Do it." Tatum barked. In the end, Nick slipped by and started leading me upstairs with Shane following. Tatum stayed in the hallway listening, his ear to the door.

Nick all but shoved me into Adam's room but thankfully Shane stopped him outside and closed the door after following me inside. She bustled around helping me out of the wet clothes and into some warm fleecy running trousers, which must have been Adam's as they weren't mine. Thankfully they had a drawstring waist or I'd have been screwed. She rolled them up at the bottoms and found me thick warm socks to wear. My top was replaced with a T-shirt of Adam's followed by a thick jumper of his. I was slowly feeling my limbs come back to life and thanked her as she let me fall back on the bed, lying face up. She sat beside me.

"Thank god Tatum was with you. He must have heard the Tracker's thoughts. Any other one of us would have lost valuable minutes until he made a physical sound." I shivered again and she pulled the quilt from the bed and covered me in it, practically rolling me up like a Swiss Roll. It helped, not only warming me, but also making me feel like I was wrapped in a cocoon. Nick knocked on the door and poked his head in, eyes closed. "You decent yet?" Shane laughed and told him to come in. He sat beside her, his hand taking hers. It would have been sweet if I weren't doomed to die any minute. Actually, if that was the case...

"You guys look really sweet together." I mumbled through lips which felt two sizes too big. Still numb I guessed. They shared a look.

"Okaayyy." Nick said. "What's your point?" I tried to sit up but looked like a floundering whale so gave up. Shane took pity and dragged me up into a sitting cocooned position. Better.

"Look after each other. Get away now if you can." Shane smiled at Nick. "She's a little bit defeatist, don't you think?"

"Um no. I'm going to die but you guys don't have to. He's found me, even here. Nowhere is safe." I shuddered, pulling the quilt tighter around me.

"We don't know for sure…"

"Oh, don't be ridiculous, Nick. Of course, it's him. Who else would it be?" Stupid thing to say but I guess he was just trying to calm me.

Shane shifted so she was sitting facing both of us.

"I know this is scary but you're surrounded by people who can protect you. Both of you. We're not going to let anyone hurt you. This is why we're here! And Halley and Eloise are excellent at tracking in wolf form. If there's a Tracker out there, he'll have to get out of dodge pretty fast or he'll be found. To be honest, I'd rather face a Tracker than those two when they're pissed off and in wolf form." I thought about that and grinned despite everything.

"Will they rip him to shreds?" I asked hopefully.

"Yeah totally. Probably play with their food a little bit first." Shane grinned at us both then turned to the side and cocked her head a little as if listening. A look of annoyance crossed her face. "Wait here." She snapped, dashing out of the room at vampire speed. The door closed so fast, we both felt a rush of air from it. Nick stared at me.

219

"She's a scary chick at times."

I grinned. "You love it." He leaned back against the headboard with me.

"You know what? I totally get it now. I couldn't see why you wanted to be with him. It didn't make sense but it does now." Did I want to know what he meant by that? I raised my eyebrows warily.

"Oh, get your filthy mind out of the gutter! I mean there's something amazingly centred about vampires. They know their limits and they treat us with respect. I guess I expected to be treated contemptuously, like food, or just as a weaker individual when I first found out. I never imagined there would be a houseful protecting you or us from danger."

"And they're good in bed." I said flippantly. He laughed out loud.

"No complaints here." I wriggled around to look at him.

"Can I ask something personal?" His eyes narrowed a bit.

"You can try. If it's about you and me, I can see now we were all wrong for each other. I think this is what we were meant for."

I thought on that for a second.

"Nice try but you haven't diverted my question. Um… have you shared blood yet?" His cheeks flushed slightly answering my question.

"Can you imagine ever getting tired of that?" I asked, eyes dropping so he couldn't read my expression.

"Don't get me started. The rush I get when Shane feeds on me is out of this world. I mean literally, she fills my head with the most amazing images and well, obviously, there are other feelings too. And she fed me her blood last night. She said she wanted to reciprocate. It tasted incredible; better than Adam's did, no offence, and today I feel so strong and powerful."

"Yeah, their blood is pretty potent. I guess you know she can't change you?"

"Yeah, she explained. She's going to try and find someone though. If that's what I want. And I'm pretty sure it is. Wow, it feels so weird confiding in you after all the time we've spent hating each other."

"Tell me about it. I was sure you were just a complete dick. Oh, no offence." His laugh told me he wasn't holding a grudge. "You've been so different since you've been here."

"I feel like I can relax and be me at last. I think I've been trying for so long to impress people, be cool and fit in… it just turned me into well, apparently, a complete dick. Nearly dying at the fists and teeth of a crazed vampire does tend to make you re-evaluate yourself."

"And yet you still have the guts to let a vampire feed on you. Impressive."

He laughed and waggled his eyebrows. "I'm so glad he didn't make me feel like Shane does. I'd be eternally confused!"

Shouting from downstairs had us clutching each other's hands. There was the crash of something being broken and then I heard Adam's voice.

"Lila? Where are you? I'm here. Lila!" He took the stairs several at a time by the sound of it and burst into the room, taking in the image of me rolled up in the quilt, holding hands with Nick on his bed. His face was angry and there was blood on his cheek. Nick leapt up from the bed with his hands up.

"All perfectly innocent here, Adam." He took in the swirls of red in Adam's eyes as he approached, looking every inch the predator, and backed into the bathroom, slamming the door as if it would protect him. Hardly! I stayed perfectly still as I watched him approach me. Much like a person would if they were being approached by a deadly wild animal.

Adam looked angry still but it didn't feel directed at me. More shouting broke out downstairs and I heard.

"I'm not finished with you, Adam, for fuck's sake!" Tatum stormed into the room and marched at Adam. He shoved him hard, causing him to stagger back a few steps. Adam shoved back with equal force and it was obvious fists were about to fly... probably teeth too with them being vampires.

"What the hell's going on?!" I screamed, trying to leap up from the bed. Typical of me and my stupid human reflexes. I stumbled off the bed, tripped over the quilt and hit the floor. Both vampires dropped down to help me instantly and I angrily brushed them away, extracting my legs from the quilt all by myself and kicking it away as I stood up red-faced. They looked straight back at each other, anger reappearing on their faces.

Nick opened the bathroom door to take in the scene, sensing he was no longer the one in danger. Two angry vampires faced each other, fists clenched, fangs bared, and eyes red and swirling dangerously.

"You'd better explain yourself right the fuck now." Tatum said evenly. Adam held up his hands suddenly, placating.

"I'm sorry. I should have let you in on…"

"Let me *in* on it? Are you out of your sodding mind? You've just brought more danger here. You're meant to be on Lila's side!" I stared at them both, stopping at Adam's face, which looked conflicted. What had he done? Was he deliberately putting me in danger?

Tatum turned to look at me. "That's how it looks, yes. And so help me, if he doesn't explain in a minute I'm going to forget we're supposed to be friends." Adam stepped back. His face lost all of its anger and his vampire features faded away before my eyes.

"Please let's all go back downstairs and I'll explain." I watched them warily as they faced off again.

"With *him* there?!" Tatum asked through gritted teeth.

Him? Oh crap, was Stig here? Was that what had happened? Adam had led him to me? Or made a deal maybe? Tatum grabbed my arm and started leading me into the upstairs hallway.

"It's not Stig." He muttered into my ear, trying to make me feel better I guess. "But it *is* a Tracker."

"Another one?!" I gasped, what the hell was going on here?

Chapter Twenty-Eight

A dam forced us all to sit in the kitchen, although we moved seats around to sit away from each other, all trust seemingly gone in an instant. Halley and Eloise were in human form again and dressed. There was, however, blood on their faces and hands. Nigel looked nervous and somehow that really freaked me out, more than anything else.

Shane looked grim and had pulled Nick over to sit just behind her, protecting him even in this room of 'friends'. My eyes fell upon someone I didn't recognise. His hair was dark blond, about chin length, and scruffy (although there was so much blood on his face and head it was hard to be sure). I gasped and stepped back. His nostrils flared and he grinned, stepping towards me. He was obviously the Tracker; if the insane look in his eyes told the truth. Tatum was instantly behind me, hands on my shoulders. His warmth calmed me but I wondered why it wasn't Adam soothing me. I looked for him. He was standing warily in the doorway. Taking in the sight before him, he strode over and pushed the unnamed Tracker further away from me.

"One metre at all times, Connor. Don't *fuck* with me." Then he pulled me along with him and moved back towards the doorway. Tatum fixed them both with a glare in turn then pulled himself up to sit on the corner of the counter.

"Time to explain yourself, Adam." The Tracker drawled, a South American accent colouring his voice and making him sound all the more out of place in the room. He pulled over a chair and straddled it. Although he was bloody he didn't seem to be hurting. I wouldn't mind betting he'd healed underneath all the mess already. A nod from Tatum confirmed my thoughts. Adam's hand tightened on my wrist as if to stop us communicating.

"I can see you're all looking at me right now like I'm some kind of a traitor for bringing in another Tracker but it makes sense if you'll just listen. Honestly."

"We're listening." Shane spat, gesturing for him to continue.

"Yes, Connor is a Tracker. I know that's not a surprise to any of you now. He's been tracking Lila for 3 days... at my request." I gasped and stepped away from him, although I couldn't break free of his grip.

"Jesus, Lila. Why are you looking at me like I'm the bad guy? I hired a Tracker to keep you safe." The room erupted in arguments, which took a moment to die down.

"Keep me *safe*?" I asked quietly. The Tracker, Connor, was staring at me in a way I really didn't like. It made me feel like he was sizing me up for a meal or worse. I couldn't help but tremble. I saw Tatum lean over and whisper something to him, slashing the air with his hand. Connor looked at him in surprise for a brief second then turned back to look at me, but his expression looked a little less creepy. I smiled a tiny smile at Tatum in thanks.

"Yes. It occurred to me that only another Tracker would know how and when he would find you and what his process would be. Connor was never told where you were or where I live. He's found you of his own volition. That was a test to see how safe this place really is."

"So Stig can find me that easily too?"

"In theory, yes." Connor drawled, standing up to lean against the wall, arms folded. "But he's probably not as good as me."

"So, Trackers are arrogant arseholes as well as psychotic and obsessive?" I asked Adam incredulously. Adam smirked for a second.

"Connor is someone I've known for almost 40 years. During that time, I've found him to be fairly bearable, all things considered."

"Back at ya, pal." Connor laughed.

"Hey, we're not cool yet." I said, backing away from Adam and Connor. "Why send a second guy to hunt me when one is already obsessed to the point of killing me?"

"He doesn't want to kill you." Connor said, studying his fingernails for a moment. "He wants to sell you. He can't sell a dead body." Tatum yelled at him and he shrugged. "Truth hurts, kid. Deal with it." Adam waved his arms to disarm the situation as if that was possible. The tension in the room was thick enough that even I could feel it. I saw Nick grab Shane's hand and grip it tightly, so he felt it too. She wrapped her other hand around both of theirs to comfort him. I wished for the same.

"I also thought it was useful to uh… have someone here who can track you in case… in case the worst happens and Stig does manage to get you away from us. Connor is locked in on your scent. He can find you anywhere. He's proven that today – quicker than I'd thought possible I'm sorry to say."

And you were going to tell us this when?" Shane asked angrily. "How do we know he won't go nutso on us and take her anyway?"

"I was going to tell you tonight, when the last one of you arrived although unfortunately he's been delayed. It's not like I hid it from you. I thought I'd have time to explain before he got here. And he won't attack Lila. I have his word. He's promised to stay a metre away at all times."

"You're willing to take the word of a *Tracker*? You're a fool!" Tatum shouted. His anger was sweet and all but it seemed to have more to do with the Tracker than my safety. His eyes locked on mine before he looked back to Adam. "This is an incredibly bad idea." He stormed from the room and up the stairs.

"Okaaaay…. I'm going to go out on a limb and say that's not the reaction you hoped for from us?" Halley asked as she got up from the table. She gestured to Eloise who got up to follow her. El met Adam's eyes apologetically as she passed. Halley's hand briefly patted my shoulder on the way past.

I backed into a corner of the room.

"I'm also going to share how I feel about this... I'm scared, Adam. How do you know he won't sell me *to* the Tracker? He's got what the other guy wants now." Connor grinned.

"You *don't* know, sweetcheeks. You're just gonna have to trust me." He stood up and looked at Adam.

"Any blood here? I didn't pack enough." I gasped and looked at Nigel, hoping he wasn't about to loan him out. The look on Nigel's face told me that he wasn't about to agree to that. Adam nodded and led him to the door to a basement I didn't even know existed.

"Help yourself to what's in storage."

I ran from the room while his back was turned. Finding somewhere to run to would be difficult. Where was safe now that there was a Tracker in the house? Upstairs, a hand snatched me from the hallway and pulled me into a room before I could scream.

A finger pressed to my lips silencing me. Tatum stared anxiously into my eyes. I calmed down a little once I knew it was him, but I couldn't help being on edge with that Tracker in the house.

He nodded in response. He removed his finger and let me walk further into the room. I sat down in the window seat of a room so similar to the one I'd used that first night, only the room was the opposite way around, if that makes sense. It was the same grey and red colour scheme throughout but with Tatum in the room, it seemed darker and more mysterious somehow. He shook his head with a sigh.

"How does a person make a room darker and more mysterious?" I clapped a hand over my mouth in embarrassment; even though the words hadn't actually come out of my mouth.

"Sorry." I mumbled. He sat on the bed and sighed heavily.

"Don't sweat it. I'm actually starting to get used to you being in my head allllll the damn time." We both laughed but it ended suddenly.

"Has he made a terrible mistake?" I asked nervously. Tatum shrugged.

"You can never trust a Tracker. I can't help but feel this is the biggest mistake we could make right now. What was he thinking?"

"Have you met a Tracker before today then?" He met my eyes then looked away, focusing on something in the corner of the room with all of his attention.

"Hey, even I don't have to be a mindreader to work that one out. You were hunted by one?" He nodded, suddenly looking so young and, dare I think, afraid?

"Yes, I'm afraid. They are the most evil a vampire can ever become. Yes, I was hunted by a Tracker. I was hunted, tormented and tortured by one before he sold me to a Creator. I was turned against my will, and then kept a slave by my Creator for years. I eventually fought for my freedom and have had to hide from people for so long with my so-called gift. If I'd stayed human I'd have died after a normal life and never suffered through all of this. So no, I'm never going to trust a Tracker. And I'm sure as hell not letting one get hold of you. I'll rip him to shreds before I let that happen."

It was the longest speech I'd heard from him and such a sad story. His protectiveness of me was so comforting but it felt undeserved.

"Why?" He asked. Damn that mind reading thing.

"I don't know. You've only just met me for a start. How do you know I'm even worth saving? Maybe it's safer for everyone if you just let it happen. Maybe it's my destiny to be captured or killed by him." He fixed an angry stare on my face.

"What the fuck are you talking about? Destiny is just made-up crap. Nothing is pre-ordained in life. You think some higher power sat down and decided to create things like me? No way! Nature went wrong somewhere and we're the result. A dirty secret hiding among the humans. And FYI within a few minutes of meeting you a person knows so much more about you than they ever need to. You can't help that. If you're not thinking you're projecting."

Oh. Something occurred to me then.

"Wait. Projecting? Like actual images?" He laughed shakily, running a hand through his blond hair. "Why do you think it's freaking me out so much? I'm seeing those hideous endings you keep picturing for yourself and everyone else. In full gory colour."

"But how? I thought that was something only Shane could do because of what she is. Does that mean I'd be a Dreamwalker if I turn?" He shook his head.

"I have no idea. It's very, very rare to get such clear images from someone without that gift, but then your mind is so over-active, maybe it's just a by-product of that."

I considered getting up and hitting him for that but it was too far and I was shattered. It had been a long day. He grinned.

"Dodged a bullet there, did I?" He got up and lifted me effortlessly from the window seat, placing me on his bed. He covered me up with the quilt. "Sleep for a while. I'll watch over you. You're safe here."

"Will you see my dreams?"

"Dear god, I hope not."

"Git."

"*Sleep.*"

I woke some time later to Adam's and Tatum's quiet voices in the corner of the room. It didn't sound like they were arguing so I didn't bother to interrupt. Of course, Tatum knew the moment I was awake.

"We're not going to fight." He said only slightly louder. Adam headed over to the bed and sat beside me. His hand gently swept the hair back from my face.

"You okay?" He asked softly. I thought I heard the bedroom door close, so Tatum must have left. I moved to sit up and Adam helped me, sitting me in the crook of his arm, with my face against his chest.

"I'm sorry this was all just sprung on you in this terrifying way. It's really the best chance we have, I honestly believe that."

"I'm so scared, Adam. I know I talk big but I've just realised today how much danger there really is." I shuddered, remembering Tatum's demonstration of my weakness compared to vampires.

Adam made soothing circles on my back with his hand. "Tatum told me about what happened in the woods. He really didn't mean to scare you so much. He just wants you to be safe. He really cares about you."

232

"I feel safe with him around me, you know, protected. I definitely don't like Connor though. He's creepy." Another shudder.

"Do you feel safe with *me*?" Adam asked, as if he suddenly doubted it.

"Of course. You're my safe place." He hugged me tighter and kissed the top of my head. With a sigh, I finally relaxed and must have fallen asleep again.

It was dark in the room when I woke again, but Adam was still there, cradling me in his arms. His breathing was slow and peaceful and his heart was beating a steady rhythm. I moved to look into his face. He looked so serene while sleeping, although he seemed to wake instinctively. Or maybe I dug him with my elbow. As you know, I'm not the most graceful girl. He smiled at me.

"Been awake long?" I stroked his face with my thumb.

"Seconds." I whispered. He moved so that my thumb was on his lips and kissed it softly.

"Feel better about things? I promise you are safe here with me, with us. All of us."

I nodded. Who couldn't feel safe with this man? I kissed him and felt him respond. Then my damn stomach growled and he laughed against my lips.

"Another time maybe?" he asked, moving to get up and dragging me with him. I groaned as my muscles complained. I guess my legs were punishing me for that kneeling in the snow incident today.

We headed downstairs to voices in the kitchen. There was food. Oh, thank god. I made for the plates and served up a plateful of roast chicken and sat down. I was next to Shane, with space beside me for Adam. Tatum was already eating his food and gave me a mouth-full smile. I returned it. I thought the words 'thank you' to him and saw him acknowledge it with his eyes. Oh, and we didn't have sex in your bed, I sent too. He choked on his mouthful and took a few moments to compose himself. We all giggled a little. His glare afterwards told me he didn't appreciate being choked with his dinner, but hey at least he knew his bed wasn't tainted. He groaned and slumped his shoulders a bit. Damn. He was still hearing me, of course.

Connor walked in and the room silenced immediately. I felt a pang of sympathy before remembering who and what he was. Tatum's eyes followed him across the room to the food. When Connor brought a full plate to the table, Tatum got up and dumped his plate in the sink before leaving the room. It was a little awkward for a moment.

"I think he was here first." Shane offered weakly as Connor sat down. He shrugged and tucked into his food. I looked at Adam and saw he looked troubled.

"Yeah he was nearly finished when I got here." I muttered. Connor met my eyes and stared a little too long for my liking. He didn't reply and just went back to eating eventually. I turned wide eyes to Adam and he nodded as if this was normal behaviour for Connor.

Chapter Twenty-Nine

"So, Connor. Any thoughts on what we should do to keep Lila hidden?" Connor swallowed his food and stared at each of us as we turned to him.

"You want me to say there's an easy answer? There ain't one. He has your scent, and he'll follow it 'til he finds you. We can't stop him finding her but we might be able to offer up a bargain when he does get here. Find out what the Creator's paying him and up it maybe?" He stuffed more food in his mouth while we all just stared at him.

"That's it? Your answer is let him find me then pay him to go away?" I looked at Adam in horror.

"Well, we talked about methods for hiding our trail. You want to talk us through that?" He tried.

Connor shrugged. "Not really. I told you before it's all a waste of time."

"Adam, why the fuck is he here if he can't actually do anything to help?" I snapped, dumping my knife and fork down and slumping back in my chair with a heavy sigh. Connor scowled at me.

"Stop having a tantrum, sweetheart. Knowing how quickly I could find you helps. Also, I'll be able to track you when he snatches you away."

I gasped, tears springing to my eyes. "*When*? So, it's just a given that he'll find me and snatch me without anybody being able to stop him?"

Adam put his hand on my arm to calm me. I winced. It felt like he was gripping me hard, or maybe my arm was just tender in my fragile, freaked out state. Adam noticed.

"What?"

I shook my head. "Just gripping me a bit there." He frowned, pulling at the sleeves of his jumper that I was wearing. "No, I'm not." His search revealed dark bruises on both arms, from when Tatum had grabbed me earlier. They looked horrible and vivid against my pale skin. Adam's eyes narrowed and I could see him getting angry.

"He was only trying to help." I said, pulling my sleeves back down.

"By hurting you?" I stood up with my plate, appetite gone.

"That's what it took, Adam. Because I was too stupid and naïve to realise just how serious all of this is. I thought I could run, or fight back. He proved me wrong. I bruise easily – I am, after all, just human." I dumped my plate in the sink and turned to lean against it with a sigh. Connor looked up at me, mouth full of food.

"Well there's your answer right there. Find someone to turn her before he finds her. She's no good to him then." He took in the open-mouthed stares aimed at him once more, then went back to his food, stopping again after a mouthful.

"Seriously, you people all want an answer and then when you get it, you're pissed. Make up your damn minds." He drawled, heading over with his plate, mirroring my movements. I backed up into the corner hurriedly as he approached. I saw Adam start to stand up from his seat.

"Don't worry sweetheart. One metre, remember?" He left the plate on the side and, with a last long look at me; he walked out of the room.

I shuddered. That man creeped me out, make no mistake. But he made a good point. If we could find someone to turn me before the Tracker found me, he'd have no need for me. I'd be safe and better yet, I'd be less helpless. I looked at the group of people still sitting.

"So... anyone know a good Creator around here?"

"No! Out of the question." Adam snapped, slamming his chair back and getting up. "And no, not because I don't want you to become a vampire but because I don't know which one he's in league with. We could end up taking you straight to Stig's partner!"

"What alternative do we have? How many do you know?"

"I don't know any! What do you want me to do?!" I noticed the room quickly emptying behind him, which was annoying because they could have helped.

237

I sighed. "What about *your* Creator? Why can't we ask him or her?" His eyes darkened.

"My Creator is dead."

Oh. That stopped me in my tracks.

"I'm sorry, Adam. I do think Connor has a point though. The only thing Stig wants me for is to sell me to a Creator. If we can find someone to turn me first, there's no sale, right? And no sale means he'll leave me alone." He sighed and sank down to the floor, sitting with his knees pulled up, leaning back against the kitchen cupboard.

"I know he's right, but I just don't know how to find one. The sad truth is I don't know many vampires. The ones I know are here, or on their way. None are Creators. They're exceptionally hard to find." He leaned his head back against the cupboard door, staring up at the ceiling in defeat.

I crouched beside him. "We'll find one. He did it. So, can we."

Chapter Thirty

 was really irritated by my still-missing iPod.
How could it just disappear in a house? Shane
caught me looking around and asked what I had
lost. I explained and she offered to help me look. We
searched the TV room, library and kitchen but nothing. I
didn't want to check the office as Adam and Nigel were
in there doing some kind of 'worky' stuff. I'm sure I
hadn't taken it in there anyway. Then there was the
sitting room but we barely used it so I didn't think it
would be there either.

"Want to borrow mine?" She offered. I smiled,
thinking what a sweet offer it was.

"Depends…do you have anything by *30 Seconds to
Mars*? I'm going insane without my fix." She grinned
and led me to her room. Her iPod touch was by her bed.
She scrolled through and found the *This is War* album

and handed it to me. My saviour. I loved this girl. Platonically of course.

"You just saved my life, Shane. Thanks so much." I hugged her, then pressed play and popped in the earphones, tucking her iPod safely into my jeans pocket. There was no sound. I frowned; realising as it was switched on and playing that the volume must just be really, really low. I couldn't hear it at all so cranked it up.

She pulled an earphone from my ear and said. "Wait 'til you're a vampire. You'll understand." I grinned, then disappeared into the library, determined to find something to read, anything to take my mind off my doom.

I settled down on the window seat with a book about vampire history and relaxed with the sounds of one of my favourite albums. By the time I got to *Hurricane*, I was engrossed in the book I'd found. It wasn't the one Adam had shown me but it gave more insight into different vampire types. Maybe this would help us to work out where to find a Creator. Maybe I could find a way out of this and keep everyone safe. Yeah right.

Sometime during *Closer to the Edge*, a hand snaked suddenly across my mouth and I was yanked from the seat in a rush. The iPod earphones fell from my ears in the struggle and something hit the side of my head knocking me unconscious.

I woke up somewhere pitch dark and cold and I was chained to something I couldn't see. I wanted to scream, and cry and panic and yell for Adam and Tatum but I was also too terrified to make a sound. He'd found me. He'd taken me away. It was over.

Chapter Thirty-One

A light flicked on, blinding me, and forcing me to squeeze my eyes shut against the painful brightness. A chuckle sounded in the room. A chuckle I recognised with a wave of deep panic. He was here in the room with me right now! Oh, my god! I hyperventilated. He was going to kill me!

"Breathe, you pathetic human. I don't want you passing out on me." A gruff voice said, and the figure in the corner moved towards me. As the light stopped attacking my eyes I was able to focus. He was a large hulking man, with dark rumpled hair and a beautiful face. Beautiful that was, except for the cruel twist of his mouth. He crouched beside me, watching me try to scoot back in panic. He grabbed the chain joining my hands and held me still, dark eyes staring into mine.

"Well, here we are at last, Lila. I must say you were a disappointingly easy prey. I've been around you for days with none of your protectors even figuring it out." He leaned close, pressing his face into my throat and taking a deep breath, as if he was inhaling my scent. I whimpered. When his face came back up, his eyes were red and swirly and his fangs were prominent. "You smell divine." He stared at me for a long while watching me freak out and struggle against his iron strength.

"What, no witty comments or comebacks? I'd heard you're quite the talker. Seems I've been misinformed. Disappointing, Lila, very disappointing. I'd hoped you would fight me… at least a little." He stood up, dropping me to the ground as he moved. I made an oof sound as I hit the floor with my hands under my stomach. I rolled to sit back up, not wanting to be prone on the floor, well as much as I could be any less prone. I wished that Tatum could be miraculously in earshot of my thoughts. A terrible thought hit me then, as I stared fearfully up at Stig. Had he hurt anyone when he took me?

"Come on little one, I can tell you want to ask me something. Go ahead." He was very obviously gloating; waiting for a question he knew was coming.

"Are they okay?" I whispered. He blinked stupidly. Clearly not the question he was waiting for after all.

"Who?"

"The others, at the house when you abducted me? Did you hurt them?" A grin crawled across his face, like a creepy critter with way too many legs.

"Ah… more concerned about others than yourself? How sweet and pathetic... and human. *They* are not your concern now. Forget about them." He watched me as I fretted about Adam and Nick and the others.

"Please. At least tell me they're okay." He held his hands up as if in supplication to a deity.

"They're okay?" He said mocking me. A sound outside the room (cell?) distracted him for a moment and he left me alone, door clanging in the frame, and a lock turning. I looked around me in the light. I had already lost any chance of hiding or running from him. I was already trapped, locked in chains connected to a loop in the wall. I tried pulling at that but it was obviously going to be impossible. Human strength sucks.

I was sitting on the thinnest mattress you can imagine, which was resting directly on the floor against the wall the chain led to. The rest of the room revealed only something that looked like a prison toilet. I really hoped he'd kill me before I had to use that. It looked ancient and gross.

I remembered then that he wouldn't kill me. That was the whole point. It did beg the question though. What would he do if I managed to somehow kill myself in this room? I reviewed the contents of the room again, trying to work out how I would do it. I guess I could try and suffocate myself with the mattress but heaven only knows where it had been. I didn't want to accidentally survive but have TB or something even worse. The chains could probably choke me but I think that would take more strength than I have. Like it or not, my only way out would be to goad him into killing me. It was sure to be nasty and vicious and painful. Would it be

243

better to wait it out and see who he sells me to? They might not be all bad. And I might be able to get away once I'm a vampire. My thoughts were interrupted by voices outside the room.

He was arguing with a woman. She sounded young like me. With an angry shout, he dismissed her and came back into the room. He stared at me from just inside the door, watching me gaze up at him in terror. His face went into full vampire glory as he surged towards me with a loud growling roar, sending me into a panicked, defensive ball on that horrible mattress.

He came to a stop directly in front of me... so close, too close. I tried to scoot back further but he just followed me until I was backed up against the wall. He dropped to a crouch in the blink of an eye, his face mere inches from mine. He breathed in again taking in my scent.

"You know, the more afraid you are, the stronger and more beautiful your scent. It's like a drug to me so feel free to give in to the terror, Lila. Or I can help you to be more afraid..." He breathed in again, suddenly dragging me close to him by my hair. His face dipped into my hair while he breathed in again. It was so creepy and intrusive.

"Stop, please!" I cried, hoping he'd listen. Instead he laughed into my hair and then he tilted my head up, still holding my hair so that our faces were close.

"You want me to stop, little girl? I'll stop when I want. An hour from now... a week from now... You're mine now. I'll do with you whatever I want. I'll feed on you, I'll use your body and I'll kill you when I'm ready.

Or not." He laughed harshly as he watched tears run down my cheeks.

"Please just kill me." I sobbed. He grinned.

"But we're having so much fun, Lila! Why would we stop now?" He lunged in and I felt his breath on my neck, then teeth sank in fast and without warning. I screamed. He wasted no time making it feel good or even painless. It hurt the whole time he was drawing my blood out through my neck. He groaned as the first taste hit his tongue and sucked hard to get more. He gulped away while lowering himself over me 'til I was pressed down flat on the mattress with his weight on top of me. I cried silently the whole time he fed.

My neck throbbed from the pressure of his teeth and the sensation of him pulling my blood through my skin. It felt like he was biting down still harder while drinking. His body pressed along mine and I could feel he was aroused. It occurred to me only then that there were many awful things a crazy man could do to a captive woman, and so I prayed he would just drink too much in his frenzy and kill me now. He pressed himself against me as he drank, rubbing against me in a way that was far too intimate not to terrify me. I cried harder and begged him again to kill me. All too soon he stopped feeding, teeth sliding abruptly out of my skin. I felt his vile tongue swirl over my neck, catching the last drops of blood before they escaped. He lifted his head to look at me, still pressing me down with his body. His cheeks were flushed with my blood and his eyes a vicious red. His fangs rested on his lower lip, as if to draw my attention and fear...

"Was it good for you?" He laughed. He ran a hand up my leg from just below the knee to my hip. He watched the fear and disgust in my eyes as he swept the same hand up further to cup one of my breasts. I shuddered and he laughed. "What to do with you now, little one? We have all the time in the world. There must be something we can do to entertain ourselves…" His hand slid back down to my waist as I trembled beneath him.

"Please." I whispered, praying he would suddenly grow a conscience and leave me alone. He laughed softly, leaning forwards as if to kiss me. With his face far too close, he smiled.

"You're mine, Lila. I will make the most of you before I sell you on. Where shall we start?"

There was a massive bang against the door and he looked up, anger crossing his face. He was up and walking to the door in a flash. I scurried back across the mattress into the corner of the room and curled up with my knees up to my chest. One hand cupped my throbbing neck. Surely it would stop hurting now. It never hurt at all after Adam fed. Why did it hurt so much now? And how much had he taken? It suddenly seemed like he'd taken a lot. I felt a heavy lethargy flow through me, and my arm dropped to my side weakly. Who had interrupted him? And how could I find them to thank them? Whatever he had been planning had been interrupted for now. I had to get away before he returned and picked up where he left off. I couldn't stop trembling, partly from fear and I think partly from shock. My body felt cold, like the loss of blood had taken all of the heat out of my body. That was probably a bad sign, or in my case a good sign. Maybe he had taken enough to kill me after all.

There was yelling outside the room. I prayed someone was here to rescue me but was horrified when the door opened a few moments later and Michelle was thrown into the room. Oh shit, he's got Michelle too. She *had been* dating Stig. That bastard. I couldn't even find the strength to get up and go to her. It turns out it wasn't needed. She leapt up and was pounding on the door yelling at him.

"You bastard! You come back here and I'll kill you." It was like she didn't know I was there, yet why else would she be mad at him?

"Michelle." I spoke quietly and she stopped instantly. How she heard me with all that noise was a mystery. She turned to face me and I saw with horror that her eyes were glowing and swirling and she had fangs. He'd turned her. The bastard had…. Wait… he wasn't a Creator! How was that possible?

"What the fuck? How are *you* a vampire?" I screamed, finding strength from somewhere. She tossed her hair back in the way that was so familiar and made me want to cry then sat on the floor across from me.

"Well, turns out Steve *was* actually someone called Stig after all and he's an *asshole!*" She shouted that last part for his benefit. "He fucked me a few times then took me to some freaky guy who bit me as well. Then I ended up like this. It's not so bad I suppose except when I get hungry. It's a bit hard to stop when I start feeding." She sighed and covered her face with her hands taking a few deep breaths. When she took her hands away she was Michelle again.

"God I'm so sorry, Michelle. This is all my fault."

"Um contrary to popular belief, not everything in this world is about you." She snapped. "He liked me. He wanted to keep me." From the look on her face I wasn't completely sure that bothered her. I wanted to know more.

"How did you meet him?" She shrugged. "I was walking out of work and he started chatting me up. He was hot and something about him made me want to drag him back to mine so I agreed to go out with him."

"Magnetism." I groaned and she looked at me in surprise.

"You know?" I nodded. "I found out some stuff about him after I found out he was tracking me."

"Tracking you? That's not what…" she got up and pounded on the door again. "You lying *bastard!*" I tried to get up and go over to her but couldn't for two reasons you already know. I was weak from blood loss and chained to the wall. She sat down again.

"He said that Adam was the one hunting *him* and you were working with him. He made me believe that he was in danger and needed me. You know how I like to be needed. And you were nowhere around to talk to about it. Damn him, he played me. All along all he wanted was *you*." She said that as if I disgusted her.

I sat up more and felt my head swirl as dizziness set in.

"Um how much blood loss is fatal?" I asked, sort of offhand as if it didn't matter because I guess it didn't. Better if it killed me now before he returned to pick up where he left off.

"I don't know!" She snapped, then her face softened as she looked at me. "He fed on you. He didn't hurt you, did he?" I stared her in the face.

"No, it was a fucking ball! Of course he hurt me. He also kind of assaulted me." The last words faded into sobs as I cried into my hands. She moved over to sit by me and patted my shoulder as I cried. When I calmed down a bit, but not much, to be fair, she spoke.

"It usually feels good when he feeds. Mind you, I'm usually having sex with him when he does. Not that he does that much now, guess my blood isn't good enough for him now I'm like him."

"Like him? You're a Tracker too?" I asked in horror, feeling the room tilt around me. She stared at me.

"How the hell would that be possible? Anyone can be made one?" She didn't know any of it.

"You don't know what kind of vampire you are?" I asked. She stared at me half annoyed.

"What the fuck are you on about?" I think I must have passed out around then because I was suddenly aware she was sitting against the opposite wall and looked like she had for a while.

"Awake again are we?" She asked mockingly. "You better hope he brings food or lets me out soon, or when I get hungry I'm afraid there won't be any stopping me. I mean I love you, babe, but I also need to eat. Sorry Lila. It's a vampire thing." I felt my heart thud. She was like Michelle but she wasn't really her anymore. Was this how I would have turned out?

"Please don't feed on me. I don't think I have much left." And yet I was still alive. Why? Why couldn't I just die now?

249

"Give me an alternative." She snarled.

"Bite the prick who locked us in here." I snapped back.

"Won't help."

Damn it. I wondered where the others were. If they were okay. If they were alive. If they were even looking for me. I suddenly realised that the only hope might be if Shane could reach me in a dream. That meant I had to fall asleep or pass out again. I had no idea if she'd already tried or succeeded but me being awake helped nobody. Climbing unsteadily to my feet, I looked around for options and eventually just threw myself headfirst at the wall. I heard a shriek from Michelle but it faded into oblivion with the last of my consciousness.

Chapter Thirty-Two

I was outside Adam's house. It was snowing, as always, and I walked along the deep snow on the path towards the door, noticing I was not leaving footprints. I also didn't feel the cold. Was I already dead? Had I travelled back here as a ghost to find him even in death?

I became aware of someone standing before me. It was Shane. She looked upset and tired.

"Where are you, Lila?" She asked sharply. I realised it wasn't the first time she'd asked. I shrugged.

"In a cell somewhere. Dying I think. If I'm not already dead." She grabbed my shoulders and gave me a sharp shake. She could touch me in a dream? That's what she meant by 'interact'... oh... gross...

"Snap out of it, Lila. You're alive, or you wouldn't be here with me. Now you need to tell me where you are."

"I don't know! It's a metal room with a locked door and no windows. I've not seen outside of the door. Michelle is there." I suddenly remembered. "I work with her." She nodded impatiently.

"Is she okay? Is she a prisoner too?"

"No…" I sniffled. "She's a vampire now…" Her face reflected shock.

"The Creator is already there?!" Oh shit, that hadn't even occurred to me in all my terror. I thought he'd taken her somewhere to change but maybe the Creator was here the whole time. I stumbled in the snow and fell to my knees.

"I'm dying, Shane. At least I hope I am. I have to. Before *he* comes back… before he… oh god… Tell Adam I love him. I love him so much. You were all amazing and I'm so glad I met you. I'm sorry."

I woke up on the mattress with an unwelcome face staring at me. I saw him tear at his wrist with his teeth and he forced it over my mouth. "Drink, damn you!" Again, I was sure it wasn't the first time the words had been spoken at me. I tried to refuse but he put pressure on my throat and caused me to gasp, sucking in a mouthful of blood. "Drink or I'll force you." He snapped. I complied, knowing he'd only keep doing that to me. His blood didn't taste sweet like Adam's, and I gagged several times as my senses rebelled against the taste. It was bitter, almost acrid and tasted exactly like you'd imagine the blood of someone evil would.

Eventually he wrenched his arm away and stalked across the room. He pulled Michelle into the corner and I saw him kissing her. It grossed me out that she was totally kissing him back. Magnetism again, I guess. I wondered why it didn't work on me. He sent her out of the room, locking the door behind her. I guess she'd had her punishment, having to stay here with me. He came back to me and sat down.

"Trying to kill yourself won't get you out of here, Lila. I'll revive you a million times if I have to. It'll help to break you anyway."

I gulped. Break me?

He grinned harshly and nodded. "Yes, I said break you. I want you compliant and well behaved for my buyer and I'll do to you whatever it takes to break your spirit until that's exactly what you are." His hand shot across and gripped my throat. I struggled to swallow and breathe.

"What will it take to break you, little girl? Pain? Fear? Disgust? I think you gave me a little hint earlier." He pressed me down on the mattress and dropped on top of me again. "I could take you right here. Force you into submission. Would that do it?" He released my throat to let me speak and I tried to spit at him. He slapped me. My ear rang with the force of it. I felt blood in my mouth and it wasn't his. Bastard.

He forced my head to one side and sank his teeth into my neck again.

I screamed in shock, then realised with horror that he wasn't holding back on me this time. I felt tingles run down my body and felt a warm feeling pooling in my stomach and below. "No! No!" I screamed. He couldn't do this to me. I felt myself gripping him with my chained arms and legs while he started to rub against me once more.

His hand slipped over my breast as it had before and squeezed at it. Damn him, it actually felt good for a moment before I forced myself to remember who I was and who he was. I kicked at him, screaming for him to stop. He laughed into my neck as he released me.

"I guess you didn't expect to like it when I do that to you. See, little kitten? I can make you want me, lust for me. When I take you it'll be because you beg me to. I think that'll probably break you faster than if I just force you now." He laughed at my fear and grabbed my face, pressing his lips against mine. I squeezed them tightly shut, desperate not to let him kiss me and he laughed as he released me. I felt dizzy from blood loss again and opened my eyes to spotty vision, which slowly cleared.

Adam's face looked back at me. How was that possible? I'd obviously passed out and he'd found me, thank god. I pulled him to me, leaning in to breathe in his Adam smell. I stiffened instantly, realising my mistake. What the hell? I pulled back to see Stig's grinning face. He licked his lips.

"You'll want me soon enough." He laughed as he left the room. I passed out again. I didn't see Shane this time. Maybe it was just as well. I wasn't ready to talk to anyone after that. How had he convinced me he was Adam? What would happen if he did it again? What if I didn't realise next time?

When I woke the next time, my missing iPod was beside me. How? It had been missing for ages. Was this his proof that he had indeed been in the house before he snatched me? Did it matter at this point?

I picked it up quickly with shaky hands and found a *Mars* track to listen to. I felt the music soothe me a little but it couldn't calm me down like it normally did. Nothing would. At least there was good music to die to. At least I got to listen to it one last time. I could feel my body was shutting down. I must have so little blood left. It was a little hard to breathe but that just gave me a sense of relief that it would end soon. I'd be free. I realised he must be keeping me weak and half dead on purpose, perhaps to try and keep me from trying to escape.

Michelle didn't return to my cell and I was glad. I didn't want to see her like that again. I used those hours alone to run the battery down on the iPod listening to *Mars* over and over.

Chapter Thirty-Three

I woke in the dark, unsure for a moment where I was. My body was so cold and numb I wasn't sure I was even alive. My iPod battery had long since died but I didn't dare let go of it. It was my last tie to my life, to who I was, to Adam. I felt like I'd been alone here forever. How long had it been? Was Adam even real? Nothing seemed real any more. Was Adam just Stig the whole time? It was hard to convince myself of anything else at this point.

Sounds outside the room were of no interest to me anymore. Was there even anything outside the room? Was there even a room at all? I drifted in a daze, barely breathing and waited for death to come. It wouldn't be long now, I could tell. The sounds grew louder but I felt the world fading away as the door crashed open so hard it flew across the room.

Even in death I felt some awareness. No longer breathing, or pumping blood through my veins, I somehow felt warm arms snatch me up from the ground, and horrified screams and crying. Everything sounded distant, unreal, and the warmth did nothing to bring me back. The last of my awareness limped away into oblivion.

Chapter Thirty-Four

I first became aware of being, well, aware, when I felt warmer than death. I'm not sure how I made that distinction, but I was suddenly also aware of the sensation of blood rushing through my veins, my heart pumping away in my chest and tingling in my extremities. I deduced that I was lying in a warm soft bed, and someone was sitting beside me, close enough that I could feel the warmth seeping through from them to me. There was no brightness glaring at my closed eyes so the room was mercifully dim. I was afraid to open my eyes. Maybe it wasn't a good thing that I was back. Maybe he'd revived me with his blood again. Maybe he was waiting to mess with my head again. It was probably him sitting beside me now. Fear kept me faking sleep a little longer.

"I know you're awake, Lila. Please open your eyes. You're safe now." Adam's voice was soft and shaky. He sounded scared. I didn't dare open my eyes. His fingers stroked my face softly, but I flinched from the contact. I didn't trust my ears to tell me the truth. I wished so hard that it would really be him, but I'd been fooled before (several times if the flashbacks I had in that moment were to be believed).

I felt him move and sensed that he was now crouching beside the bed, giving me space. It felt like a proper bed and not the grungy thin floor mattress but I still didn't let myself believe.

"Please, please look at me. Or just say something. Lila?" He begged. I drew in a shuddering breath, tears leaking from my eyes, which I squeezed tightly shut.

"Lila? It's me, I promise. You're home and safe." I shook my head, choking back a sob. I wished I could open my eyes and find Adam sitting across from me, his blue eyes so expressive and full of love, his brown hair slightly rumpled as if he'd run his hands through it many times. My soul ached for him and it sounded so much like him that I wanted to give in but I just couldn't trust that it was. Eventually I felt him move away from me and the door opened and closed softly. I gave in and cried like a baby, although hopefully quieter. When the door opened again, I knew he'd be someone else, another trick to break me. I turned my face away from the direction of the steps coming towards me. Please just stop, I thought. When would he stop? When would he let me die?

The footsteps stopped a short distance away. I heard the person pull what sounded like a wooden chair across

the floor. I didn't recall a wooden chair in that place…
but other things came back to me then – chains and pain,
and blood and terror. A pained gasp came from the
visitor as I heard them sit down.

"Jesus, what has he done to you, that bastard?"
Tatum's voice asked softly. His hand covered mine and I
shuddered and tried to pull away.

"I know, I know. I can see what he did to you in that
place but he's gone, Lila. You're safe now. You're
really home with us now, I promise. Lila?" I wanted to
believe, so much. He squeezed my hand and I felt some
comfort but at the same time it repulsed me. It could be
Stig, pretending again. Fooling me, playing on my hopes
and dreams. I didn't recall him pretending to be Tatum at
any point, but it could just be a new trick to fool me into
believing.

I stayed rigid and silent the whole time whoever was
there and I heard the heavy sigh as they too left. I didn't
know how much longer I could hold off – it's impossible
to keep your eyes closed indefinitely. The natural urge is
to open them, especially when you've cried so much they
burn. Eventually, knowing I was alone, I slowly opened
my eyes. The room was dim, as I'd known from feeling
no light shining at my eyes. I took in the room. It looked
like Adam's room. Our room. I turned my face to the
pillow and took a deep breath. The pillows smelled like
Adam's cologne and shampoo so I took another breath
and curled up, the pillow in my arms. Huge gasping sobs
poured out of me as I hugged that pillow. I didn't sense
anyone in the room with me so I just gave in to it, crying
out my fear and horror. Eventually I heard a sound in the

room but soothed by Adam's scent on the pillow I didn't react.

I didn't freak out when I felt someone climb onto the bed and pull me into his arms. Pressed hard into Adam's chest I kept crying, feeling his hands rubbing my back as he tried to calm me. I wished I could smell him while I was so close but my nose was so bunged up from crying I couldn't smell anything. As I calmed eventually, hyperventilating as is my way, I realised he was crying too.

His beautiful face was wet with tears and his eyes were so full of sorrow and pain. I trailed my fingers down his cheek, wiping away tears. He just stared at me.

"Tatum told me. I… I'm so sorry… Lila." He didn't need to say any more. I got the point. Tatum lifted from my head what that animal had done to me and had told Adam. I couldn't be angry about it but I still felt ashamed.

"I'm sorry too." I muttered. His eyes narrowed at me.

"Sorry for what? Nothing that happened was *your* fault. We were all here to protect you and *none* of us even knew he'd been here. Talk about feeling completely fucking useless! He just slipped in, grabbed you and waltzed back out and how did we even know? We found Shane's iPod smashed on the floor. That's it. Son of a…"

"Adam." He stopped instantly and looked at me, using a thumb to brush tears away from my eyes. What the hell? They were still leaking? I'd shrivel up from dehydration at this rate.

"It's nobody's fault. He'd been here before. I know that now."

"What? No. That's not possible." As he said it though, I saw it dawn on him. "How do you know? He told you?"

I wriggled to get more comfortable facing Adam without budging at all from his side. Now I was mostly sure it was him I didn't want to be even an inch away from him. He helped me sit up higher facing him.

"No... well yes at some point he bragged about it but I'd already kind of guessed. My iPod went missing a few days ago. He gave it back to me when I was in that... in that... ugh..." I shuddered as a wave of horrible, vivid memories hit me and heard something drop outside the room with a crash. I jumped and Adam's arms tightened around me.

"Tatum?" He called out and the door opened. Tatum was covered in something, a big splash-mark down the front of his shirt. I wanted to offer him a smile but I had nothing to give.

"It was supposed to be coffee. I'm sorry." He wiped at his shirt and groaned. "Nope, no good. It's ruined." I cast my eyes down.

"I'm sorry. I didn't mean to." He shot me a weak smile.

"I know."

He gestured to Adam to follow him and left the room, pulling off his shirt as he walked. I heard the muffled drone of them talking outside and Adam's voice raised at one point then I heard a loud thud. Did he just punch someone? Or something? When he came back a few minutes later I was sitting on one of the pillows with my back against the headboard, knees drawn up, arms wrapped around.

"What happened?" I asked as he sat down across from me, crossing his legs so he could face me. The knuckles on his right hand were bloody.

"Jesus Adam! You hit Tatum?!" He blinked for a moment then made an 'oh' face.

"Oh god no. I um, slipped." I glared at him.

"So, I get myself kidnapped and come back an idiot? Don't lie to me, Adam. I don't need lies right now." He looked like he wanted to cry. Oh no, someone was dead. I couldn't believe I hadn't asked about the rest of them; I'd been so wrapped up in myself.

"Adam, you're scaring me. Is someone hurt?"

"What? Yes, you. Dammit, Lila. Tatum just told me what you had a flashback of. That sick, fucking bastard. I'm going to kill him." The room swam and I sucked in a gasp of air.

"Kill him?! **KILL HIM**??? Oh, god he's alive? He's still out there… Oh god, oh god." I backed across the bed and hopped off, backing into the corner of the room; the most defensive position I could find. Stig was still out there. He'd find me again. I'd end up back in that room again with him hurting me, and touching me and feeding on me. Pretending to be Adam… Messing with my mind… Breaking me down into nothing. A slave. A shell. I sucked in shallow breaths, gasping and sobbing. Adam approached me slowly, palms up as if to prove he wasn't a threat.

"No no no no no no…" I just kept saying it over and over, like I was broken. Maybe I was. I folded into the

264

tiniest shape I could make and buried my face in my arms, which were rested on my knees. Adam tried to comfort me but I didn't even really feel his touch or hear his words. I shivered uncontrollably. I couldn't stop. I couldn't stop saying it over and over. He'd done it. He'd won. He'd destroyed me.

Chapter Thirty-Five

here were heavy footsteps in the hallway.

"Adam? What did you d…" Tatum dropped to his knees, hands over his ears as if he was being deafened by a terrible noise. His face was locked in a grimace as he dropped and writhed on the floor in pain. "Stop…please…" he begged, gasping and rolling, tears running from his eyes. I watched from under my hair, seeing his pain, knowing he was actually feeling mine. I couldn't help him. I couldn't stop. My hysteria kept building and I heard others coming into the room and shouting and anger and fear and pain and screaming and yelling and insanity…

Someone approached me quickly and placed hands roughly on my temples. A wave of peace hit me and I blacked out.

"I told you she would be severely damaged. I *told* you not to tell her." The voice insisted in the corner of the room. I half understood the words being spoken in the corner but I didn't recognise this voice. He was a stranger.

"She seemed okay though, you know like maybe she was dealing."

"Dealing? Really?! With what she's been through, at the hands of that sociopath, nothing is certain. Kid gloves I told you, Adam. Not blunder in and tell her the one thing that'll absolutely send her over the edge."

"Fuck… I didn't mean to say it. It slipped out before I could stop myself. Tatum told me what that bastard had done to her. Jesus, I wanted so much to protect her from him; from *that*. I failed her. Jesus, she might never feel safe or trust anyone again. What do I do?"

"You back off is what you do. You give her time and space and security."

"I thought I was."

An incredulous laugh sounded. "That's what you thought you were doing?! Telling her he's still alive and at large? That's not helpful. The kind of psychological trauma she's experienced means we have to tread very, very carefully if we want to help her regain herself. It could take days, weeks or even years, Adam."

"Please tell me you'll stay to help. I will do whatever it takes." Adam sighed and I opened my eyes.

"It's not his fault." I whispered. Two people moved quickly over to the bed. Not vampire quickly, but normal quickly, if maybe a little cautiously. The other man was a grizzly bear of a man really. He looked huge and beardy and yet he was somehow comforting, almost exuding calm. I couldn't help but give him a little smile. He smiled back.

"Nice to meet you, Lila. I'm Nero. I'm a Shapeshifter like Halley and Eloise." I believed him; he seemed cuddly like an animal.

"What's your favourite animal to change into?" I asked softly. He tilted his head.

"You ask this because you think you might know. Tell me." I shrugged.

"A bear?" He laughed out loud, a jolly, friendly sound that put me instantly at ease.

"She's good." He commented to Adam. "Bet you're hungry, girly. Nigel's cooking for you. You want something to eat?"

I nodded, realising I felt like I hadn't eaten in days. Nero sat beside me but Adam had retreated to the seat over by the window, looking conflicted. I sat up in bed slowly, keeping the blanket high, a thin layer of protection.

"How long have I been out?"

"Since we found you?" He kept things simple; I liked that.

"Yes." I nodded. I kept looking over to Adam but he stayed far away. Out of reach. It was no good. I wanted him beside me. I needed him.

"Adam, when I said give her space I didn't mean sit across the room. She needs you here." Nero murmured without looking at him. Adam did the vampire speed thing, like he'd been held away from me while attached with elastic and Nero had just told him to let go. In a few seconds, I was sitting back against Adam, leaning against his chest with my shoulder. His arms encircled me and made me feel warm and safe.

"See? You feel better already don't you?" I nodded.

"I don't want Adam away from me. Not even for a minute. I don't feel safe without him." Adam's heart thudded in his chest. I actually felt it. He felt so guilty about what had happened, I could tell.

"Adam's been in pieces since you were taken. He's been inconsolable; crazed you might even say. If I didn't know it was impossible I'd say a part of him had been missing too." It sounded a little corny coming from a huge bear of a man like Nero, but I appreciated the sentiment. I also sensed he didn't bother saying anything that wasn't true. He was too down to earth, almost spiritual. I gripped Adam's hand, which was on my stomach. He gripped me back.

"How long? You were going to tell me I think?" I asked, perking up when I suddenly smelled food. Nigel appeared as if by magic in the doorway with a tray. I could see a steaming bowl of some kind of soup, wafting a terrific aroma in my direction. I could see a huge hunk of bread and some butter and coffee. My mouth watered and my arms reached out almost of their own volition. I may have even moaned or drooled. I say that because Nero the bear laughed and helped Nigel place the tray on my lap. Adam reluctantly released me so I could lean forward to eat. Nigel hovered a moment, placing a hand over mine.

"I'm glad to have you back." He said quietly. I smiled up at him.

"Thank you, Nigel. I missed you too." He patted my hand and hotfooted it out of the room but I saw the pink in his cheeks.

"A lot of people are glad to have you back. They're itching to see you but we thought quiet was best. For now, at least." Oh shit. I dropped the bread I was holding.

"Tatum? Oh god, how is he? Jesus... he was actually *IN* my head with me! Is he okay?" Adam and Nero exchanged a glance. I took it as a bad sign.

"He uh, left." Adam said grudgingly, jabbing a thumb in the direction of the window.

"Left? He left us?" Panic rolled through me.

Nero made a shushing sound and pointed to my food. "Eat. Just focus on eating. I'll talk." I started shovelling food back in my mouth obediently.

"Tatum is out in the woods, meditating. He needed silence and calm and he's getting it out there away from us all. He'll be fine." I groaned, and went to speak. Nero made an ah-ah gesture with his hand so I carried on eating like a good girl. I'd realised almost immediately that you don't argue with this man.

"None of this is your fault. But you accepted the blame pretty readily, didn't you?" Adam's hand was stroking my back, as if he couldn't bear to lose contact with me. "Tatum knew the risks. Being here with you in the state you were in when we found you – he knew it was dangerous for him but he wouldn't leave you. He was sure he could help you."

I polished off the food and settled back in Adam's arms, which he wrapped tightly around me immediately. Nero moved the tray away.

"Well, you certainly put all that food away fast. You will start to feel better immediately." His voice was melodic and relaxing and I felt immediately calmer. My eyelids felt heavy and as he carried on speaking to me in that even, soothing voice, I drifted off into a deep sleep, wrapped in the safe cocoon of Adam's arms.

Chapter Thirty-Six

When I woke, Adam was still holding me. It was such a sharp contrast to waking up in that room. I couldn't let myself think about it. Thinking about it just made me freak out to the point that I'd even taken poor Tatum along with me last time. I really wanted to see him, to make sure he was okay but I was afraid to. Looking into his eyes and knowing he'd seen everything would make it real and I could only function at the moment by believing it was a terrifying nightmare. The worst a damaged mind like mine could conjure up out of nothing. I tried to gently turn to see if Adam was awake. I leaned on my wrist to turn. My wrist twisted and I slipped, elbowing Adam in the stomach. He woke with a grunt. I laughed. I couldn't help it. His face was so surprised and it just made me feel normal just for a moment. He rewarded me with a half smile.

"Good morning to you too." Morning? I had no concept of time, had we slept through the night? Was it night when I ate that yummy soup. My stomach growled. Yes, I guess so. Adam laughed and smoothed my hair with his palm, skimming his thumb across my cheek. I was starting to understand it wasn't that my hair was sticking up. He just wanted an excuse to touch me. I liked it. I threw myself into his arms and he hugged me tightly. His warmth gave me comfort and made me feel protected. He buried his face in my neck and breathed me in. I stiffened with a gasp. I couldn't help it. It made me think of Stig, inhaling my scent over and over and then doing stuff to me to freak me out. I heard a thud across the upper floor of the house and Adam let go of me, pulling back.

"What? What did I do?" He didn't show any concern for Tatum, who must have just picked up on my thoughts. He was more worried about my reaction to him. I felt sick and dirty as I looked at him.

"He did that to me…. A lot. He seemed to not be able to get enough of my smell. Ugh…" I shuddered and Adam cupped my face in his hands.

"He was a sick twisted bastard but he's gone. You're safe here and I'm not going to hurt you. Ever." A door slammed in the hallway and footsteps approached our room.

"Now Tatum, on the other hand, might be feeling a bit pissed off but don't worry about that, I'll protect you." The door flew open and Tatum stood there. He looked awful. His skin was pale and drawn, his cheeks slightly sharp looking. His blond hair was sticking up in all directions and he looked mad as hell.

I actually drew closer to Adam feeling afraid of Tatum for the second time since I'd met him.

"Will you get her the hell out of here or get her mind on something else before I go fucking insane?" Tatum snapped. I'd never seen him like this and I hated it. I was so sorry I'd done this to him. I made to speak but he cut me off.

"And don't keep saying you're sorry. For fuck's sake, I get it that you're sorry. I completely fucking get it. Cos you're thinking it. When you're not thinking about that sick fucker and what happened when he took you, that is. And I can't get that out of my head because you can't. I can see everything he did to you and I can fucking *feel* it too." His tirade upset me for several reasons. Mainly though it was because it was only natural for me to dwell on what had happened. Was it my fault he couldn't stay the hell out of my head?

"Who the fuck do you think you are?!" I roared at him, shooting up from the bed, leaving a stunned Adam sitting there, arms still up as if holding me. I didn't give Tatum a chance to reply. I got in his face and I mean, *right* in his face. I poked him in the chest as I spoke; anger giving me courage.

"If you can't keep your nose out of my freaking business then get the hell out of my life and go back to being sad and pathetic and alone! Go on! Fuck off back to your hermit cave and leave me alone!" I finished it with an attempt at a slap but he caught my hand and held it in mid air. His grip was tight and that just pissed me off more.

"Oh, nice move! Why not give the victim some more damn bruises to worry about! Really, Tatum, I mean it. Don't hold back. Why don't you kick me some more while I'm down?" He grinned suddenly, and I felt suspicion creeping in.

"Thank god for that." He exclaimed, pulling me into a crushing hug before I could stop him. "Our girl is back." He laughed triumphantly as I tried to elbow him away, angry with him for drawing me out. Eventually I gave in and let him hug me. He pulled back to look at me.

"See? That's much better! Anger I can deal with! Hit me if you want, blame me if you want. If it helps you, I don't care what you do to me. Just please don't hold it in and let it fester." His face turned so sorrowful as he said the last words and I couldn't help but think an apology. He grinned. I shrugged.

"And speaking of festering… you might want to grab a shower…. No offence." He backed up quickly before I could try to slap him again. I closed the door behind him and turned to Adam. He was still sitting on the bed staring, mouth open a little.

"I'm going to take a shower." I said with as much dignity as I could manage.

I grabbed some clean clothes and headed into the bathroom. Adam didn't follow me and I appreciated that. A little quiet and alone time should help. I was only in the shower about five minutes though when the shakes kicked in and I dropped down to sit in the shower, letting the water rain down on me. I sobbed for what felt like hours, only becoming aware of Adam's presence as I quieted down to hiccups and sniffles. He was just sitting opposite the bathtub. It didn't feel creepy at all – just like I was being protected, watched over by a guardian angel. I held out my arms to him and he stepped fully clothed into the bathtub and wrapped his arms around me. He pulled me up to a standing position and we just stayed there holding each other while the water poured over us both.

As we dried ourselves off and dressed later I felt able to talk to him properly at last. I don't know why, maybe it was the release from all the crying or finally feeling clean with no trace of Stig left on me - on the outside at least.

"I thought I'd never see you again." I said quietly. "I was so afraid of never seeing your real face again. Never feeling you hold me again." His face was so sad.

"I thought the same. It was killing me. How could I let you be taken like that?" I walked over to him and took his hand, pressing it against my cheek and holding it there.

"You couldn't have stopped him. I don't think anybody could have. He would have reached me no matter what. I'm just so glad you all found me. Although I have no idea how you managed it." He nodded, taking both of my hands in his. He walked us over to sit in the window seat. The heavy curtains were open a few inches and I could see outside into the snowy garden. Tatum and Nick were standing chatting while Shane was building a snowman. It looked so normal and innocent it was hard to believe that two thirds of the participants were vampires.

"Shane got into your dream." Adam said, distracting me.

"I know. I even tried knocking myself out to get to talk to her. But in the end, I couldn't tell her anything." I sighed. "I was useless."

"You were delirious from blood loss. But you managed to tell her about your friend."

Oh crap – Michelle. Michelle was a vampire!

"Oh no, Adam. How could I forget about Michelle? Where is she?" I was distraught at my selfishness. How could I just forget she was caught up in this?

277

"We were able to get Connor to track Michelle. It took almost two days, I'm so sorry for that, but we needed to find something of hers, which meant finding her home and letting him get her scent. If not for Connor, we'd never have found you." I stared at him. Who would have thought Connor of all people would have been instrumental in my rescue? I suppressed a shudder at the thought of him tracking me or even vampire-Michelle.

"Is he still here?"

"He's packing. He wants to keep tracking her so she can lead him to Stig." I gasped. A Tracker after my best friend who was now a vampire? How had everything gone so wrong?

"Will he hurt her?" I stared at Adam, watching his face for truth. He bit his lip.

"Stig or Connor?"

"Both. Either." He shrugged.

"It sounds like Stig wants her around so he'll probably not hurt her. She's of no interest to him in the way you were. Connor is fixated on her now, like he was with you." I felt a twinge of relief.

"So, he won't be staring at me anymore or being creepy?"

"Well he's still a Tracker and he's still Connor so honestly I have absolutely no idea." I grinned and hopped up from the window seat.

"I want to see him." Adam led the way, holding my hand tightly the whole time.

I knocked on the door. "Yeah?" Came the muffled southern drawl so I opened the door. He stared at me in surprise.

"Well if you ain't the last person I expected to be standing there." I walked over and, putting aside my nerves and revulsion, pulled him into a brief hug. He looked even more surprised when I stepped back and instantly put a comfortable distance between us.

"Thank you for finding me, Connor. For saving me." He nodded, struck dumb I think. I liked it. "I heard you're following up on Michelle." I stated it as calmly as I could manage, staring at him.

"Yeah. She's gonna lead me straight to the crazy sonofabitch." I nodded.

"Promise me you won't hurt her, please?" He smiled widely. "What do you take me for, sugarpie?" I folded my arms, and glared at him. He laughed and held up his hands.

"I promise not to hurt your little friend. But I am gonna rip the fucking head off of that sick bastard she's with. Just so you know."

"Please do, Connor. Slowly." I told him, turning to leave the room. Adam was smiling at me as I walked towards him.

"And don't stare at my ass." I snapped, feeling Connor watching. His laugh told me I'd been right.

I wanted to go out in the snow with the others so Adam helped me wrap up in extra warm clothes, mostly his as mine were all at my old place. Yeah, that's what it was now. I'd be moving in here as soon as I had the guts to leave Adam's place to get the rest of my stuff. We hadn't discussed it but somehow, I knew we wouldn't have to. I knew I belonged with him forever.

Outside we were met with a welcoming cheer and hugs, which suddenly somehow descended into the chaos

279

of snowball fighting extreme! There's no escaping a vampire with a snowball trust me. I was drenched and freezing by the time we'd finished dowsing each other with snow but it was such fun that for a little while at least, I felt like a carefree child and enjoyed watching the others just kick loose and enjoy themselves. Seeing Adam and Tatum running around laughing and pelting each other with snowballs made me feel kind of warm inside. I loved Adam so much but in a way, I loved Tatum too. We had a connection, which meant I'd never want him too far away from me; if his sanity could take it, of course. Damn it, I hoped he was too distracted to hear those thoughts.

Over the next few days, everyone filled me in on how they'd rescued me, each proud of the part they'd played. They were gutted that they'd allowed me to get taken (their words not mine although I thought it from time to time I admit) but they were proud of pooling their gifts and resources to find me.

Tatum had used his gift to pick up on me as soon as they were in range. Shane's Dreamwalker abilities had helped, as she'd found out Michelle was the one to track to find us. The Shapeshifters had spent most of their time in wolf form, trying to find my scent to find me.

Once Connor was tracking Michelle and led them to the right area, they very quickly hunted us down and with Tatum's help they were able to pinpoint us and surround the place. They'd stormed it using brute vampire force and a huge battle with Stig and his three vampire minions had raged for more than twenty minutes I'm told. Michelle wasn't there at the time so wasn't involved in the fight. I remember little more than a bit of noise out in the hallway as I died. Tatum was able to warn them there were more vampires there than expected so they weren't ambushed.

Finding me at death's door was another matter. Adam and Tatum apparently would have fallen apart if not for Nero. I was quickly realising his spirituality wasn't just something I'd imagined. He was deeply at one with himself and others – virtually a shaman or high priest to the other Shapeshifters. I could feel a sense of peace whenever he was around me. He'd managed to get the others to focus on the task at hand... giving me enough blood to bring me back before it was too late. I don't recall any of that of course. All I remember is dying, or so I thought, and waking up in bed with Adam watching over me, so protective and terrified. I knew I was going to spend eternity with him... just as soon as we could find a trustworthy Creator, assuming such a thing existed.

Nero was spending time with me, teaching me the extremely valuable art of meditation in an attempt to help me centre myself so that the fear of Stig finding me again didn't cripple me. At times, it still did. I couldn't help it.

I'd be sitting chatting with one of the guys or doing some mundane activity and terror would wash over me so completely and intrusively, like that monster's hands on my skin and I'd be a crying, shivering wreck. Tatum would normally be the first to know if I was alone when it happened. He had a terrible habit of dropping things when it happened, so Adam had finally given in and purchased plastic dishes to try and save Nigel's sanity. The good and expensive items like vases had been packed away long ago! Well, the ones Tatum hadn't already broken of course.

Of course, the nightmares were awful; very few contained scary flights of stairs as they had in the past, which was the only good thing about them. I'd relived what had happened so many times in my sleep that I woke screaming often. Adam would always comfort me and help me settle back to sleep but it was taking its toll on him and everyone else who woke each time with us. It didn't happen every night but when it did it was horrifying. Sometimes in waking from those terrifying flashbacks, I wouldn't believe it was really Adam beside me, trying to calm me, and a few times Nero had been forced to use his 'peace power' on me and put me back to sleep.

Chapter Thirty-Seven

I sat at the window seat in Adam's and my room. We were going over to collect my things from my old house. I'd already advised my estate agent to put it on the market and there was already some interest in it so I just wanted to get my belongings back here and leave it to them. Once it was sold, I'd have money to keep me going while I looked for something else to do with my life. Career wise, that is.

Unfortunately, it would be my first time away from home since the abduction. I won't lie – it was a terrifying feeling. How do you feel safe away from home after something like that? We were going together, every last one of us. Except Connor, of course. He'd left a few days ago. We heard from him now and then. He had spotted Michelle here, or tracked her there. He didn't know if she was with Stig but figured she'd lead him there eventually. I've asked that Michelle be brought to us once Stig is dead. I'm sure she just needs good friends around her to get her back to who she was. I can't leave her to live like that. I want her back.

My house looked so empty with everything packed and carried out. I didn't take any furniture with me, well apart from a comfy recliner chair of mine, which Adam said he'd put in the library for me instead of having to use that god-awful chaise (his words not mine). My books, DVDs, music, etc were all loaded already, and the last boxes of clothes were just being loaded. It was great having a gang of vampires helping – they could carry so much at once!

I'd packed a few favourite things from the house and was taking all of my memories with me, like photographs, but otherwise I left the place furnished. It still looked strangely empty though. As if we'd removed its heart and it was just sitting waiting for a new heart to beat there. I cried. I couldn't help it.

"Lila? You want a minute alone?" Adam's hand soothed me, stroking my back. I leaned into him. "No. Thanks, but I'm fine. I just need a minute to compose myself." His hand moved and I spun around to watch him.

"You're not leaving?" I asked, my voice going a little high. He smiled. "I promise I'll be right in the hallway. You're safe."

Bless him. He'd had to say that to me so much over the last week or so. He'd had to deal with panic attacks and flinches and shudders. The flinches and shudders seemed to occur most often when he tried to be intimate with me. He was so patient. I was lucky that he was so amazingly patient. The last time he tried to show me some attention in bed I'd frozen like a rabbit in front of headlights. He was hurt, I could tell, but he knew I couldn't help it. Stig had messed with my head, so much more than he knew. Pretending to be Adam, touching me, leading me to believe I was safe and rescued. He'd always pretended to be Adam, almost like he was making sure if I ever got out I'd never trust the man I loved again. That bastard deserved to die slowly and in agony. Thoughts like that are far more common for me now, by the way. I now had the dark thoughts and anger to match the goth style of my dress. I prayed Connor would find him and make him pay… for a few days or weeks at the very least.

"Lila? Seriously let's go… you promised us pizza!" Nick laughed, coming in and hooking his arm through mine, leading me out of the house, pulling me out of my dark thoughts. We crossed the empty drive – my car with the dead battery had been towed to a garage and was being sorted out for me. I allowed myself one last backward glance as we reached the gate and then handed the keys to the Estate Agent. He looked at us all a bit warily – probably imagining I'd joined a cult or something and I guess I had in a way.

That night at home at Adam's I tucked the last of my clothes into a random drawer, crammed in with his. I knew he'd tut when he saw it, and maybe the mischief in me was recovering a little as I grinned picturing his reaction.

"Lila." Adam made me jump, caught in the act. "I wasn't making a mess." I said quickly, trying on a grin. His relief was palpable.

"It's your home now. Make any mess you like." He held something amazing in his hands. I followed my feet over to him as they seemed to be on autopilot. Two steaming mugs of hot chocolate with marshmallows and a dusting of chocolate faced me when I reached him. I met his eyes.

"You're my god." I said, reaching to take a drink. He let me take it, then headed over to sit in the window seat. He'd been doing that a lot. Staying away from the bed until it was time to sleep. Letting it be my domain. It was sweet and at the same time so sad. It was his room. I followed him and sat down. We angled ourselves so we were facing each other, sipping at our drinks and slurping up marshmallows, never taking our eyes from each other.

"Good?" Adam asked finally, reaching over to wipe a smudge of chocolate from my upper lip. I grabbed his hand and licked it from his thumb.

"Really good." I replied watching his eyes swirl as I released his hand. He finished his drink and set it down on the floor.

"Can I ask you something?" I noticed his teeth were fanging at me a little. I hid the shudder that threatened to come out and smiled, focusing on my inner calm (thank you Nero).

"Of course." I said, finishing my drink. Adam took the mug from me and put it on the floor then he cupped my face in his hands.

"Can I please kiss you? I know why we're keeping our distance, and of course I respect that, but it's killing me not being able to kiss you." I felt tingles in the right places at his words and nodded. His eyes swirled with about a million colours as he leaned forward and pressed his lips so lightly against mine. I didn't want to close my eyes, didn't want to not see his eyes looking into mine. His lips worked lightly against mine, before he pressed closer, his tongue easing inside. I accepted the deeper kiss and returned it, my heart starting to pound heavily in my chest. He stopped and pressed one hand over my heart lightly.

"You want me to go?" He'd heard my heart thudding away like that. Damn vampire hearing. I shook my head, having no words at that moment.

He leaned forward to kiss me again, the contact becoming more desperate as our breath came faster and I knelt up to lean into him. He pulled me closer and I ended up draped over him inelegantly. He didn't seem to mind so neither did I. Our kisses went on for ages, but I could feel him becoming more aroused and knew he wanted more. I pulled back to look at him and saw his face drop, just for a split second before he pasted a passive look in its place. I grabbed his hand and pulled him up to stand beside me.

"Lila?" He asked, as I led him to the bed. I shook my head, pushing him so he fell backwards onto it. I didn't want him to distract me. I needed to focus on the here and now. My feelings and his. What we both wanted so much. What I needed to find again.

I dropped on top of him, straddling him, and kissed him. His hands came up around my back and then slid under my top. I pulled away from our kiss a fraction, his bottom lip lightly caught between my teeth, and the groan it elicited from him made me feel more confident. I laughed as I kissed him again, harder. His hands pulled

287

at my top and I allowed him to help me remove it. Since it was a *Mars* T-shirt I didn't let him damage it. I think he was tiptoeing around me too much to try anyway. Lucky for him!

My bra was off in seconds and his hands tentatively cupped my breasts, making me shiver deliciously at his touch. It had been too long for both of us. The dark red dominating the other colours in his eyes told me he was close to taking control, needing to take me and my blood so I pulled his hands away from me and pressed them over his head.

"Stay." I commanded, letting go. I was gratified to see he kept his hands above his head but the twitching of his fingers as I touched his chest under his T-shirt told me he was really forcing himself to stay that way. I tried tearing his T-shirt the way he'd done to me in the past but I didn't have the vampire strength. It was a little embarrassing.

With a growl, Adam snatched up the fabric and tore it away, instantly putting his hands back above his head while I laughed excitedly. His bare chest tempted me and I pressed kisses up and down, making sure to pay attention to each nipple. He shuddered beneath me and his hands moved several times before he stopped himself reaching for me. Eventually they curled into fists. His discipline was incredible. I loved him so much for that.

I moved off of him briefly to remove my leggings and underwear and then pulled at his trousers. I was so incredibly glad that he'd worn drawstring pants today. I was equally pleased when he helped me slide them down, along with his shorts. I stopped for a moment to absorb the complete beauty of the man lying at my mercy.

Naked, aroused and glistening with sweat, breaths heaving, hands above head as instructed. It made his chest stand out more and his muscles strained in his arms as he fought to control himself.

"You're just going to leave me like this?" He asked desperately. My mouth smiled without my control. I straddled him once more, raining kisses down on his face, his neck and onto his chest. He grunted beneath me.

"You're killing me, Lila." He said gruffly as I leaned forward to press against him chest to chest. His hands moved and then stopped abruptly as I met his eyes.

"Patience." I told him, feeling so turned on by the control that I wasn't ready to relinquish it just yet. I wriggled on top of him, feeling his arousal bounce against me as his body flexed. His eyes narrowed at me, almost entirely red now. I was in two minds about biting. On the one hand, it always felt amazing when he bit me, but the memories of Stig crowded my memory, making me gasp before I shook my head, forcing them away. Adam's hands were instantly on my face. He'd seen it in my eyes.

"You don't have to do anything you're not ready to do, Lila." He gasped, trying to cover his fangs with one hand as he fought to retract them. I pushed his hand away and kissed him, letting his fangs brush against my tongue.

With a little careful pressure, I managed to cut my tongue on one of them and listened to him hiss in a breath as he tasted my blood. Our kiss deepened as I felt him suck at my tongue and the feelings that raced through me to every inch of my body rushed me to want an orgasm now. I tried to sit on him, tried to get my climax but Adam stopped me. He pulled back from the kiss.

"Not like this, Lila. Not from the feeding, please." I understood. I let him kiss me some more, giving up control as his hands tightened around me. With a quick motion, he flipped us over, resting his weight onto his arms as he hovered over me, lust turning his eyes the darkest red I'd seen yet.

"Can I make love to you now?" He asked softly, leaning down to run his tongue around my ear, making gooseflesh travel down my neck. I nodded, mutely and then gasped as he flexed and was inside me in one smooth motion. I wrapped my arms around him and let out a sharp breath. He stilled, meeting my eyes. "Okay?" He mouthed. I nodded and kissed him, letting him know I wanted him too.

He began to move, in and out so slowly and reverently. I felt climax creep closer and moved with him, letting him plunge deeper inside me with each flex of his hips. As our breaths became louder and harsher, our hearts sped up together and I felt myself clench inside as I came. I gasped and Adam caught my gasp with a laugh, covering my mouth with his. I felt him thrust harder a few times as he too came with a groan and a laugh then he collapsed on top of me, breathing hard and smoothing my hair with his thumb, before resting his hand on my cheek. When he felt wetness there, he lifted his head to look at me, concerned.

"Shit, Lila. What is it? Did I hurt you?" I shook my head.

"It was perfect. I'm happy, Adam, really." He didn't look convinced but let it go, knowing I wasn't going to talk more right now. He kept stroking at my cheek, brushing away tears as they trickled silently from my eyes. When he went to move away, I locked my arms around him, and one leg over his.

"Please don't." I begged, not wanting to lose the closeness and intimacy of the moment. He stared at me a moment, trying to work me out, but settled back into place. I fell asleep like that, Adam draped over me, his warmth leaving me feeling protected and comforted.

For the first time since my ordeal at the hands of Stig, I felt completely safe and slept deeply, dream-free.

Be sure to pick up
Conflicted, Lila Casey Book 2

Writing Playlist

As a favourite author of mine has done in the past, I also wanted to share with you the amazing music which helped to motivate and inspire me while I wrote this book. As you might have guessed from the book, I'm a big fan of 30 Seconds to Mars, and really feel their music played a big part in my journey, unlocking creativity I never knew I had.

The albums below are awesome and available via iTunes and all other good music retailers.

30 Seconds to Mars – 30 Seconds to Mars
30 Seconds to Mars – A Beautiful Lie
30 Seconds to Mars – This is War
30 Seconds to Mars – Love Lust Faith + Dreams
Awolnation – Megalithic Symphony
Bruno Mars – Doo-Wops & Hooligans
Fall Out Boy – Save Rock & Roll
Imagine Dragons – Night Visions
Marilyn Manson – Lest We Forget – The Best of Marilyn Manson
Maroon 5 – Songs About Jane
Maroon 5 – Overexposed
Olly Murs – In Case You Didn't Know
Placebo – Battle for the Sun
Placebo – Once More with Feeling (Singles 1996-2004)
Placebo – Meds
Panic! At the Disco – Vices & Virtues
You Me At Six – Sinners Never Sleep

Printed in Great Britain
by Amazon